PRAISE FOR *GUILE*

"His long career in government and politics has given Craig Snyder an inside look at how things work. His lively mind has transformed his knowledge into a gripping novel. Read, reflect...and enjoy!"

– **WILLIAM KRISTOL**, Director, Defending Democracy Together

"Written by someone who knows the way Washington works, *Guile* is an action packed adventure with twists and turns to keep you guessing."

– **CHRISTINE TODD WHITMAN**, former GOP Governor of NJ and Cabinet member for US President George W Bush

"I've been a Washington journalist for decades, but there are events and moments you just can't reproduce unless you were in the room. This is the behind the scenes story I've always wanted to read, by an author who has been there and done that. A gripping, propulsive roman a clef. Have fun guessing the real-world names of the characters. Craig Snyder knows them all.

– **BARTON GELLMAN**, journalist and author with awards including the Pulitzer Prize, an Emmy for documentary filmmaking, and the Los Angeles Times Book Prize.

"Craig Snyder knows the inside world of politics. He's been there. His novel skillfully captures the relationship between the candidates and their consultants. Snyder outlines how ethically compromised these relationships can be. How tough... how impossible... when they find themselves flying too close to the flame. There is sizzle and scandal. They get so far, they can't turn back and typically they're convinced that they must win at any cost... that the ends justify the means. It's ripped from the headlines, you will recognize the players. Sometimes it becomes a battle between the bad and the worse. Snyder provides a surprising and rather uplifting ending. If you like political intrigue, this is the book for you."

– **MARJORIE MARGOLIES**, former Democratic Congresswoman

"Snyder has been a national political insider and highest level operative for three decades and it shows in the authenticity and details on every page of this gripping 'House of Cards' style novel."

– **JAMES GREENWOOD**, former GOP Congressman

"*Guile* is impossible to put down. As you read lightbulbs explode in your brain as you realize Snyder is flinging the door to the real political insiders and their machinations wide open. If you've ever watched the news and wondered 'How the hell does that happen…,' this book is your answer in fictional form. Snyder's political experience and uncanny ability to show his readers both the big picture and also the tiniest details (which is what makes this book really come to life) brings his readers the best approximation of our current situation, complete with people you feel you know and situations that, while larger than life, ring true. "

– **ROBIN DAVIS MILLER**, former President, The Authors Guild

"*Guile* is one of the most interesting and important novels I have read in years. It takes an unsparing look into the inner-workings of contemporary Washington DC in ways that only the author, Craig Snyder, can do. Over the past four decades, Snyder has moved through a number of top positions on the Hill, at political consulting firms and at various think tanks, and he knows the ropes ; the cynicism, the intrigue, and the maneuvering which are features of business done in DC; the ambitions and aspirations that draw people to DC in the first place and which drive national politics. With amazing skill, Snyder builds characters and tells a story that depicts the realities of DC, realities which have almost—but not quite—suffocated the yearning by many in Washington and beyond for a spirit of greater optimism and idealism in government. Can an American political renaissance ever happen? What are the limitations and possibilities in public life today? For all those interested in these questions, my recommendation is to sit down and read *Guile*."

– **DAVID EISENHOWER**

GUILE

GUILE

CRAIG SNYDER

Guile

© 2024 by Craig Snyder

Editors: Jorge David Remy, Noëlla Simmons
Cover and Interior Design: Emma Elzinga

Indigo River Publishing

3 West Garden Street, Ste. 718
Pensacola, FL 32502
www.indigoriverpublishing.com

Ordering Information:

Quantity Sales: Special discounts are available on quantity purchases by corporations, associations, and others. For details, contact the publisher at the address above.

Orders by US trade bookstores and wholesalers: Please contact the publisher at the address above.

Printed in the United States of America

Library of Congress Control Number: [Insert number]
ISBN: 978-1-964686-05-9 (paperback)   978-1-964686-06-6 (ebook)

First Edition

With Indigo River Publishing, you can always expect great books, strong voices, and meaningful messages. Most importantly, you'll always find . . . *words worth reading.*

"For what shall it profit a man, if he shall gain the whole world,
and lose his own soul?"
—King James Bible, Mark 8:36

"It's a fucking valuable thing, you just don't give it away for nothing."
—Then-Illinois Gov. Rod Blagojevich on naming a successor to fill
President-Elect Barack Obama's Senate seat.

CONTENTS

PART 1 1

1   Operation Cabot 3

2   Partners 8

3   Red Meat 13

4   The Hessian 19

5   Charles Town 23

6   Cuba Libre 31

7   Squash 40

8   Olga 49

9   Strike Price 54

10   Death from Below 63

11   Epping Forest 71

12   Brains 78

13   Oppo 88

14   Corner Table 91

15   Snorkeling 102

16   A Thing of Value 113

17   Rough Riders 121

18   Albuquerque 133

19 Leaks 142

20 Cactus Lan 153

21 Mount Vernon 164

22 Fish 176

23 Lafayette Park 187

24 Drake 194

25 St. Thomas 205

26 Auto-Da-Fé 211

PART 2 221

27 General Aviation 223

28 Guile 230

29 Centreville 236

30 "What's Going On?" 241

31 Pasta Salad 251

32 The Resistance 259

33 Things of Value 266

Acknowledgements 271

PART

ONE

1

OPERATION CABOT

Pete Vankov shot his cuffs, to expose just the right length of linen. He stepped in front of a window in his office, stood before Washington's K Street power corridor, but the sky was too gray to give him a halo.

"Look," he told Olga, forcing his gaze from the curves in her agora sweater to her jade green eyes. "This is geopolitics at its apex. The cloak-and-dagger shit you watch on TV after Pilates, when you're eating your organic fig yogurt with asparagus protein booster.

"We're walking with Jesus on this one, God and country, against the communist hordes. We represent the new President of Argentina, the first reform-minded, democratically elected Argentine head of state since your mother was blowing commissars in Odessa, or whatever hellhole you crawled out of."

Before she could reply, Vankov turned to Yair, a former Mossad agent. "The first non-Peronist Argentine president. This guy pushed out that Peronist scum who used to harbor ex-Nazis and shrug at bombings of Jewish community centers in Buenos Aires."

Vankov rolled his neck until he heard a crackle, dulling the pain shooting down his arm. A reminder of the stud he'd been and was no more, ended by dropping a barbell on his head, compressing a nerve.

He turned back to Olga, mostly because he couldn't help himself. When this meeting ended, he'd walk straight to Thirteenth Street, to an upscale bordello. Maybe his new favorite, a strawberry blonde, would be available.

"The stated scope of work," he said, hoping formality would ease the pressure building in his pants, "is to build a positive image for the Argentine president, and that country more broadly, in the US Congress, the media, and on Wall Street, to help Argentina sell more beef and wine in the US, get military aid restored, and attract US private investment."

Olga raised a sculpted eyebrow.

He ignored her. "We'll call it 'Operation Cabot.' After Sebastian Cabot, the first European to reach Argentina. An Italian."

"Venetian," Yair said.

"Whatever." A wop was a wop.

"Technically, Cabot was the second European explorer to reach Argentina," the commando continued in a schoolmarm tone. "The first was eaten by natives."

"Don't let the facts get in the way of a good story. You just redraw the narrative. Operation Cabot."

Vankov settled back into his sofa, savored the full-grain leather's give. He let his eyes wander to Olga's sweater. Then to her golden hair cascading onto the downy wool. Then to her perfect teeth framed in those glistening cinnamon lips. He wished he'd scheduled her half an hour early, before this Israeli thug had shown up.

The former Mossad man, now a mercenary private eye, or "global security contractor," was wearing a glen plaid suit and looked like a banker with a gym membership, which Vankov supposed was the idea. Yair might know European history, but he didn't know how to dress. Vankov was wearing a bespoke double-breasted, pin-striped navy suit, paisley pocket square, white shirt with starched cutaway collar, woven blue silk tie. Blue projected authority. With a gold howling wolf's head glinting on his diamond-studded pinkie ring to sharpen the point.

"Peter?" Olga's voice sliced through his thoughts.

He snapped toward her. "Our client is a 'good guy,'" he said. "An earnest new presidente."

"And he has signed off on the 'stated scope of work'?" A grin played on her moist lips.

The horse-faced Mestizo client was so naïve, there'd been no point in detailing the operation to him, not that Vankov felt bound by contract terms, anyway. "Christ, the only thing worse than a communist is an amateur."

"Sounds like we're exposed here," Yair said with that command voice they teach in military knife-and-fork schools.

"We're covered." Vankov nodded and held Yair's gaze. After a silence, he added, "We have a signed contract."

"I'd like a copy."

"I'll get you one." For your next birthday.

Yair turned to Olga, who shrugged.

Vankov had insisted on signing the contract with the Argentine secret intelligence service. That way, the contract and its ample payment terms weren't disclosed in the Argentine press, which let Vankov avoid registering with the State Department as a foreign agent.

"Operation Cabot has to stay low-key," Vankov told the commando. Technically, he'd probably violated some statute. But he'd have a tough time pitching to run jingoistic Republicans' campaigns if he got a name as a foreign-government shill. And he hated the onerous FARA paperwork.

"The client won the presidency, but his defeated opponent controls the Argentine Senate and is determined to block and ultimately humiliate him," Vankov continued, his eyes fixed on Olga's fuzzy gray sweater.

"Your job is to get close to the opposition leader in the Argentine Senate," he told her. He pointed at Yair. "He'll go with you, to keep you safe."

Olga's lips parted, showing those luminous, absurdly straight white teeth. She angled forward as though to ask him something, reminding him of his second wife, before that had gone to hell.

Vankov's cell phone blared in his pocket.

He reached into his suit coat, careful not to scrape the lustrous wool.

The phone's display showed "Unknown Number," but Vankov knew who it was as soon as he heard the first words. He'd been waiting a week for this call, had nearly given up, begun to question his strategy.

"Hey, kid." The voice floated into Vankov's ear, deep with a faint twang. Ven Hess seemed to call everybody "kid," even those with a few years on him, like Vankov at fifty-two. Some baseball thing.

"Mr. President," Vankov said to the candidate, trying to hit that perfect tone, neither sarcastic nor suck-up.

Vankov motioned to Olga and Yair, pointed to his office door and the anteroom beyond, raised his finger to suggest he'd be only a minute.

Olga's eyebrow raised and parted those glistening lips, about to speak, but he backhanded the air as though shooing them.

"How's the boy?" Hess drawled.

Maybe Hess's question wasn't purely perfunctory. Vankov had bonded with Hess the first time they'd met; two hardball hustlers with artistic bents: Hess as an actor, Vankov as a painter.

"Pete, I need to revamp my media operation, redo the lineup, the plays, the signals, the whole shebang." Businesslike now. "We could use your help. I'd like you to come aboard for a couple of months, shouldn't take you more than that. You'd be deputy campaign manager, reporting directly to me."

Vankov grinned. But that "deputy campaign manager" part scraped his eardrum. Hess hadn't said "the deputy manager," which implied he had a troop of deputy managers scampering around.

"I appreciate your thinking of me," Vankov said as though fielding an unexpected barbecue invite.

"Destiny is calling, kid." A tinny echo popped.

"There are some details we'd need to discuss," Vankov said.

"We can work all that out later."

Vankov let silence scratch through the line for a few beats. "Sign me up, sir. I need to wrap up some stuff in the office, but I should be able to start Monday."

"That's fine, Pete. We'll see you on Monday." Hess sounded like Vankov's high school wrestling coach.

"Yessir. Freedom and prosperity."

The line clicked dead.

Vankov pumped his fist, and then again. "Yes!" he hissed. Hess had a good shot at the Republican presidential nomination and a fair shot at the presidency. Better than a fair shot with Vankov's help. Though Thomas Venable "Ven" Hess had no business anywhere near the White House, some second-rate brushback pitcher turned radio motormouth and hack actor and pitchman. Still, Hess wouldn't be the first dolt to occupy the Oval Office.

Vankov rolled his neck again and noticed his nerve pain had vanished. Where was Olga? He'd figure a way to dispatch Yair, get her into the conference room with the black leather couch.

2
PARTNERS

When Pete Vankov's turn came to update on projects and prospects, he angled his Knoll chair toward the mahogany conference table, chosen like the rest of the office design to embody seriousness of purpose and success, adjusted the wide lapels of his double-breasted, pin-striped suit, and spewed minutia. Vankov's nasal voice slid into a monotone as he detailed payment schedules for a direct mail piece and lauded a printer who'd done a nice job on a brochure.

David Gruber took note that several other partners had begun doodling or poking cell phones. One worked a *New York Globe* crossword on his lap. Gruber craned his ears to Vankov's grating voice. He waited for the Dark Angel to slip a bombshell into this stream of banality. Gruber figured he knew Vankov better than any of the other partners at Drayton, Nesbit, Fitch and Vankov. After all, Gruber and Vankov had been partners before DNFV had settled into its current incarnation. And the Dark Angel, even though only a year older than Gruber, had been a mentor. That all seemed eons ago.

Vankov was droning now about a young aide who'd proven a star deputy finance director on a gubernatorial campaign. Vankov wanted to recommend the prodigy as a deputy campaign manager for a Senate race the firm was handling. Vankov kept leering at the black leather couch against one wall in the windowless room.

Gruber picked at a thread of flesh alongside the cuticle of his left middle finger, prying up the flap with a nail, then tearing it off, a painful process that left an angry pink strip half an inch long. He sighed. He hadn't picked at his fingers for months, and not like this in more than a year. Scars and shiny skin around his fingernails attested to bouts of dermatillomania during earlier periods of stress.

Gruber grinned at Vankov's Al Capone outfit. Gruber was also a clothes horse, but to gain that edge of intimidation. Gruber had lost hair and gained weight, but he wouldn't follow Vankov down the road of plastic surgery and fad diets and supplements. Gruber thought of Vankov as his own portrait of Dorian Gray.

Vankov was still droning, maybe trying to induce comas.

"Pete, excuse me," Gruber said, interrupting with an innocent mien. "That bill you just mentioned, is that related to your bill to expand casino gambling?"

"Unrelated," Vankov said, locking Gruber's eyes. "Now, getting back to the direct-mail house . . ."

Gruber picked at his thumb again. He made eye contact with Ezra Fitch, the closest friend he had in the room, and the closest to a landsman; Fitch was married to a Jew.

"That's it for pending projects," Vankov said. "Now, one prospect: I've just gotten an offer to do some work for a campaign. Housekeeping, really, for a few weeks, sharpening a press operation. For Ven Hess."

Gruber shook his head. Around the table, he heard a few grunts, one chuckle. No gasps. Well, what the hell, the firm was known as "The Hangmen's Lobby" for its clientele of African strongmen, Asian civil rights abusers, and Middle East despots.

"Really, Pete?" one partner asked. "Ven Hess, for Crissakes?"

Gruber glared at Ezra Figlare TVU.

"You and Hess are tight?" Fitch asked Vankov.

Vankov shook his head. "No. Recommendation from a mutual friend. Caught me cold."

Fitch shrugged at Gruber.

Couldn't Fitch see it? Couldn't the others? Pete Vankov wasn't going to settle for a temporary gig, a few weeks of press therapy, on what might prove a winning presidential campaign, Gruber knew. Vankov wanted to ride Ven Hess to glory, and they'd blithely screw up the Republican Party, the country, and the planet in the process.

"This offer has a short shelf life," Vankov said. "I've got to move quickly."

Around the table, a few murmurs, some grimaces and raised eyebrows, then a collective shrug.

"All right, then," Vankov said and leaned back in his Knoll chair.

Gruber pictured Ven Hess guffawing in the Oval Office as he did on TV, cinnamon hair bouncing over his tanned face and a double-knit plaid sports coat. Gruber's hand began to throb, and he looked down to see he had pulled off several layers of skin around his thumb, blood dotting one side.

Vankov was leering again at the black couch, now with a celebratory sheen.

Another partner was shuffling papers, preparing to deliver his report.

Let it go, Gruber told himself. You knew what you were getting into when you signed on here. And they gave you a good deal; don't screw it up. They'd let Gruber establish a separate practice within DNFV—his own little island—sharing the firm's address, support staff, and photocopier, but otherwise doing his own thing. Let it go.

Gruber's hand rose almost by itself in a stop sign. "I object," he said. He stood, his limbs thrumming. All eyes were boring into his face. "Ven Hess is not the kind of client this firm wants or, for that matter, the kind of president the country needs."

"You 'object'?" Vankov asked. "Whaddya think, you're back in court? Back with that white-shoe weenie law firm pushing zoning variances in suburban Philadelphia? Presidential politics ain't beanbag."

Vankov was angling his head back, which expanded his neck like a cobra. Gruber just glared back. This wasn't a schoolyard stare-down; Vankov's steroid-pumped wrestler's build wasn't going to cow him, even if Gruber looked like a balding wimp. Gruber scanned the room and found a couple of smirks and some slack jaws. When his focus returned to Vankov, he saw taut shoulders, in apparent preparation to lunge, give way to mere annoyance and eyes that seemed to scream disappointment.

"This firm owes some responsibility to the System, not just to its clients." Gruber squinted at Vankov's wolf-head pinkie ring. "In more mercenary terms, by taking such a high-profile role, you're inviting scrutiny, especially with your track record, which also puts the firm at risk."

"What track record is that?" Vankov met his glare.

Gruber smiled. "Where should we begin? No need to go back too far. How about Egypt?" Gruber scanned the table again and found more grimaces. "The Muslim Brotherhood's candidate won a fair election as President of Egypt. Which made the emir of the UAE soil his pants over the prospect of Brotherhood power spreading through in the region. So what did the emir do? He organized a military coup in Egypt. And he hired our Mr. Vankov." Gruber raised a finger. "Now the emir was no Boy Scout, either. But you wouldn't know that from the international press. After Mr. Vankov went to work, the media didn't look too hard inside the UAE, at dissidents imprisoned and tortured, at slave labor building its gleaming skylines and world-leading per-capita carbon footprint, at its vanity projects like indoor ski slopes and flower gardens in the desert."

Gruber wagged his finger. "Now, US law required curtailing military aid to a country whose military seized power, so I would never suggest that Mr. Vankov here lobbied the White House to look away. But look away it did." He scanned the room again. "None of this bothers anyone here? The United States cries for democracy around the world, but that kinda only means when we like who wins an election, eh?"

"David, my good friend, you have it all backwards," Vankov said with a smile that didn't reach his eyes. "We should get some attention out of Ven Hess.

DNFV should be involved. We're supposed to be players. You'd rather have those press weasels sniping at us for not getting a seat at the winning table?"

Gruber rubbed a temple.

"As for the rest of it," Vankov said, "Don't be a weenie."

Gruber eyed his partners, felt like he was looking at a firing squad. He locked on Ezra Fitch. "You're okay with this, Ezra?"

Fitch shrugged. "Pluses and minuses."

Vankov leaned down behind the table, and a pulse shot through Gruber's chest, worried for a moment that the Dark Angel might come up with a weapon. Vankov rose hefting a small carton. He reached inside and tossed an impossibly white baseball to one partner, then another ball to another, and on. Finally, Gruber got his, thrown so hard it passed through his hands and plunked against his sternum. A certified Major League baseball, with a signature in bright blue ink: "For David Gruber, Keep Fighting—Ven Hess."

After the meeting ended, Gruber sat for a while, thinking. Then he went back to his office and shut the door, leaving his new ball on the conference room table.

3
RED MEAT

By the time the house salads arrived, an ache was pounding Vankov's eyes. Across their corner table at The Prime Rib, Flip was slathering a roll with so much butter it nearly dripped onto the fading faux animal print carpet of this aging "power left lunch" spot. The Fox News producer's gleaming double-knit suit screamed "Tourist" or "bureaucrat." And who went by "Flip" anymore? Vankov drained his martini.

"We're doing fine, executing our plan," Vankov said, looking away as Flip crammed buttered bread into his maw. "But some of the staff is untested, and you never know how that's going to break." Vankov caught a waiter's eye and raised his empty martini glass. "Hess is an antiestablishment candidate, running a guerrilla campaign, and in the beginning he couldn't attract high-profile, seasoned hands vetted by the press. Even for the top spot, campaign manager. But you go to war with the army you've got."

"I'd say that's worked in your favor so far." Flip buttered another salted roll.

"How's that?"

A faint grin spread above Flip's wispy goatee. "Two of your predecessors as comms director flamed out, one right after the other. For number three, Hess did reach out for a top pro. He hired you."

"First, I'm not Hess's 'comms director.' I'm his deputy campaign manager. And what of it?"

"A rose by any other name. What I mean is, after two scandals, you'd think Hess would bring on a replacement who had less . . . baggage. No offense."

Vankov nodded. "How many married couples you see, where you wonder what the hell she's doing with him, or vice-versa?" He eyed Flip's goatee. "Or he with him, whatever. When the chemistry works, you go with it."

"Yeah. But now you tell me Hess's campaign manager is untested, who knows how that's going to play out, and the way it played out with his comms directors."

"I'm not following you."

Flip scratched his temple with a greasy finger as though to coax his memory, then grinned again. "A month ago, Fox gets documents about Hess's first comms director and his divorce. These papers—from a sealed court filing, by the way—allege Hess's comms guy slapped his ex around and sent her some . . . colorful, threatening texts. The story breaks—other outlets apparently also got copies—and Hess fires the guy and hires a replacement."

A waiter set down a fresh martini. Vankov gave him a nod and swirled the olive.

Flip crammed another hunk of bread and spoke through it. "Next thing you know, the entertainment trades run a story that Hess's new comms chief is funneling campaign contracts for digital ad placements to a company he set up in the name of his new husband. Ven Hess, it turns out, paid for the couple's $250,000 gay wedding at the National Botanical Gardens—though apparently unknowingly. Not so good when you're courting the evangelical vote, though. So Hess fires his new press guy." Flip wiped his fingers on his napkin. "And hires you."

"Yeah. So?"

Flip shrugged. "So nothing. I just find it strange when you start telling me Hess's campaign manager is green. I wonder how long that guy's going to last. And who's going to succeed him."

Vankov nodded. "I told you, Hess had to hire amateurs in the beginning. Bottom-feeders and sycophants like those two press weasels, and it was just a matter of time until they imploded. You asked me how things were going, and I told you. And I'm not talking about dirty laundry, I'm talking about performance."

"Okay." Flip flashed another grin.

Vankov sipped his martini and his lips puckered. Not dry enough.

"I'm not sure what you're getting at, but it's certainly not in my interest for more Hess aides to implode. Too many blow up, and people get the idea that Hess hires losers—crooks and scoundrels." And Hess might get wise that Vankov was behind the implosions. So far, Torpedoing Hess's first two press guys had been cheap, cost Vankov only a bottle of eighteen-year-old Glenmorangie single malt and a box of Cuban cigars, for a friend in the Arlington County courthouse to leak the records.

"O-kay." Flip finished another roll. "Hey, cheer up. It's your birthday. Well, nearly."

"Yeah." Now this guy was gloating about a factoid he'd probably plucked from Wikipedia? Vankov should appreciate the gesture. He'd been born on Veterans Day, and jingoistic hoopla always drowned his milestones, turning each birthday into a reminder of Vankov's lack of military service.

A speck of butter clung to Flip's wispy goatee, and Vankov stared at it until he felt bile rise. He held a deep breath, released it slowly.

The waiter swept by with their entrees, setting a heaping oval platter before Vankov.

He cut and chewed a bite of T-bone, from the more succulent tenderloin side, shot the blood against his cheeks. He'd love a Cuban Cohiba Robusto. A T-bone was made for a fine cigar, but today that would be a felony. Vankov's stomach was still bouncing. He watched the producer hack at a slab of roast beef. "What's your story, Flip?"

"You mean, how did a nice guy like me get into a racket like this?"

"Not exactly. But go ahead if that's how you see it."

Flip began prattling about his days in the Christian press. Vankov tried to figure how he was going to torpedo Hess's campaign manager now that even Flip seemed to suspect Vankov's hand in the press guys' departures.

Vankov rolled his neck, trying to stop a needle shooting down his trapezius. He began doodling on the tablecloth with a charcoal pencil he always carried, a topless take on a babe sitting a couple of tables away gnawing on some red meat. He expanded her cup size and gave her a toga sliding down one arm, like a Greek goddess.

Now Flip was yakking about Jesus, how we should all be more prayerful. The producer began lamenting the loss of the legions of innocent unborn, the most precious and vulnerable among us.

Vankov looked up, gave Flip a nod, and began sketching a car-wreck scene, with a child's shattered body lying in a road.

Last week was his kid sister's birthday. Or would have been her birthday. She would have turned what, forty-nine? He tried to picture her in middle age. The best he could do was morph his father's features onto her five-year-old face. That's as far as she'd gotten, five. She would have resembled their father, at least had the old man's broad Bulgarian face, thick lips, and bulbous nose. His siblings all looked like his father, like Slavs; he was the only one who'd gotten their mother's sharp Irish nose, hazel eyes, and chestnut hair. Though what was left of his hair was sandy now, from a bottle.

It wasn't only that his sister was dead; that was cliché tragic, the treacle of Hallmark afterschool specials. It was the absurdity of it, the pointlessness, the obscenity. She'd been bouncing a Spaldeen against their Hoboken row house, all their parents could afford, a plumber with a tenth-grade education and a part-time grade-school math teacher. She dashed into the street after the ball and was flattened by a car. Skull cracked, never regained consciousness, didn't die for a couple of days, so they could all savor the agony.

What got him most was the car that hit her, a beater Pontiac wagon covered with New York Giants stickers and packed with locals rushing to a sausage-eating contest. The episode was an exquisite digest of his entire déclassé boyhood. He hadn't been big on God since then, came to see the church and his Catholic parochial school as another racket, and a pretty good one.

Flip's monologue halted, and Vankov looked up to see the producer was aghast.

"A habit I picked up when I heard that Picasso used to doodle on napkins and tablecloths and present his scratchings to cover the checks."

"I don't think you're quite in that league."

Vankov shrugged. "I could probably do a sketch to cover the tab at Mickey-D's, but they don't have tablecloths. Hey, friend, I've had stuff shown in New York galleries."

Vankov studied his sketch of the woman. He'd captured her, the look in her eye that said she was available for the right price. Everybody had a price. "They don't like it, they can wash it out," he told Flip. "Go on with what you were saying."

Flip swallowed his indignation a few beats. "I was saying that radical feminists are driving the abortion debate, and they try to shut down anyone who disagrees. Even Bill Clinton said abortion should be 'safe, legal, and rare.'"

Vankov admired his sketch. Maybe he'd draw his wife with a Double-D cup, give him something to picture when they went at it.

Flip was saying how America was a Christian nation. Vankov cut him off with a head shake.

"The most beautiful sight I ever saw," Vankov said, "was a pro-choice rally on the National Mall. A magnificent summer day, lush lawn, and a legion of babes in tight T-shirts, all protesting for the right to have recreational sex." He shoved his plate aside and lifted the tablecloth to show Flip the full drawing of the woman. "That's what nobody understands. Abortion isn't about female autonomy or the rights of the unborn or the Bible. Abortion is about fucking."

Flip recoiled, as though Vankov had slugged him.

Christ, he hadn't even gone for the kill yet, on Hess's campaign manager. Vankov slid his plate over his sketch. "Got a little carried away there. No disrespect intended." He'd better fix this, fast, before old Flip did an exposé on him.

4

THE HESSIAN

Ven Hess folded a stick of Wrigley's Double Mint into his mouth and leaned back in his desk chair. Through his window, he admired the Capitol under a sky the color of faded denim. The US Capitol. Smart move, he decided, putting his campaign headquarters here at the Hall of the States Building. Decent digs, with a riot of colored flags in the marble lobby that gave the place some style, some heft, some gravitas. He actually liked Washington, even more now that it was a baseball town again.

He wished his father could see him now. Renowned heart surgeon, dead at seventy-five from a stroke; go figure. When Hess was a kid, his father had called him "jock," "bully," "yahoo," "boor," "lout," all sorts of crap. The old man laughed when Hess thought "boor" meant a wild pig, as though that proved the point.

Hess mashed the gum, savored the initial mint blast. What a metaphor, flavor ebbing from chewing gum until you're left with a bland glob. He'd tell his speechwriter to do something with that. At least he wasn't still mixing the Wrigley's with a chaw of Red Man, the way he did a few years in the

Minors, in Peoria and Charlotte. That stuff will give you cancer; look what happened to Tony Gwynn.

He punched a button on his desk phone. "Send in Bobby," he told his secretary. "And have Pete Vankov stand by."

A few minutes later, two raps on his door, louder than they had to be, Bobby playing macho.

"Yeah," Hess called.

Bobby stepped in, head high, chest out, but reeking of fear. Like a batter stepping to the plate with that little hitch of hesitation after Hess had brushed him back or knocked him down.

Hess pointed to a couple of matching leather chairs in front of his desk—low-end, from some office supply store, they'd have to upgrade those. "Sit down, Bobby."

His campaign manager had finally stopped wincing at the nickname. The guy went by Robert and was actually a Robert the third or fifth or sixth, blueblood Ivy League prick, but Hess renamed everyone. He'd learned that in a classics class at Arizona State, all he could remember from that course: the power of naming. Something to do with Odysseus saying his name was Nobody, and then the cyclops wailing that nobody had blinded him. Bobby eased into one of the cheap chairs, wary, like a dog told to sit before getting swatted on the snout with a rolled newspaper.

Hess stood to his full six-four, six-five easy with the thick heels on his cap-toes, and stepped toward a wall covered with jumbo glory photos. Now Bobby would also have to look at a younger, snarling version of The Hessian in a Cubs uniform, leg raised as he began his windup. They'd taken that shot during the last of his five games in the show, his "cup of coffee," before they sent him back to Triple-A in Des Moines. Still, he was a Major Leaguer. Didn't matter how many games you played, that was a title you kept for life, like Mr. President.

He glared down at Bobby, a respectable five-ten, but never ripped enough for a day in team sports. "It's time to change pitchers." He raised his hand. "I'm not going to take away your rice bowl. We can use you in another position. Like moving a catcher to first or right when his knees go bad. Lots to do around here, kid."

Bobby gazed at him, mouth quivering. Hess felt a pang, like when he had to put the dog out in the rain. He reminded himself that Bobby was trying to ride him to glory, then cash in. Even if Hess lost, Bobby would win, could shop himself as a seasoned presidential campaign chief.

"Look," he told Bobby, "this campaign isn't being managed right. For Crissakes, you hired those two bozos in the press shop, the one who slapped his wife around and the other who charged us for his homo wedding. And the spending. I'm out there bleeding for every nickel—You know how many calls I gotta make, how much rubber chicken I gotta eat, just to keep the lights on? And you're pissing it away on giant-screen TVs and crab cocktail." He nodded. "I heard that on Fox."

"It's bullshit. That TV in the main room was refurbished, less than half price. I'll show you the invoice."

"We're not debating. When the manager holds out his hand, you surrender the ball."

Bobby's lip puckered again. "You know who started that BS rumor about the spending, and spread it, don't you? Pete Vankov."

Hess stepped closer, toward a photo of himself snarling into a mic, neck cords bulging, from his sports radio days shortly before he jumped to TV. "That's a strong charge, kid. You have proof?"

"Just what I heard. From a solid source. Even more reliable than Fox News, right-wing-nut radio, and that Christian rag you read."

Hess glared at Bobby the way the way he'd glared at batters crowding the plate before giving them some chin music. "You're not interested in the outfield, you can clear out your office. Today. Now."

He walked back around his desk and picked up his phone. He locked on Bobby's eyes again and waited for him to turn and leave. Then he buzzed his secretary. "Send in Vankov."

A minute later, his door flew open, no knock, and there was his press maestro. The Dark Angel. That was almost as good as The Hessian. And that outfit—He'd never seen pinstripes like that outside a gangster film or a circus tent.

"Pete, how are you, kid?" He extended his arm, angling his wrist down to protect his pitching hand against a bone-crusher grip, which Hess's size and the Hessian thing seemed to invite. Vankov's grip was firm but light. He looked into Vankov's cold hazel eyes and saw the savvy and savagery that Bobby lacked.

"I'm redrawing the lineup," he told Vankov. "You're now campaign manager. How's that sound?"

Vankov smiled broadly, the kind of gotcha grin Hess used to give batters when he was ahead in the count and could afford to throw close heat. "That sounds great, Mr. President."

5

CHARLES TOWN

Inside his new office in Hess's headquarters at the Hall of the States Building, Pete Vankov narrowed his eyes against the blinding gesso white of the sheetrock walls. The venetian blinds were drawn against a view of other wretches in similar sheetrock cubes in the other wing of the colossus.

He aimed his ears at the closed paperboard door and listened to aides scampering and shouting in Hess's suite beyond. He shook his head.

Vankov read a phone number from a memo and dialed. As he waited for the *New York Globe* reporter to pick up, his heart pounded, mouth dried, pits sweated, the whole thing. He reviewed the dossier he'd had his assistant prepare on her after he'd caught a couple of her cable-news talking-head bits. Grew up in Omaha. English major at the University of Pennsylvania, then a master's at Columbia Journalism School. A couple of small papers, then the Philadelphia Inquirer, then the *Globe*.

When she was working out of the *Globe* (Trenton) bureau, the New Jersey governor banned her from his office for what he called biased coverage. Mostly for her reporting some of the governor's offhand remarks about his challenger's wife. The paper backed her, and she kept covering the governor, right up to the point her stuff helped sink his reelection. That got her promoted to the paper's Washington bureau.

She'd been married to a Democrat consultant, a weasel Vankov had run into a few times. Word was, he cheated on her and she dumped him.

Jane Berglund. Scandinavian, probably Swedish. She looked it, cobalt eyes, fair skin, sunflower hair. Early forties, but with a youthful glow, at least on the tube, though that could be makeup. She looked tall and fit, maybe five-nine, nearly his height—he hoped she wasn't taller than he was—with a runner's body.

She didn't hype her looks, though. She parted that natural blond hair—it looked natural, anyway—in the center and let it hang straight down like a Dustbowl Oakie farmgirl, and wore simple, sensible business suits. She could use a few pounds, and it wouldn't hurt if some of them went to her rack, but still a type Vankov liked. One of several types he liked.

There was a brusqueness to her, though, and an underlying sadness. He'd seen her laugh only once on camera, and it was dazzling. If Berglund ever picked up the phone, he'd make her laugh. Maybe make her howl one day; she looked like a screamer.

Careful, Vankov warned himself. This was a tigress, not a housecat.

The line clicked. "Jane Berglund."

Vankov liked her voice, even better than it sounded on TV, now that it was directed only at him. Midwest flat with a throaty edge. He also liked that she played games. That officious "Jane Berglund," even though she had to know damn well who was on the line; she wouldn't have taken the call unless the receptionist had told her.

"Miss Berglund," he said. "Pete Vankov with the Hess campaign."

"Mr. Vankov. What's up?"

He slid his hand down the front of his pants. "Well, I'm managing Ven Hess's campaign, and I understand you're covering us, so I thought I'd introduce myself. Was hoping we could just chat for a couple of minutes, off the record."

They bantered for a while, and he let her throaty voice tickle his ear with its flat Midwest tones. She even said "pop" instead of "soda." He felt his breathing deepen and angled the phone away.

He did get a titter out of her. Then, when she was primed, he said, almost by-the-way, "You might want to look at Alec Maynard's financial disclosure report, it's due tomorrow. Specifically, at contributions from some private-equity guys and venture capitalists who are big into fossil fuels and big-box sweatshops." Maynard—Admiral Alec Maynard—was the Dem who most worried Vankov.

"Kind of hypocritical, don't you think?" Vankov asked. "Maynard hollers about climate change, fossil fuels, Wall Street, and income equality, and then, lo and behold, he's taking serious dough from guys in bed with the oil companies and Walmart."

"I'm assigned to cover Mr. Hess's campaign. I can have another reporter give you a call about Senator Maynard."

"Don't play bureaucrat, Jane—I hope you don't mind my using your first name. Your paper hasn't assigned a reporter yet to cover Maynard, or I would have called him—or her. You want to give this scoop to some general-assignment dweeb?"

"That's not how it works around here."

Silence scratched over the line until he heard her sigh. "You have names?"

Vankov grinned. "Let me see what I can nail down; I'll call you back this afternoon. Freedom and prosperity." He pulled his hand out of his pants.

He plucked a file from his new metal desk. Or new to him; the thing looked like a floor sample from an industrial supply house. He found his list of bigfoot investors and dialed a number in Chicago.

"Just wanted to give you a heads-up," he said when the guy picked up, a money man with a big portfolio who'd contributed over the years to dozens of campaigns Vankov had worked. "You're probably going to get a call this afternoon from the *New York Globe* about your donation to Alec Maynard's campaign. You just need to tell her what we discussed."

"Refresh my memory."

He sighed. He didn't want to do this over the phone again. Too many ears around, on both ends. He lowered his voice. "You just say, 'I'm in the business of American energy and I want America to have strong energy, and I give to candidates in both parties who are best for that.' Or you can make it broader and say 'sound business.' Or 'sharp finance.' Or 'good products.' Whatever."

"Guys like me, we spread our chips across the table because we want to be with the winner, you know? We want people in power to take our phone calls, and we can afford to hedge our bets, you know? Nothing wrong with that. A *Globe* reporter will understand that."

"No!" Vankov hissed. "Yes, she may understand that, but No, you don't say that. You don't say anything that even hints that you sometimes donate to a candidate you don't want to win, on a bank shot. Just stick with the script and keep it simple, will you? Please?"

It had taken him weeks to enlist donors who might get past Maynard's screen. The admiral's staff would be on alert for donations from Wall Street or Walmart execs because Maynard had made a stink that he wouldn't take Wall Street money, fossil fuel money, sweatshop money. The trick was to line up bundlers who gathered money from fossil-fuel honchos or financiers, but who wouldn't have to list an occupation on their contribution forms that set off alarms in Maynard's finance shop.

Vankov hung up and sighed. "Amateurs."

The next afternoon, Vankov rocked in a rattan chair and enjoyed the porch floorboards' groans. The air was warm and thick in Charleston, even in November, and birds warbled in lush trees. Maybe he'd come here more often. If not for a Lincoln parked by the carriage house, the view must have been the same 150 years ago. He sipped his mint julep, careful to hold the pewter cup by the top and bottom edges, the way Colonel Sanders was doing in a matching rocker. An older Black man in a Wedgewood-blue jacket and black bowtie set a tray of biscuits on a glass-topped table.

"I appreciate your coming down." Stockton even looked like Colonel Sanders, with his white mane, jowls, and paunch. All he needed was the goatee and hornrims. And he should trade that green linen jacket for a white suit, or anything else, on general principles.

"I haven't been to Charleston in ages," Vankov said. "Forgot what I was missing."

"You know, when Charleston was founded in 1670, it was located at Albemarle Point, on the Ashley River's west bank." Stockton pointed past some sycamore trees in his backyard. "It was called Charles Town then, two words. Half the Africans brought to this country arrived in Charles Town. Which was known as 'the Jerusalem of American slavery.' I've got an eighteenth-century map in my study. When we go inside, I'll show you how the city was laid out then." Stockton collected old maps for a living, a hobby, both, whatever.

"Love to see it."

"So you think this fellow Maynard can win the nomination?" Stockton's lip curled.

Vankov shrugged. "He's crafty. And he's got the resume."

Stockton scowled.

"Did you see that stink a week ago about his campaign contributions?" Vankov asked. "The *New York Globe* broke the story. Turned out Maynard was taking Wall Street and Big Oil money while he was hollering about one-percenters and climate change. He's like a lot of Democrat saints—Look close enough, you see he's running a 'do as I say, not as I do' operation."

Stockton sipped his julep and shook his head. "My father was a naval officer during World War II. On a destroyer. Back then, the Blacks were cooks and cabin boys. Now they're admirals." Stockton snorted, and the sound sent a wave of nausea through Vankov's guts, where he hadn't thought the world could still reach.

Vankov looked away so Stockton couldn't read his face. He noticed one of the column capitals had warped, near a window with wavy glass. The house probably went back before the Civil War, built by Stockton's great-grandfather's slaves.

"The fellow's wife," Stockton said. "There's a history of that kind of thing here." Meaning Maynard's wife was white.

"Claudia Maynard is a history professor at San Francisco State. She's been making more campaign appearances for her husband recently."

Stockton emptied his drink and sighed. "What's this thing called? Sisters and Sisters?"

"The Super PAC is going to be called 'Sistas for Sistas.'" Vankov let the phrase sink in, waited for Stockton's chuckle.

"Isn't this a long way around the barn? I thought you were going to find another Black to run in the Democrat primaries and siphon votes from this Maynard."

Vankov shook his head. "Too late in the cycle for that."

Stockton nodded and reached for a biscuit.

"The single most important constituency in the Democrat Party is women of color," Vankov said, trying to steady himself with the formal tone. "Black women. They vote overwhelmingly for Ds and their level of turnout can spell the margin between victory and defeat. We need to poison this group against Maynard, and soon. The Sistas for Sistas Super PAC will hammer that Alec Maynard is married to a white woman, and that he's always preferred white women." Vankov held out his hands. "But first we need to fund the PAC, with dark money—no pun intended—whose source will never be revealed."

Stockton eyed him, then grinned. "How much do you want? This is too good."

Vankov smiled back. He felt bile rising and hoped he wouldn't puke.

Stockton fished into his green jacket for a checkbook.

"Now there are some protocols here," Vankov told him. "After this conversation, we can't coordinate anymore because the Super PAC has to be independent of the Hess campaign." He paused a few beats, watched Stockton's forehead wrinkle. "You need to hire a guy named Rivers to run your Super PAC. He's a genius. I'll get you his contact info." He gave a reassuring smile.

Stockton smiled back, seemed to get it. "I respect your judgment and expertise."

Four hours after he left Colonel Sanders, Vankov was sitting in a booth in the Busy Bee Café on Martin Luther King Boulevard in Atlanta, a soul food fixture since the forties, digging into an oxtail platter. The warm, heavy air carried scents of fried meats and vegetables, and a din peppered his ears.

The oxtail had looked decent on the menu, hand trimmed beef tails, slow-cooked and smothered in gravy over white rice. He'd ordered a corn roll, what the heck. Not bad, except they'd drowned the meat in gravy. He would have preferred a gravy boat he could pour himself, but the place didn't look like it had a suggestion box.

Across the table, Georgia State Senator Laronda Tibbs was working on a plate of fried shrimp and catfish fillets and a yeast muffin. Vankov had traded his glen plaid suit for khakis and a striped oxford button-down, but he still felt obscenely white, and patrons' glances said he looked it.

"How's your food?" Laronda Tibbs asked.

"Best oxtails I've ever had." Vankov popped a morsel of corn muffin into his mouth.

Tibbs was shorter than she looked in the photos Vankov had seen, she must wear platforms, but otherwise about what he'd expected. He'd found her on the web, visiting online chat rooms and touring Facebook and Instagram gaggles looking for comments about Alec Maynard and white women. He needed a public face for the Sistas for Sistas PAC. A Black Democrat woman who was as pissed at Maynard as Colonel Sanders was for marrying a white woman, if for different reasons.

From what Vankov had gleaned online, during her senior year at Spelman College, Tibbs was offended by a male friend dating a white woman. The man opened his door one morning to find a bottle of bleach on his doorstep.

Much of the recent material on Tibbs involved her support for Fahringer, the Minnesota socialist vying with Maynard for the Democrat nomination.

Tibbs seemed to like Fahringer's pinko policies. But she also didn't want a betrayer of her race as her party's standard-bearer. "The core Democratic constituency that delivers power is African American women," Tibbs had said, "and I think we need to stand together and send a message."

Vankov had come to Atlanta to confirm that Laronda Tibbs was what he was looking for, what she might call "the real deal."

"As I was telling you on the phone," Vankov said, "I have a client who's working on a ballot initiative to legalize casino gambling in Georgia. He'd like to build a casino in Atlanta, and while I'm down here I'm trying to enlist some support. His casino would mean more jobs, good jobs, for people in the area." Some truth there. Vankov did have a client who owned casinos, and maybe someday the guy would consider trying to expand into Georgia.

Tibbs began a spiel about set-asides for minority contractors and workers.

Vankov leaned back and smiled. Laronda Tibbs was perfect.

When Vankov's plane landed at Reagan National that night, the local temperature had dipped into the forties. Well, should be a quick dash to his car; his driver should be waiting. As he was walking through the concourse, his iPhone pinged. A text from Rivers, a protégé now running Sistas for Sistas, asking him to call. He found a quiet spot by a column.

"Your friend from Atlanta is in," Rivers said.

"She give you any trouble?"

Rivers laughed. "The conversation lasted thirty seconds. I said, 'Would you like to be the public face of Sistas for Sistas?' And she said, 'Hell yeah.'"

"Freedom and prosperity." Vankov hung up and shook his head. God help him if Laronda Tibbs ever found out she was now the public face of an organization funded by Colonel Sanders.

6
CUBA LIBRE

David Gruber put the lawyer on speakerphone, then jogged over and closed his maple office door on a corridor lined with photos of DNFV partners beside presidents, senators, governors, and kings.

"You understand this is completely confidential," the lawyer, Michelson, said.

"Absolutely. I appreciate the call."

Michaelson began describing a Super PAC he'd set up for Pete Vankov, something called Sistas for Sistas. A couple of technical terms eluded Gruber. Michaelson was a legal and accounting whiz steeped in federal election law, one of a handful who did the compliance work required in modern, supposedly regulated Republican campaigns.

Gruber killed the speaker and lifted the handset to his ear. He began picking at a flap of dry, dead skin on his forefinger left by an earlier round of picking. Was this call a ruse, some Vankov jujitsu, to spin up Gruber and send him on a tangent? No, Gruber knew Michelson, who'd done work for him, for both him and Vankov over the years, often at the same time, for different clients. The guy was straight—or as straight as they came in this line of work.

Actually, Gruber knew Michaelson longer and better than Vankov did. They'd met during Gruber's stint as a white-shoe Philadelphia lawyer when Gruber was networking within the incestuous world of GOP politics in the deep-blue City of Brotherly Love, and Michelson was advising some local candidate. When Gruber moved to Washington as a Senate Judiciary Committee staffer, Michaelson took him to dinner and gave him a primer on the town.

Gruber pried at what was left of the cuticle on his ring finger as he listened. He ripped open a flap and ripped it down, shooting a pain through him. "What kind of stunt did my partner ask you to pull?"

"No, nothing. It was clean. The compliance work was straightforward—I mean, it's always arcane and complex—but this PAC is fairly basic, as they go. It's the concept of the PAC that started to bother me, so I decided to give you a call." Lawyers like Michaelson weren't supposed to say anything about the jobs, under a political omerta.

As Michaelson spewed specifics about Sistas for Sistas, Gruber studied framed photos of his daughters on his desk. Two failed marriages, each lasting ten years and producing a child, now twenty-five and seventeen. Two angels.

Finally, the lawyer finished.

"Wow," Gruber said. "Really appreciate your call. You're a patriot."

In a presidential election year, Michaelson was probably setting up dozens of PACs. And Vankov, maybe alone, had pinged his conscience enough to make him talk. The Dark Angel still had his touch.

Gruber stood beside Ezra Fitch at the Lincoln Memorial marveling at his partner's height. Six-five easy, at least an inch taller than the Great Emancipator, America's tallest president. Probably even taller twenty years ago. And close to seven feet with the homburg over Fitch's thinning hair against a gray chill and winds whipping through the marble columns.

He was surprised that Fitch had agreed to stroll to the Mall when they left a client meeting at the nearby Watergate.

"Lincoln is nineteen feet high, seated," Gruber said. "Awesome—literally."

"Okay, David, what's on your mind?"

Gruber took a deep breath. "The firm needs to sever ties with Pete Vankov before we go down with him. We need to make it crystal clear that DNFV and its partners are not on the Hess train. We need to preemptively avoid liability for what we both know is coming, Vankov doing worse and worse stuff to get this . . . cretin elected."

"What do the others say?"

"You're my first meeting."

"And your mind's made up, eh?"

Gruber nodded.

"So you've started with me, not that you want advice, but you think I'm low-hanging fruit, eh?"

"I think you're a reasonable man who wants to do the right thing."

Fitch smiled.

"I'm going to talk to the other partners, in turn." From easiest to toughest.

"And then?"

"When I have the numbers, I'll call for a vote." Gruber stepped back to reduce the angle he had to look up at Fitch. "Even Vankov's most loyal friends have no emotional bond to Hess, can't actually think Hess should be president. They're just calculating interest, handicapping Hess's odds of winning and what his victory would mean to them and their entities." He shrugged. "I can shift their calculus."

Fitch flexed his jaw.

Gruber gazed up at Lincoln. "I was raised to believe that patriotism means more than waving the flag. My grandparents fled Russia and Ukraine, had a little shrine to FDR in the sole hallway of their small apartment. My father fought in World War II as a grunt—he'd quit school in eleventh grade—and made a career as an Army civil servant. My older brother was also a grunt, in Vietnam. He's now a DOD senior civilian employee at the Pentagon—incredibly bright, though; I think he settled for less than his talent allowed. We've stayed close, my brother and I, 'twins separated by eleven years,' despite judging each other to have made poor life choices. I still ask myself at moral crossroads, 'What would Jake do?' That's what I've been asking myself all week."

He met Fitch's eyes. "It should be relatively clean. Vankov's already on leave of absence, working full time for Hess."

"A vote, even if you lose, would weaken Pete," Fitch said. "Make a statement that his partners think he's unstable, eh?"

Gruber nodded. "I'm playing offense and defense at the same time."

"That's a high price for the firm to pay." Fitch gazed at Lincoln, maybe figuring odds. Could they stop Vankov and Hess? How badly would the firm suffer if they made a stand, but Hess got elected? What would befall the traitors if Hess won the crown, with Vankov the most powerful and influential minister at the new king's court?

"Inertia also carries risks, Ezra. Hess needs to be stopped or he will win the GOP nomination and maybe the presidency. Where would that leave the firm?"

"Ven Hess has connected with Middle America. He's become the voice of guys who go to baseball games—white, older, socially conservative. People resentful of where they stand in the pecking order. People wrapped in a culture war. People you understand abstractly but have a tough time connecting with, eh? Ven Hess is a hurtling freight train, and you're asking me to hold hands and jump in front of it."

"I'm not proposing suicide; I'm outlining a practical, strategic effort to stop the train." Gruber scratched his brow. "Though the odds are admittedly poor."

Fitch cocked his head. "This is a bigger risk for you than for me. I'm pushing seventy, and I've made my bundle; I can walk away without too many regrets. But you're still a wunderkind on the way up—and able to attract clients and charge accordingly. You lose that, you'll never get it back. You see the looks Nicole Kidman gets these days? Not the same looks she got when she made Eyes Wide Shut."

Gruber nodded. "If this doesn't work out, I'll be like Zero Mostel in *The Producers*, 'Do you know who I used to be?'"

They both smiled.

"I need to move ahead on this, Ezra. Do I have your vote?"

Fitch looked past Gruber, maybe at the engraved text behind Lincoln: "In this temple, as in the hearts of the people for whom he saved the union, the memory of Abraham Lincoln is enshrined forever." He sighed. "Yeah."

Two days later, Gruber welcomed Bob Snead, a junior partner, into his office for his final meeting. Gruber gestured at a leather nail-headed chair in front of his desk. Snead eased into the chair like a cowboy onto a bull in a chute. Snead looked a little like the cowboys Gruber had seen in bull-riding contests during late-night channel surfing. Rangy and sinewy, with thick brown hair and an outdoorsy complexion, though in Snead's case the body came from a downtown gym and the tan from a Caribbean beach or a Connecticut Avenue bronzing salon.

"Crazy weather, huh?" Gruber said. "One day it's winter, next day it's fall or even summer." Washington was forecast to hit seventy that afternoon, in late November. The central air was off, and his office felt stuffy.

Snead plucked the framed photo of Gruber's eldest daughter from the desk and leered.

Gruber felt himself tighten. "I'm going to move to expel Pete Vankov from the firm, and I'd like your vote."

Snead smiled, more a smirk. Which said he'd known what was coming, thanks for letting him score points with Vankov and Hess by demurring.

"You may get some short-term gain, but you'll have long-term pain."

Snead shrugged.

"You're joining the jackals. At some point, this is going to blow up. Corruption is going to get exposed, along with all sorts of improprieties and plain old incompetence. And that toxic brew is going to become part of your brand."

Snead just gave another shrug. Was he recording their talk on his iPhone under his glen plaid suit, to turn over to Vankov? Was that why he was saying so little, letting Gruber prattle and threaten?

"If that's your calculation, I want to make $10 million in the next four years and go buy an island and go away, okay." Gruber continued. "But if your idea is you want to make $10 million a year for the next twenty years, your strategy ain't gonna work."

Snead smirked again. "We see things differently."

Gruber felt blood pounding in his neck. He snatched his daughter's photo from Snead's hand. "Let me try another tack. Ezra Fitch is already with me, and so are Drayton and Nesbit, and all but two of the other partners. I saved you for last because I knew you were going to be a pill. But you're outvoted. So don't fuck with me."

Snead's jaw shifted as though weighing a response.

Gruber stood, stepped to his door, and held it open.

Snead popped out of the chair like a bronco buster after a long ride, adjusted his lapels, and sauntered out.

Gruber arrived early at the Cuban café in the heart of Miami's Little Havana so he could settle before Vankov arrived. He also wanted to scout the place, since Vankov had picked the venue. That had been Vankov's prerogative, Gruber supposed, like the man challenged to a duel getting the choice of weapons. Gruber had forgotten how warm and humid Miami could get, even in late November. He thought about loosening his tie or taking off his jacket, but didn't want to show any discomfort, any weakness, like a football lineman wearing short sleeves in December.

He shifted in a metal chair on the patio until he found a position that didn't press his spine. He began to pick absently at a finger but caught himself before he did much damage. He ordered a Cuba Libre and took a few slow, deep breaths. From his bag, he pulled a thick file folder with "P. V." printed in red on the tab and set it on the table by his water glass, angled so Vankov would be able to read it.

Gruber studied the menu as he waited. He thought back to first meeting

Vankov, when Gruber was on Senate Appropriations staff. By then, he'd seen—and coveted—the lifestyle of top Washington lobbyists and political consultants. Vankov had hired him for a campaign. How young and green Gruber had been, how thrilled at a chance to learn from a grandmaster.

Noon came, then five past, and still Vankov hadn't shown. Gruber walked into the dining room. He was sure Vankov had said the patio, but who knew with him? Old's Havana Cuban Bar and Cocina was a tribute to pre-Castro Havana. Black-and-white photos covered the walls amid vintage memorabilia. A rumba popped from a soundtrack. The place was filling, a mix of locals and tourists. But no Vankov. Gruber went back to the patio.

He was debating between a dressed-up pork sandwich and a grilled fish entrée when a shadow crossed the table. He looked up to see Vankov, resplendent in a beige linen sportscoat over an open blue button-down.

Gruber stood, partly courtesy, partly to look down on Vankov. Gruber stood six feet, hardly towering, but he knew Vankov was self-conscious about his height, and even a couple of additional inches gave him an edge. He braced for Vankov's crushing handshake.

The Dark Angel settled into a chair across the table and reached into his bag, a black leather thing with long straps, like a designer shopping bag. He fished out a blue file folder, nearly as thick as Gruber's folder, and set it unopened beside his own water glass.

Gruber smiled. He'd forgotten that he'd learned the file ploy from Vankov. Still, he couldn't help wondering what Vankov had in that blue file, which bothered him, because that was the point of the ploy. Maybe just blank pages or a prospectus on rat poison. No, Vankov probably had something on him. The Dark Angel had probably been collecting tidbits on him for years, anticipating a moment like this. That was Vankov's MO. He didn't concoct attacks out of the ether; he built from a germ of guilt or impropriety.

A waiter swept by and Vankov ordered a Classic Mojito. Gruber nodded for another Cuba Libre. The waiter, a young guy with slicked-back hair, gave a dimpled smile and sauntered off. The guy must slay the middle-aged women tourists.

"Dave, Dave," Vankov said, shaking his head. "What are you doing?"

Gruber drained the rest of his first Cuba Libre. "You're out, Pete," he said, and realized he'd lifted the line from *The Godfather Part II*, Michael to Tom Hagen, one of Vankov's favorite films.

"Maybe you have the votes, maybe you don't," Vankov said, and waved away whatever assurance Gruber might offer. "But you're sure you want to go this route?"

"Meaning what? You'll ruin the sandbox if the other boys chase you out? You'll sue the firm and tie us up in ten years of litigation?" He angled his head at Vankov's blue folder. "You'll run dirty tricks on me, Fitch, and the other partners and blow it all up?"

Vankov scowled.

"I do have the votes, Pete. But you already know that. That's not what I wanted to tell you." Gruber gave a theatrical look at his own folder.

The waiter returned with their drinks. "Gentlemen, are you ready to order?" A sensuous voice, light accent.

Vankov gave the waiter his own easy smile. Glancing at the menu, he ordered a small Potaje de Frijoles Negros—black bean soup—and Tasajo Criollo. Salt dried beef with Criolla sauce, peppers and onions. The entrée had intrigued Gruber on the menu, and now he found his mouth watering. But he wouldn't ape Vankov's order.

Gruber looked at the menu to check the name of the fish and gave it his best accent from eighth-grade Spanish: Filete de Pascado al Grill: Grilled fresh white fish fillet, topped with butter, lemon, white onion, and parsley. "No appetizer."

"Excellent," the waiter said and strode off.

Gruber waved a hand at their dueling file folders. "We're looking at 'Mutual Assured Destruction.' We each have enough firepower to blow the other out of the water. Ten times over with the ammo I've got. That's the detente that kept the Cold War from erupting."

Vankov sipped his drink, and the waiter swept by with his soup. Gruber wished some of the firm's staff had that sense of urgency.

"The best we can do is go our separate ways and avoid a nuclear war," Gruber continued.

Vankov spooned some bean soup. "They know to put the full dose of salt in for me. They serve it bland for some of the tourists, porkers and winos in 1950s plaid who watch their sodium."

Gruber sipped his fresh drink. The rum and Coke mix was too sweet, drilling a molar.

"Dave, how many times, when we were working together, did you see some sweaty-palmed, pencil-neck asshole try to strong-arm me? You ever see one of them of get over on me?"

"They didn't have what I have." Gruber glanced again at his folder.

Vankov smiled and looked at his watch. He pushed his soup aside, lifted his folder, still unopened, held it aloft a few beats, and slid in back into his leather tote. "I've got to run. Take care of the check, would you? Freedom and prosperity."

7

SQUASH

You've got to break this old bastard," Pete Vankov told himself as he followed Ezra Fitch onto the court at the Capitol Hill Squash Club. "Or in a couple of days he's going to break you."

Fitch was point man on Gruber's weasel move to oust Vankov from the firm—Did Fitch really think Vankov wouldn't figure that out? They wanted to oust Vankov from the firm with his name on it—not Gruber's—that Vankov had built and put on the map, at least as much as the old man, or any of them.

Did Fitch really think they could load up and shoot Vankov in the back and that he wouldn't see it coming or do anything about it? Anyone who let himself get bushwhacked like that deserved to have his head on a pike. Did they really think that was Pete Vankov? It was insulting, not just unfair, the more he thought about it.

Vankov was full of rage, but took a deep breath. Calm. You played best when you were dispassionate, loose. You play angry and tight, you flail and miss and burn yourself out. He'd learned that on the high school wrestling mat.

"Usual stakes, Ezra?" Vankov asked as he set down his Tecnifibre squash bag. "Winner buys drinks afterward?"

"Sure."

Changing Fitch's vote—those were the real stakes—would make all the difference. Gruber had lined up four partners, including himself and Fitch, to vote Vankov out. Vankov had only two to oppose—Bob Snead and himself, if they'd even let him vote. Snead was a sweaty-palmed asshole, and his vote would cost Vankov, but it was worth it. Shifting one aye to a nay would make the vote a tie among the six partners, and a tie went to the runner, as Ven Hess might say. A tie would mean no action, no eviction from the firm.

Fitch didn't look like much mincing onto the court, his long frame bent with age, his legs gaunt and stringy, making his knee joints look swollen, like a diseased caribou. His hair looked grayer and thinner. These old guys never let go of their glory days, though, like the Springsteen song. Fitch's white "DC Open 1998" shirt with a tournament number on the back had holes under an arm and on the gut, the thing now hanging on Fitch's shriveled frame. Did the old man think that rag intimidated Vankov? He felt the rage stir.

This was Vankov's court, his favorite at the club, his club. This was the court he liked to use in early mornings after sleepless nights to burn off tension, to smack balls around and place them just so, to sharpen his game and his mind. With less muscle now after the pinched nerve, he'd shifted his game and his approach from power to finesse.

He could probably skunk Fitch, take three games straight in their best-of-five match, maybe hold the old man to a few points per game. But that wasn't the humiliation Vankov was after. He'd torture the old bastard, run him around the court until he dropped. Vankov could go hard for the forty-five minutes they'd rented the court. Easy, at these stakes. His wrestling coach's adage echoed in his head, that once you grab hold of an opponent's leg, you own it, and you should rip it out and beat him to death with the bloody stump.

Vankov reached into his bag and pulled out a Dunlop Yellow Dot box. He made a show of opening the box and tossing the ball to Fitch, like a card shark letting his opponent cut a new deck.

Fitch had wanted to play hardball, on a smaller court with a faster ball, demanding less running around. Nothing doing, Vankov had said; hardball went out in the 80s, along with ghetto blasters. They'd play International Softball, which is what players played. Now Vankov watched the old man bounce the softball, trying to get used to it, and hid a grin.

Vankov pulled his Tecnifibre Carboflex Airshaft racket from his bag, unsheathing it like a blade. Fitch had a decent weapon, a Dunlop Precision Pro. Smart racket for a placement game. Which was fine; no glory in gunning down an unarmed opponent.

Fitch began volleying against the wall, warming up the ball and limbering his old bones. Vankov stepped over and joined, the two of them enjoying the squash equivalent of a game of catch.

As the old man loosened, Vankov could see the player he'd once been. The Oakley goggles gave Fitch an athletic air, aided by his height. Guys six and a half feet tall naturally looked like athletes, which had always bothered Vankov, an unfair, unearned presumption.

Vankov adjusted his Boast microfiber shirt, part of his performance whites that would wick away sweat. Another advantage. He flexed his feet in his Salming squash shoes and glared at Fitch's scuffed New Balances. Jesus.

The match began the way Vankov had planned. The older man hogged the T in the center of the court, which let him reach most shots, especially with that long arm—the limb extended like an orangutan arm—and that long stride. Fine. Vankov ran him across the court, relentlessly, on the diagonal from back corner to front corner, keeping the ball in play so Fitch was always running. Vankov peppered shots into the back of the court that Fitch could reach but couldn't do much with, couldn't make his old man drop shots or reverse corners, just had to keep the ball in play with lobs that Vankov smacked, sending Fitch running to the other corner. Following that old squash precept: "If they're behind, hit in front of them; if in front, hit it behind."

In ten minutes, the old man's mouth was hanging open. In fifteen minutes, his ratty old shirt was plastered to his concave chest, a thatch of chest hair showing through, pink flesh glistening through a hole.

Fitch began calling lets, chickenshit moves, pansy moves, claiming Vankov had blocked his path to shots, that he deserved the points. Vankov let him get away with the first one, playing the gentleman, hoping it wouldn't become a pattern, but it did.

"Come on, Ezra," Vankov said the second time Fitch called a let. "You never could have gotten that."

Soon, Vankov was arguing, "I cleared that shot" or "I gave you a direct line to the ball." Meanwhile, Fitch was doubled over, catching his breath.

Which steamed Vankov all the more. Fitch carried himself like an aristocrat, an honorable man in a shady profession. Ezra Fitch, senior partner, tall and straight and fair, you can trust him, looked like a seven-foot mandarin with a stick up his ass. But Fitch played to win like anyone else, even if he had to resort to pansy chickenshit now that he was old. Except that Fitch wouldn't admit he was playing pansy chickenshit, would play the victim. That was the difference between them. Vankov would tell you politics wasn't beanbag, don't be a weenie, but he wouldn't defend his moves with moral relativism bunk, he didn't try to have it both ways. He did what he did, and he got results, no apologies. Yeah, he'd deny everything if he got caught, but that was just theater, tactics.

The old man hogged the T to give himself maximum latitude and minimal work. That was Fitch's approach on the squash court, in the office, and in life.

"Come on, Ezra," Vankov cried, after Fitch called yet another let. "Play the damned game."

"I am playing the game. You should try it."

Vankov got an idea. He'd hog the T, just for a while, to bump Fitch from his comfort zone, and to take a quick breather himself. He was getting more winded than he'd expected. He hadn't been sleeping well for a week, since learning about Gruber's play to oust him.

He'd sensed that Gruber was up to something, seen it in Gruber's smarmy grin. So he'd given Gruber's young admin fifty grand—more than half a year's pay—for Gruber's passwords, then monitored Gruber's email. He'd even installed keystroke copying spyware on Gruber's devices so he could watch everything Gruber did.

Could he have saved the money and just bent Gruber's aide over the conference room sofa? She wasn't much to look at and might have considered it a bargain. Well, it had paid off. He'd not only learned of Gruber's move against him, but he'd found some exquisite gouge digging through Gruber's email archives.

Vankov had learned that Gruber had an "arrangement" with a young woman who worked as a curator at the National Museum of Natural History and was paying for her Woodley Park condo as a corporate expense of the firm. Since the money was available to Gruber under DNFV's "eat what you kill" compensation distribution formula, Gruber wasn't cheating his partners. But he was cheating on his taxes and exposing the firm to audit scrutiny it couldn't survive. And, of course, puncturing Ezra Fitch's aura of rectitude.

Vankov was looking forward to wiping the luster off Fitch's protégé—who had once been his own protégé. In time. Meanwhile, Vankov was having fun hogging the T. Fitch was so predictable, it was easy. He could anticipate the old man, knew when a rail shot was coming, and could slide over in plenty of time.

Vankov had just smacked back the fourth or fifth rail shot when he angled to watch Fitch's return, just in time to see a follow-through that sent the ball flying right at him. He lunged, but not in time. The ball thudded into his kidney, sending a stabbing pain through him and down his prick as though he were pissing Tabasco. His whole body pulsed and tightened. The ball dribbled in front of him.

Fitch was beside him now, looking down, offering regrets, but arguing something else. The old bastard wanted the point. Fitch was saying that any ball going to the front wall that hit an opponent was a point. The stones on the old goat.

"Are you out of your mind?" Vankov said, the vibration from his voice scraping through his prick. "I was clear, I wasn't in your shot."

"No, you were crowding me. You shouldn't be that far up."

They went around for a while, and Vankov saw Fitch was defending his honor, didn't want the shame of hitting an opponent, even if he'd done it intentionally. Of course it had been intentional; the old man played a placement game.

"Okay," Vankov said. "Your point."

Vankov moved back, gave Fitch the T, went back to running the bastard from corner to corner, no mercy this time, bam, bam, smacks of the ball interspersed with slaps of the ratty old New Balance shoes. Bam, bam, bam. No time between serves. No pretense, no perfunctory "good shot," or "good lay," or "nice drop" if Fitch made a decent play.

As they passed half an hour on the court, time winding down, the old man huffed as he lumbered. He looked like he might ask for a break or worse, concede. Vankov was ahead 5–1 in the fifth game, the tie breaker.

Vankov waited a couple of points, until he was up 7–1. Four more points and he'd win the game and the match, but the torture would end, and Fitch would escape. Now or never.

Vankov was back in the court retrieving. Fitch, on the T, was sliding over to cover a ball he was anticipating would go back down the rail. Vankov waited for Fitch to turn his head to watch Vankov's shot.

Vankov smacked the ball, sending it six feet up. Right into Ezra Fitch's mouth.

Fitch's goggles flew off, and red spittle splattered the wall. The old man crumpled, holding his face.

Vankov watched Fitch settle on a locker room bench after a shower, the old man's gray hair looking even thinner, like baby-rat fuzz. He waited until Fitch tossed his bloody towel on the carpet and stared at it in horror.

"Look, Ezra, I feel terrible." Vankov stepped closer.

Fitch glared at him with narrow gray eyes.

"You get through to your dentist?"

"I'm heading over as soon as I get dressed." Fitch sounded as though he had marbles in his mouth.

"Well, that's great."

But Fitch just sat there on the bench breathing hard, occasionally shifting his damaged maw, not even putting a T-shirt over that concave chest with the graying hairs around the sagging nipples.

Vankov loomed over him. Showed that big old bastard what it felt like to be looked down on. Vankov shifted his file folder from one hand to the other, noticed a salsa stain from the Miami Cuban café.

"Great game, Ezra, until the end. Sorry I beat the crap out of you. We have to talk a minute."

Vankov opened the folder as Fitch looked up. He pulled out a crisp sheet and handed it to the old man. A printout of a Gruber email to his archaeologist mistress.

Fitch gazed at Vankov, at the page, and back at Vankov, like a driver's ed student before proceeding through a hairy intersection. Finally, he took the page and began reading.

"I'm not going to tell you how I got this, and it's best for you not to know," Vankov said. "But trust me, it's authentic. And if I need to prove that to the world, I can."

Fitch gazed at the page.

"Ezra, no need for this to go any wider. I don't want to publicize this scandal; my name's on the masthead, same as yours. I don't want to ruin Gruber, though he deserves a good spanking. I don't even want to circulate this more widely in the firm."

The old man's face tightened, even the damaged mouth. Finally, Fitch shook his head. "Oh, David."

"Disappointed?"

Fitch looked up. "Not in you, Peter. You've behaved as I've come to expect."

Vankov laughed. "Yeah. Well, I'm used to that. I've been getting my whole life from country club Republican pricks who sneer at me like I'm shit on your shoes.

"When you brought me on at the firm, you figured you were making a deal with the devil, but you could keep yourself out of the fire, keep your own clients above reproach, keep your silo clean. You'd get my ferocity, creativity, determination to win, but not my darker aspects.

"I told you what you wanted to hear, sold you that I sometimes went up to the line but never over it. And you accepted 'up-to-the line,' even if you didn't play that way. You convinced yourself that there actually is a line, and that I'd stay microscopically on the right side of it."

Vankov shook his head. "The thing is, you're greedy, which is why you took the risk on me in the first place. For decades now, you've been looking away when you saw me cross whatever lines you thought we'd agreed not to cross. You'd stuff yourself with caviar and Champagne and enjoy the spoils I brought in—money, power, influence, headlines—in the ways you didn't want to know."

Vankov wagged his finger. "But if you're good at this type of arrangement—and you are good, Ezra—you recalibrate periodically. And now you've been recalibrating. It must have seemed a gift from Heaven, Gruber's weasel play to vote me out, and you leaped to sign on; let somebody else do the dirty work. Well, you've made a mistake you can't recalibrate." Vankov flicked the email printout with his finger.

Fitch kept gazing at the email.

"What bothers you more, your boy's moral judgment or his sloppiness, letting me get over on him to put you in this spot?"

Fitch glared up at Vankov, eyes even narrower.

"Ezra," Vankov began, but the old man raised a long arm, stilling him.

"You've made your point." Now Fitch's words sounded as though they were passing through water. "I need you to give me a couple of days to go to David and see where we are."

Vankov smiled. "Two days." He adjusted the knot of his tie, a lustrous woven foulard he'd picked up on Savile Row, pressing the dimple just so. "Freedom and prosperity."

He left the old man on the bench with his hairy, concave chest and his bloody towel and the email printout.

As Vankov strode out of the locker room, he felt rage brewing again.

Was Gruber going to go nuclear, trigger Mutual Assured Destruction? Over what? Vankov's move to maintain the status quo?

That was the whole point of MAD, that you didn't shake things up. Even if Gruber thought Vankov's embrace of Hess was akin to Khrushchev's building and arming missile silos in Cuba, you don't tell the Russians to pack up their nukes and go home without offering something in return—not that Gruber had anything Vankov wanted that badly. JFK anted up, publicly promising not to invade Cuba again and secretly agreeing to dismantle US nukes in Europe. Come on, Dave. At least put something on the table. You think you can get over on me, and for free? Think again.

Vankov stormed through the club door into a sunny afternoon.

8
OLGA

The miniature donkey, adorable with its big brown eyes, long mane, and lustrous gray coat, leaned down to nuzzle a nugget of manure. As the animal began nibbling the turd, Jane Berglund turned away, though the smell was inescapable.

The Kids' Farm at the National Zoo was a shrewd place to meet, Berglund supposed. The area, at the zoo's eastern end, was nearly deserted on a crisp November morning. Though Berglund wondered how natural she and Olga looked, two thirty-something women in business attire strolling the hay strewn paths ogling goats, llamas, and miniature donkeys.

Berglund waited for Olga to continue. But the woman kept studying her, like a cop or a shrink. Olga. That was the only name the woman had given her, and Berglund assumed it was an alias. A nom de guerre, maybe, in this case.

A lion roared in the distance, and the mini donkeys stiffened, the white one taking a couple of stiff-legged steps back. Berglund could feel the presence of wild beasts, setting off alarms in her brain's primitive recesses.

Berglund crossed her arms. The gesture was textbook nerves, defensive posture, something she watched for in others. She gave Olga a silent salute for putting her on defense in a contest in which Berglund had most of the advantages.

"You did a fine job on that financial story," Olga said. "The campaign contributions to the senator. That is why I phoned you."

She nodded, wanted to say her *Globe* colleagues hadn't been as enthusiastic. The only Truth some reporters knew, or cared about, was that Alec Maynard must defeat Venn Hess for the White House.

"You have talent for looking under the covers." Olga's eye narrowed, almost a wink. "With Peter Vankov—We will call him "V"— you will find plenty. I'll point you in the right directions."

Finally, Olga began her tale. Berglund nodded occasionally, not agreeing, merely acknowledging. She focused on Olga; the recorder in her jacket pocket would catch the words. Washington DC had "one-party consent," though Berglund normally told sources when she was taping them.

Olga had a face and figure akin to a Hollywood starlet, Scarlett Johansson perhaps, but how much work had she undergone? Olga seemed the type to strap a derringer inside her garter belt and wedge a stiletto in her panties. And maybe a knifed-edge credit card in her wallet; Berglund had met a CIA operative who'd had one of those. Berglund wondered what kind of childhood would turn a little girl into a political honeytrap. With Olga's accent, maybe she was the rebellious East German daughter of a former Nazi youth.

"They groom each other," Olga said, pointing at one donkey nuzzling another's wither. "They are both jacks. Males. But they have none of the hang-ups that so inhibit most men."

Berglund shrugged.

"V breaks his promises, fails to honor his contract, and then threatens you if you dare complain." Olga spat the words, emotion inflecting her voice for the first time. Her accent, usually faint, also thickened. Eastern European? French?

"Threaten you how?"

Olga smiled. "He owes me a 'performance bonus.'" Her voice was calm again. "Six figures. I did what he asked." She paused, as though weighing her words. "I 'got close' to the Argentinian opposition leader and extracted from him useful information." She eyed Berglund. "Well, useful information about him. His preferences in bed. He is creative and . . . unconventional." She shrugged. "Recorded by an Israeli Mossad man who went with me."

Berglund gave another reporter's nod.

"I asked for what I was entitled to, what I had earned. Perhaps the phrase 'I demanded' is more precise. If you let others walk all over you, you get known as a doormat, which is not good for business, either. V refused to pay. He told me he'd ruin my reputation, paint me as a whore, if I persisted."

Now Olga reached into her handbag, and Berglund anticipated a photo or document or some other evidence. Instead, Olga produced a pack of Dunhill cigarettes.

"No smoking here," Berglund said. She was glad not to have to breathe the toxins, but also glad to see that Olga was also nervous, reaching for a sedative.

Olga put the smokes back in her bag and closed the cinch with a snap. Her lush lips spread into a gleeful grin. "Look, the fat one is mounting the other."

Berglund turned to see the gray mini donkey with its forelegs propped on the brown one's back, swiveling around behind him. "They're both male?"

Olga laughed, more a titter. "Yes. Does that bother you? They are not homosexual, not really. It's a dominance thing."

Berglund nodded. Well, that's why call them animals.

"You should do something with your hair." Olga was studying her. "You wear it like a girl, not a woman. And your clothes. They shout, 'Stay away.' Beauty is a gift from God. You should not hide it." Olga squinted at her. "Do you try to avoid men, to deliberately make yourself unattractive to them? Well, less attractive? You are still an attractive woman. Anyone can see that."

Jesus, is she hitting on me? And what was wrong with her clothes? A simple tweed jacket over an oxford blouse. Classic, professional. Some jewelry might have softened her vibe, but she didn't like objects hanging from her body or affixed to it, another reason she'd been glad to shuck her wedding ring. She varnished her nails, gave them a gloss she'd always considered femme. Maybe not to Olga, with her red lacquered claws.

She disliked Olga. Who was eyeing her again and seemed about to speak. Berglund stilled her with a raised hand. "Let's stick to the subject."

Olga mock-recoiled, followed by a smile, her perfect lips parting moist and full, showing even white teeth. "You are quiet, for a reporter."

Berglund shrugged again. "Better to remain silent and be thought a fool than to speak and remove all doubt." A line her father had quoted to her repeatedly during her teen years.

Olga cocked her head. "You should call one of V's partners at his firm. David Gruber." She spelled it.

The "V" shorthand was beginning to bother her. A Comic book *Cloak and Dagger*, like the horny little donkeys. Berglund didn't pull out a notebook to write down the name. Let Olga think she had a stellar memory or wasn't interested enough to bother. The tape recorder would catch it.

"He was V's helper on the Argentina account."

Berglund shifted her weight and waited.

"Argentina was V's account, but he needed Gruber to get Argentine wine tariffs reduced in Congress, do other journeyman work." Olga's tone was brusque now. "We had team meetings, what they called 'an open line of communication.' Gruber was at those meetings and knows all about this. You find this interesting?"

"Sure. But this Gruber doesn't seem a very promising lead. I might as well call Van—call 'V'—as call his partner, who'd tip him off. And why should I expect a straight story, or any story, from this Gruber, if he was involved in the same seedy Argentine arrangement?"

"V and Gruber used to be very close but are having a falling-out. I hear it is very messy."

She eyed Olga. "Where are you from?"

"I am a citizen of the world."

Berglund nodded. About what she'd expected.

"Gruber knows much about V. Maybe you need only ask him. Ask him about V's Mideast dealings. About some sheiks buying at least one of V's homes for him, hiding the purchases through a series of opaque transactions. Ask him these things." Olga gave another moist smile.

"Look," Berglund said, pointing at the gray donkey, who'd gone back to nuzzling turds. "Lunchtime." She angled toward the walkway back to Connecticut Avenue. "I'll be in touch."

9
STRIKE PRICE

Ezra Fitch's assistant buzzed David Gruber on the intercom to say that Mr. Fitch would like to see him in his office, promptly. The way she threw the final word—"Prompt-lay," in the British accent she clung to—echoed with foreboding. Amplified by the early hour, just after nine. Fitch rarely arrived before ten anymore.

Gruber walked a long corridor lined with jumbo shots of iconic Washington, the Lincoln Memorial and the Washington Monument displayed like so many trophies. By the time he knocked on Fitch's door, coppery film coated his mouth. Fitch's office always made him feel as though he were reporting to the British governor of the Virginia commonwealth. Mahogany paneling covered the walls, highlighted by seascapes and oil portraits of Fitch's blueblood forebears, all framed in ornate gold. An exquisite crimson Isfahan rug covered the floor, leaving only a surrounding strip of underlying institutional beige carpet to betray that they were in a 1980s K Street concrete-and-glass box.

Fitch was sitting in a leather throne behind a massive pedestal desk. He didn't come around or even stand to extend a hand. He just motioned at a leather chair in front of his desk.

Gruber sat, edging forward. Closer now, he saw a swelling and purple discoloration around Fitch's mouth, with a nasty line of crusted blood cutting across Fitch's lower lip. He was going to ask what the other guy looked like when Fitch reached into a leather tray, plucked out a crisp sheet of paper, and sailed it across the big desk at him.

"Mr. Vankov gave me this," Fitch said, and leaned back in his throne. The words came out distorted, as though Fitch had lost his teeth.

Gruber was still studying the heading, one of his own emails to his mistress, a pulse pounding in his head, when Fitch leaned toward him.

"What the hell are you doing?" Fitch raised his large hand. "Hey, I don't care who you screw or how you pay for it, as long as it's not on me, eh? I don't care about your personal life, but I do care about your effectiveness. I care about potential embarrassment to the firm and to me. And I care that Vankov apparently can get over on you."

A hot fizz climbed Gruber's neck and settled in his head. He began reading the email, which went into details about the condo he was bankrolling for the woman. Foolish to put it in writing, maybe, but how had Vankov gotten his email?

"I'm really disappointed, David, that you put me and the firm in this spot."

The fizz in his head boiled, as it had a few years earlier when his brother chided him for behaving like a "middle-aged frat boy," a lifestyle his partners boasted about.

Gruber's arms began thrumming. He'd threatened Vankov with mutual assured destruction, and the Dark Angel had fired anyway. Should Gruber follow through, dump what he had on Vankov? Right now, right here across this mammoth desk, tell it all to the senior partner? You issue an ultimatum, you have to back it up. But Fitch didn't look like he was in a listening mood. No, Gruber would get back to his office, close the door, and think. And change his passwords and find the leak; no point firing a shot that Vankov would see coming.

"The reality is," Fitch was saying, "given this information, I'm not going to stand with you in a pyrrhic effort to get rid of Pete Vankov."

Tomorrow's vote. Another hot fizz flared in Gruber's throat. "Ezra, it's not a pyrrhic effort. If you consider the damage Vankov has already done—and the far greater damage he's going to do—from inside. For Crissakes, he's running a hostile takeover of the GOP by a huckster so unfit for the presidency that he'll make Nixon, my childhood bogeyman, seem mild by comparison." He took a deep breath. " I'll take the heat for my . . . indiscretion. But without your aye, the vote is a tie, a loss, a fiasco."

"We'll keep him behind a firewall, eh? But we're not going to jigger the equity when he can bring the house down."

Gruber listened to his own shallow breathing. "Okay," he finally said. "I won't call for the vote tomorrow."

"I'm going to cancel this item from the agenda. Anybody has a question, he can take it up with me."

Gruber folded the email printout and slowly tucked the page into his jacket pocket. He stood and padded across the Isfahan rug and out of Ezra Fitch's office.

Two days later, Gruber strode into Rasika West End, a choice Indian place on M Street only a few blocks from DNFV's offices, and found Brett, a Christmas-card friend from their days together at the Senate Appropriations Committee, already waiting at a table toward the back. The section was quiet and discreet, dark tapestries and white linen, even a bookshelf. Brett was now CFO of a high-tech national startup that offered educational content by subscription.

They told each other how good they looked, how they hadn't aged a day.

"I was surprised to get your call," Brett said. "Last time we talked, your 'No' seemed Sherman-esque."

"You ever see those letters in your college alumni weekly—I assume Dartmouth has them, like Penn—from some guy in his fifties or sixties who says that after his second heart attack or his third bleeding ulcer, he finally had a chance to think and saw that he was living all wrong? They always end the same way—he's now in bliss, running a charter fishing boat in Outer Tubthump or a community vegetable garden in Hicksville." Gruber smiled. "I don't want to take it quite that far, but I figured maybe it's time for a move." He reached for his water glass. "And I like what your company does. Seems noble. So I thought I'd give you a call."

Brett nodded. "Well, your timing is terrific. We need to fill the government relations gig, and they might even go Executive VP, though I can't promise that. But Senior VP with basically the same package?" He shrugged as if to ask, What's the difference?

They ordered two courses, and the appetizers soon arrived.

Gruber sliced into some kuri kuri lamb, basically a shish kabab swathed in dough with a chili pickle, one of his favorite starters. Brett was gazing at him, still with that faint grin playing, and Gruber let himself enjoy being coveted.

"On the content end, we signed two more contracts this month with universities and one with a think tank for exclusive access to lectures and speeches." Brett sounded as though he were cutting a radio ad. "On the delivery end, we grew our subs ten percent this quarter—that's both institutional and individual subscribers. While we work mainly online, we're also partnering with TV, radio, and satellite networks to deliver in home and car, both video and audio."

Gruber nodded.

Brett began pitching the stock options Gruber would get. "You come aboard now, your strike price is peanuts."

Gruber laughed. "Yeah, Brett, but that's because you guys are on financial life support—no offense. From what I understand, you didn't hit your subscriber and revenue growth, missed your break-even date, and the market is pounding you. And you're in austerity."

"That's a temporary situation—We're sorting out the funding now. But it's part of the reason we're moving hard to fill the government relations spot."

"Okay. But here's my concern: With your stock price tanking, it seems only a matter of time until somebody scoops you up. I wouldn't want to come aboard only to be tossed out a few weeks later by new management."

Brett shook his head. "Not going to happen. We're getting everything squared away." He shoveled eggplant ginger chutney. "The stock price is going to go through the roof. You'll make a mint. You'd be able to exercise some options in a year."

The lamb soured in his mouth. He pictured a grinning Pete Vankov prowling the halls at DNFV. "Can you give me a couple of days to get back to you with an answer?"

When Gruber got back to his office an hour later, he closed his door and dialed a number from memory at the Pentagon.

His brother Jake answered on the second ring.

"I'm about to make a move that might make you proud," Gruber said into the phone. He pictured Jake a lifetime earlier, back from Vietnam at twenty with a youth's lean, lithe body and a mop of curly hair but with a man's eyes, hard and cynical. He pictured Jake as he was now, those thick brown curls combed back thin and gray, that washboard gut now lapping over his belt.

He gave Jake a digest of the education-streaming company, emphasizing its noble mission, and touted a corporate exec's more regular lifestyle. "The more I think about it, the smarter this move seems."

Silence scratched over the line. Pentagon censors or recorders? No, Jake mulling.

"It's a good move," Gruber said, filling the silence.

"Who are you trying to convince, me or yourself? You want affirmation, you should call our sister. You're still her baby brother who can do no wrong, even when she knows you're still sinning."

Gruber tensed at the mention of his sister, at anyone taking her name in vain, then reminded himself that Jake had license. Their sister was a throwback to pre-feminist ideals of selfless womanhood, but still a kickass single mother raising teenage boys on jobs available to a woman without a college degree.

And still his second mom, eight years older.

"You talk about sinning," Gruber said. "These guys at this company wreaked mayhem when their funding fell through—including mass layoffs with only hours' notice. At first, that bothered me. But then I looked at it another way: If do-gooder educational pioneers are no better, morally, than political bottom-feeders, the whole world has gone to hell. Which is liberating in a way. I figure it gives me license to pick my spot in the lake of fire."

More silence.

"I can still make money, maybe serious dough if the stock does take off, with more regular hours and less stress. And help advance a worthy product, even if conceived in greed. Doing good and doing well at the same time, the highest aspiration in Washington."

More dead air.

"You want to cash in, throttle down?" Jake finally said. "I get it, I'm the one who's been telling you for years you've been burning the candle at both ends. I've always been proud of you, even when I disagreed with the particular . . . brand of snake oil you were pushing, because you always wanted to make a difference, an impact. How much impact you going to make as a corporate tool for some egghead closed-circuit TV channel?"

He was mustering an argument when Jake went on.

"The country's in rough shape, Dave, the world. Can't you find a way to stay in the fight, maybe from further back, like a general at HQ instead of a captain in the trenches? I don't know how it works in your field, I just know when we used to discuss our dreams at Sunday family dinner, nobody brought up selling out to Wall Street for a few shekels."

"There's more to it than that. I don't want to go into it right now."

"Uh huh. Well, maybe you can at least make a complete break, register as a Democrat. Even an independent."

"I never left the Democratic Party," Gruber said, reflexively. "It left me. And you. Going back to 1968, when you were in Vietnam. The Democrats became leftists, not liberals. They decided America had become a net force for ill, requiring radical transformation. While the Republicans—formerly hidebound and isolationist—recognized and tried to advance the distinctively American way of life."

He was into his spiel, which also numbed his pain, and kept going. "What Ronald Reagan believed in—I had this epiphany in college—was pretty much what Democrats from FDR to LBJ had also believed and aspired to: A booming market economy in which government taxed to pay for what it needed to do, not to punish success; social justice based on equal rights and opportunities for individuals, not on special preferences for groups with collective grievances; and most of all, a global American role defined by saving the world in WWII and protecting humanity ever since from tyranny and barbarism."

"Sounds great, Dave. Although I don't see it in today's GOP. It's so important to you, why don't you stay and keep fighting?"

"I told you, it's complicated."

"Yeah? What are you running away from?"

"I'm not running away from anything!" The volume of his own voice shocked him. He sighed. "Okay, I'm taking on a new cause, after having to surrender my sword." He gave Jake a rundown on the Vankov situation. "The Dark Angel won. I don't see a way forward."

"You say Vankov is bent on bringing down the country, vitiating these vaunted GOP values that seem all talk to me, but let that pass. Well, you should know the guy; you've been his partner for years. Which gives you an edge over anybody else who might want to stop him. And you're just going to walk off the battlefield. Yeah, yeah, I know, they canceled the expulsion vote, they cut your legs off. But is this guy that much better than you that there's nothing you can do?"

Jake began about their grandparents fleeing Russia and Ukraine, overcoming daunting obstacles to make a life in suburban Baltimore and raise a family.

"Stop," Gruber said. "You made your point. Don't beat it to death."

Ten minutes later, Gruber phoned Brett. "I greatly appreciate your kindness and your esteem and your friendship, but the job just doesn't seem the right fit."

He pulled out a yellow legal pad and began scratching out a strategy. He'd gotten partway through a plan to wall himself off further within the firm, which didn't really feel that promising, when his desk phone blared, his direct line, shattering his thoughts.

He sighed and reached for the handset.

"Mr. Gruber?" A female voice, authoritative.

"Yes."

"Jane Berglund, *New York Globe.*"

His stomach lurched. He'd seen her byline. She'd written the story on Alec Maynard's sketchy campaign contributions. He remembered because he'd been rooting for Maynard and had groaned reading the piece, including Maynard's inept response to the charges. Was Berglund after him now? Had Vankov sicced her on him, leaking his paramour's condo arrangement to the *New York Globe*, or whatever else Vankov had in that file folder?

"Always love to talk to the Fourth Estate," he said, as lighthearted as he could muster. "What's up?"

"One of your colleagues suggested I contact you. I was hoping to run some stuff by you involving another of your colleagues. Peter Vankov."

"You're looking for stuff about Pete Vankov?"

"Yes."

He gazed at the phone as though at a burning bush. "Can you give me a sense of what you're after?"

"I was hoping we could meet, and I'll lay it out for you then. Basically, it involves an operative that Mr. Vankov sent to Argentina and some of Mr. Vankov's financial arrangements involving Middle Eastern leaders."

This wasn't the way reporters usually worked, not on something this dicey. They didn't cold-call a principal at a public affairs firm and ask him to rat out one of his partners. Was she really a *Globe* reporter? "Let me call you right back; I need to put out a brush fire."

She gave him her number. He hung up and thought. If that really had been Berglund on the phone, that meant she knew about Gruber's troubles with Vankov, that he had a reason to talk to her. But she was gambling. If she'd guessed wrong, Gruber could tip off Vankov.

He ignored the number she'd given him and dialed the *Globe*'s (Washington) newsroom. They connected him to Berglund. Same flat Midwestern voice.

"Okay, let's meet," he told her. "But our conversation, at least initially, has to be on background."

A pause. "We can start that way."

Think. Neither of them wanted to be seen, so he had to suggest a private place. The privacy might also let him get to know her. He liked this Berglund, the sound of her cool, assured voice, but maybe the same way he might like a female surgeon who was going to excise his tumor.

"I've got to close up my weekend house on Sunday, for the season," he said. "It's near Annapolis, on the Chesapeake. How about if you come by on Sunday afternoon?"

Jane paused ever so slightly. "That sounds fine. Around three?"

He gave her the address and directions. He might get that SOB after all. He'd tried the low-cost way, within the firm, and the effort had blown up. Like launching cruise missiles that missed and gave away his position. Now he might call in the Air Force.

He pumped a fist, twice.

10
DEATH FROM BELOW

Senator Alec Maynard clamped his jaw as he watched the Georgia state senator rip into him on Fox News.

Laronda Tibbs, spokeswoman for the Sistas for Sistas PAC, asked whether Maynard was a traitor to his race. "And if he's a traitor to his race, does he have any integrity at all?" Tibbs's eyes widened. "Can he be trusted by anyone?"

Maynard's senior aides had huddled him into a small utility office with nothing but folding tables and chairs, at his Washington presidential campaign headquarters, and he felt their stares as they tried to cue their own level of outrage to his. A nagging pain crept up his leg, a reminder of one of his more foolish exploits, going to parachute school at the age of 41. He stroked his trimmed beard, which was going white, enjoying the brush of the stubble against his fingers, after decades of daily shaves.

"This Sistas PAC has been making attack videos against you like this one for weeks," his campaign manager, Jeff, said. "They post them on social media and on their own website, but some of them are getting heavy play—excerpts, anyway—on TV news. Then it snowballs more. Mouthpieces like this Tibbs do network interviews, like this Fox hit."

Maynard felt his staff gaze at him as though waiting for an order to fire torpedoes or launch missiles. "Smart strategy," he said. "They turn a modest production investment into an earned-media bonanza. Don't underestimate your enemy, don't let your hatred blind you."

Above a Fox logo, Tibbs railed about Maynard's preference for white women.

"You've got to admire her courage, this Tibbs," he went on. "Going on Fox must have been a tough call for her. Makes her radioactive to some in her crowd. Even if she skips Hannity, Ingraham, and the other hardcore right-wing nighttime circuses, and sticks to the newsier daytime fare, it's still Fox. Though, of course, once she rants, CNN is going to cover her and her Sistas bilge, too." He turned away from the screen. "Enough. Turn off that noise."

Maynard looked at Jeff. "Tell me about these other PACs and the other lies they're telling about us."

Jeff raised an index finger, raced out, and rushed back in with Scott, the campaign's digital director, a pudgy kid with crumbs in his scraggly orange beard who could have popped from *Revenge of the Nerds*. Once Scott began briefing, though, he reminded Maynard of submarine sonarmen, also often chubby nerds, who used high-tech hunting tools to spot, identify, and help take out targets. "Match sonar bearings and shoot!" He felt his heart race again, as it had when he'd given those orders.

"Several other well-funded super PACs are attacking us on various fronts," Scott said, matter-of-fact. "And some of their stuff is also resonating; we've been picking up a lot of chatter."

Maynard nodded.

"These others don't have that much money and they don't have big front men—or women—like Tibbs," Scott said. "So they're microtargeting and micromessaging on social media with lies designed to sow doubts and depress voter turnout in other important D groups. Non-college-educated whites are told that Senator Maynard supports federal funding for gender-reassignment surgeries for trans prison inmates, that he wants to shorten public school Christmas and Easter breaks to require days off for Muslim holidays, and that he believes Spanish should become America's official second language."

Scott met Maynard's eyes, maybe to see whether he was nearing shoot-the-messenger territory.

"Go on," Maynard said.

"They're saying the Senator will allow American troops abroad accused of war crimes to be tried and punished by international courts rather than by the US military, and that Senator Maynard supports reparations for slavery to be paid to every African American."

Scott kept eye contact locked with Maynard, who gave another nod, this time with a glare. Maynard was trying to live by the idea that his face should never show how hard his ass was getting kicked. Wasn't working so well at the moment.

"College-educated white women are told Maynard is the candidate of Big Pharma," Scott continued, "and therefore supports eliminating all exemptions to mandatory vaccinations of their kids, that he's supported by the chemical industry and therefore supports the expansion of GMOs in food and opposes any requirements for consumers to know what's a GMO product. They're circulating a deep-fake AI-generated video 'showing' Senator Maynard telling a group of older male supporters"—Scott raised his bony fingers in air quotes—"that if women didn't want to be hit on at work, they should stop coming to work looking 'fuckable.'"

The kid paused, looked at Maynard.

"Go on. But wrap this up."

"Those disposed against Senator Maynard aren't bothered that the video is bogus. They figure it expresses a larger, general truth about him." A pause. "That's the situation." The kid stiffened into a millennial computer geek's version of attention, which made Maynard smile.

"Death by a thousand cuts," Maynard said. "These PACs, these hits can't be coincidence." Threat-assessment drills from his early submarine days came to him, when his boats patrolled the deep-ocean front line in the Cold War's hottest zone. "Our primary target," he told his team, "Is Sistas for Sistas. We take them down and discredit them. But we also direct some suppressive fire at those smaller targets, the other PACs."

"Right," Jeff said, with brio. "We can't let this stand."

"That's tough talk from a centrist, Jeff. Moderates are supposed to be . . . moderate, no?"

A confused look crossed Jeff's face and he shrugged.

"Stay centrist, Jeff. We need the balance as this campaign tacks ever leftward. But that's another subject for another time." He turned back to Scott. "Who's funding these PACs?"

Silence, until his finance director cleared his throat. "We're trying to figure that out, sir. So is MSNBC, for what that's worth. We've peeled back some of it, but it's pretty dark. The PAC officers are publicly identifiable, but they just say, 'This is a group I agree with,' blah, blah."

"Bunch of fucking cowards." Jeff again.

"So much for moderation," Maynard said. "But 'cowards'? You think a sneak attack, or an anonymous attack, is inherently cowardly?"

Jeff chewed on that. Finally, he stood straight and said, "Yes, sir, I do."

"Interesting. I built a career on sneak attacks; it's the nature of submarines. Tom Clancy called an attack sub the deadliest machine ever invented, a creature that appears when it wishes, destroys what it wishes and disappears immediately to strike again when it wishes. Submarines destroyed more than half of all enemy ships lost during World War II. A submariner's job is the give and take of death. But 'cowardice'? I've never seen it that way, Jeff."

Silence.

"I'll tell you what does bother me," Maynard told his team. "Sticking with the submarine analogy, the power base on a boat—an incredibly complex machine—is knowledge, regardless of rank, race, or social status. Or gender; when I was in, subs were all-male. If a sailor is 'heavy'—knowledgeable—he gets respect. Submariners don't ask each other where they're from; they ask what boats they've been on.

"That's the way I've tried to live and work. Merit and equality, not 'equity.'

That's what this campaign is about. This campaign can be transformational. But now Sistas for Sistas and State Senator Tibbs come along, to bludgeon us with identity politics." He locked on Jeff. "I agree we can't let this stand. What do you propose we do about it?"

Jeff lunged forward, like a fighter hearing a bell. "We get some friendly Democratic super PACs to hit Fahringer hard, with counterpoints. We can't tell them what to do, of course, can't coordinate with them. But we can encourage them."

Maynard smiled. "Why are you so sure Fahringer's behind this stuff?"

Jeff's brows scrunched.

"Fahringer's already a long shot, even this early in the race. We're pulling ahead by every metric, from polls to fundraising to straw polls, endorsements—even from union leaders. And we've been excessively polite to Fahringer and his people. From Fahringer's point of view, does he really want to taint and cripple the front-runner with vicious lies—a front-runner who's been gracious to him and might be even more generous after locking the nomination and the election? Does Fahringer really want to turn the country over to the Republicans, probably to Ven Hess?"

"Who else could it be?" Jeff snorted. "Laronda Tibbs is a big-time Fahringer booster."

Maynard raised his eyebrows. "You've got me in submarine mode, so look at it this way: A submariner lives—or dies—by reading signals and signatures from enemies he can't see. In my time, before today's advanced tracking systems, a sonarman used passive radar—listening but not actively pinging sounds off the given object, which would give away his own position—to identify a vessel and its size, range, course, and speed, just by the sound of its screws.

"These attack ads and social media posts don't sound like Fahringer's signature. For starters, the attacks seem pitched as much to conservative Republicans as to Democrats. Which suggests that somebody is trying to weaken us for the Democratic primaries and—if we survive—for the general election."

Jeff's eye narrowed, as though his brain were draining energy to think.

"I have an idea who may be behind this stuff," Maynard said. "I need you to arrange for me to talk to Laronda Tibbs. Ideally in person. By phone, if that's all you can swing."

His words hung in the air as they waited for him to elaborate.

Jeff finally said, "What are you going to tell her, if you don't mind my asking?"

"I don't mind your asking." Maynard took a couple of steps toward the door. He smiled and turned back. "We should be in Tibbs's tribe. Maybe we can make a deal with her. 'Are there policy positions we can take that would prompt you to change your mind?' 'Are there roles in the administration where you think your perspective would be of value?'"

"Senator," Jeff said, tentative. "We can't offer her a job in the administration—That's illegal, and she'll go squawking to the press."

Maynard felt pressure pound his skull. "Right. That's why we ask obliquely. That's why it's called politics, Jeff."

"We might be able to arrange something at the CBC annual confab," Jeff said. "Maybe the dinner, on Saturday night. It's at the Washington convention center again."

The Congressional Black Caucus's Phoenix Awards Dinner highlighted the group's annual legislative conference, which drew tens of thousands of African American officials, celebrities, and political players to Washington for panel discussions, seminars, and town-hall meetings.

"Tibbs should be there," Jeff said. "It's de rigeur, and you're already locked."

"Fine. Set it up."

On Saturday night, Alec Maynard sat in his tuxedo on a green plastic chair in a small windowless room his aides had commandeered at the Washington Convention Center and waited. He pulled at his starched wing-tipped collar, trying to loosen the fabric. These penguin suits were as painful as choker whites, a blinding white tunic that served as the Navy's summer dress uniform.

He glanced at his watch again and shook his head. If you're on time, you're late. The Navy had that right.

He was checking emails on his iPhone when he heard a knock and looked up to see one of his campaign aides escorting a short, solid woman who was spilling out of a blue chiffon gown. He met the woman's eyes, trying to avoid her cleavage, and she glared back.

He stood. "Senator Tibbs." He gave her the courtesy of not calling her State Senator, the way you called a lieutenant commander simply "commander." "Thank you for taking the time to meet."

She stepped forward and extended her hand, violating basic military etiquette, and maybe general etiquette, which gave the superior rank the prerogative to initiate a handshake. What had he expected?

He shook her hand, small and firm.

Tibbs rested her other hand on her ample hip, waiting for him to explain his summons.

"What the hell are you doing?" he said. "Whatever problems you have with my marriage, my personal life, let's keep that in the family, not air it for the whole country."

Her eyes widened as they had on Fox News, and she began berating him for disrespecting her, for acting like a Black plantation overseer trafficking in his own people's misery.

Maynard shook his head, letting her words ping off his skull. Eventually, he raised his hand to cut Tibbs off, finally waving it in her face until she stopped yacking, eyes bulging even wider.

"We haven't got time for this," he told her. "Look, I'm an old-school liberal Democrat who embraces colorblindness as the Platonic ideal of race relations. And you're a progressive wed to identity politics. You're never going to see me as an avatar of a brighter, more enlightened America, because you reject the idea of that America. Just as I see you as an obstacle to progress, a big part of what's wrong with the Democratic Party today." He held up his hand again. "But much as we may fundamentally disagree, we have a community of interest, a bigger common enemy."

She eyed him.

"You're being used by Peter Vankov. He's Ven Hess's campaign manager."

"I know who he is," Tibbs shot back. "But I don't know what you're talking about."

"Who do you think is financing Sistas for Sistas? Some multi-color civic improvement organization? It's dark money, and Vankov is a master of dark arts. 'The Dark Angel,' they call him."

She was still glaring at him and seemed about to launch another salvo when a look crossed her eyes and her mouth spread into an "O."

"It's Vankov's signature," Maynard said. "He finds some kindling—my white wife or my call to expand official communication in Spanish. Then he gets others—your PAC and some others this cycle—to light that kindling into a blaze."

"Wait a minute." Tibbs shook her head. "So that's what that was all about. Why that cracker called me in the first place." She met Maynard's eyes, her gaze softer. "Vankov came to see me about bringing casino gambling to Georgia." She shook her head again. "I was thinking, 'This guy doesn't seem straight.'"

Maynard's head recoiled. He hadn't thought Vankov would be brazen enough to reveal himself to Tibbs. That showed a recklessness that Maynard might be able to exploit. He felt his lips forming the same oval Laronda Tibbs was wearing.

11
EPPING FOREST

Jane Berglund downshifted and steered her Volkswagen GTI around a bend in Epping Forest, in the outskirts of Annapolis. She squinted against sun pelting her eyes through branches of shedding trees. The car bounced over a hump; she'd have to get the shocks checked. She thought she could smell the Chesapeake now, the air growing thicker. The bay should be less than a mile away.

She downshifted again, into second, at a rising hairpin, and the VW whined but gripped the road. She'd always preferred the control of a manual and lamented how scarce they'd grown. The GTI four-door hatchback was nearly the only model in her price range that appealed, a mix of sport and practicality. Some men thought a chick driving a stick was cool and edgy, while others wondered, given Berglund's stark style, whether she was a dyke. Who cared what any of them thought? She liked the car, and it had never let her down.

The GTI hugged Epping Way through a turn and into an open vista, autumn leaves and blue sky. A final turn onto Severn Road, and she could see the deep blue Chesapeake Bay. She thought she could smell the oysters, which had been coming back. She'd always thought of herself as growing up on the water; Omaha was on the Missouri River. But that stretch of water was industrial and commercial, nothing like this.

Severn Road hugged the shoreline, and she looked for Gruber's house. Can't miss it, he'd told her, the only modern amid a cluster of Cape Cod cottages. She smiled, spotting it. A gray-and-black assault of angles and windows, like something Frank Lloyd Wright might have designed, then ripped up and tried again. Not the biggest house on the strip, maybe $1 million, but more distinctive than the $5 million mansions.

Researching Gruber and asking around, she'd found Olga had been right about his falling-out with Peter Vankov. Supposedly over Gruber's principled objections to Vankov's excesses. But this chateau looked like someplace Vankov might live. It demanded notice. As Gruber himself had said, she couldn't miss it. How different, she wondered, could Gruber be from Vankov?

She felt a twinge of disappointment. She liked Gruber, wanted to like him. There was something about him. Sure, for starters, he might help her nail a big story. She'd found that though Gruber was right of her politically—big surprise for a Republican consultant—he wasn't a Neanderthal. She liked one of his lines, his call "to lower both the deficit and the decibels," to find common ground, to make deals in the center.

Something else about Gruber, though, sparked envy: They both toiled broadly in public affairs, but Gruber made things happen, while she merely reported happenings. She sometimes felt the same envy shoving a mic in some pol's face or to scribbling in her notebook, asking them what they thought, what they felt, what they planned. Yes, she investigated and interpreted, ordered and portrayed the world. But, ultimately, as Columbia J-School had taught, journalism in its highest form, as a public trust, exposed systemic flaws so that others—such as presidents or Congress or prosecutors or even school boards—could correct them. And, yes, Berglund believed in sunlight as the best disinfectant, saw transparency as vital to democracy. "That the people shall know," Pulitzer's words carved on Columbia's wall. But she ached, increasingly, to be an actor, too. A participant, a player, not merely an impartial observer.

Gruber also seemed upbeat, even cheerful, amid the political mayhem in which he toiled and trafficked. She liked to be around upbeat people, needed to be around them, to temper her generally dour outlook.

She wondered how David Gruber would look in leisure wear; the clips she'd seen all showed him in suit and tie. He was packing up a house today; he wouldn't be in a blazer, ascot, and loafers. She was guessing a V-neck sweater and faded jeans, maybe something Gold Coast nautical, like a cable-knit fisherman's sweater from Orvis. Had she overdressed in tweed jacket and slacks? She looked like a Talbot's ad.

Jeez, this was a dicey interview for a big story, and she was treating it like a blind date. The perils of an anemic social life, especially since she'd uprooted to Washington, alone and past forty. She shook her head to clear her thoughts.

She pulled into Gruber's driveway and parked behind a Jaguar XJ, a $90,000 sedan left at a rakish angle like a casually abandoned bicycle. She locked her GTI, force of habit. She took a couple of deep breaths before knocking on the heavy front door.

Seconds later, she was facing Gruber, who exuded the spirit she'd imagined, big smile and country prep duds. Faded green canvas shirt, corduroys, and boat shoes. He'd probably spent a fortune to dress down. His watch looked like a Rolex, probably worth more than her car. She tried to smother her disdain. She could have had such trinkets and trifles if she'd studied law or business instead of journalism and climbed into some fancy firm. But she'd never chased money and comfort, maybe partly because those had been her father's values, the great Midlands industrialist.

Gruber's house seemed an extension of its owner, casual comfort at luxury prices. The kitchen and dining area, where Gruber led her, was done in Carrera marble over grooved wood cabinets and a tumbled stone floor.

"Nice place," she said, settling onto a bar stool at a marble counter. "And nice wheels. That's your Jag outside?"

"Whoever dies with the most toys wins. That's a prime credo in my line of work."

"In my line, we say, 'Comfort the afflicted and afflict the comfortable.'" That drew a glare. "Not that I buy in completely. I've never owned a weekend house, but I can see why you'd want a refuge like this from the Washington circus."

He nodded. "Thanks for making the trip."

"Thanks for making time," she said, businesslike, as Gruber slid a mug of hot cider in front of her. The cinnamon tickled her nose.

His easy smile made him seem cool, unflappable. Then she noticed his fingers, the tips red and angry, bitten or pulled around the nails. He caught her gaze and slid his hands under the table.

She pulled a digital recorder from her bag and set it on the counter. "I assume you don't mind."

He shrugged. "Fine."

She pressed a button and a red light ignited.

He lifted his mug of cider, wrapping his fingers around the handle to hide the mangled tips in his palm. He sipped and waited.

"Your firm has been providing services to the president of Argentina," she said. "I have that on solid authority, even though documents that would normally be filed for a contract like that don't seem to exist."

She paused, made sure the "Record" light was still on.

He sipped cider and gazed over his mug at her.

She outlined what Olga had given her. Gruber kept sipping cider and listening. Her heart rate quickened, the way it used to when she broke for a pass in a high-school basketball game.

She reached for her cider to signal she was done, surprised to find her hand unsteady. The juice had cooled to lukewarm, a poor temperature for cider, she decided. Cider should be either chilled or steaming. She gulped from her cup.

"On background, as we agreed," he began. A statement, not a question. She nodded.

"I can confirm that what you've just described is accurate." He pushed his mug aide. "Are you going to run a story about Argentina?"

"Not sure yet. We're looking broadly at Peter Vankov. We may hold off and run a larger piece encompassing his various other . . . efforts."

Gruber smiled. "Pete Vankov's greatest hits."

Literally, she wanted to say.

"Argentina is a pretty big story," Gruber said, and she tightened. She hated when those not in the business, even sources, told her what was news and what wasn't, what would make a great story, what she should write about, or when she was wasting time and ink.

"This guy is trying to be a Svengali puppet master on a global scale." Gruber leaned across the table, toward her. "Complete lawlessness. If he's doing that over there, you don't think he'll do it here?"

He smelled nice, some understated manly cologne. Focus!

"You say 'complete lawlessness.' Would that also apply to his work on the Hess campaign?"

Gruber shrugged.

"Would that apply to some of Vankov's efforts in the Middle East? I understand oil sheiks bought at least one of Vankov's homes for him." She glanced at the digital counter on her recorder, made sure it was advancing, so she could note the number if Gruber said anything seismic.

Gruber winced. "Let's stick to Argentina for today."

She squinted at him. "Why are you holding back?"

"I'd like to limit today's discussion to Argentina. That should give you plenty."

Her muscles pulled at her bones. Now he was telling her how to report a story, that she already had enough for a solid standalone piece.

"That's not how I work. You're the one who volunteered the term 'global,' as in global puppet master. Now you don't want to talk about it?"

"First, I want to see what you do with Argentina."

She was a *New York Globe* political writer, not some cub reporter on a tryout, she wanted to say. She weighed her options. "Fair enough," she finally said. "In the same vein, I'd like to know why you're talking to me at all. Reflects on your credibility as a source. Especially since you insist on being anonymous."

He swirled his cider. "You might say I looked hard in the mirror one day. After looking hard at my colleagues."

She waited, but he sipped his cider.

"Can you be even more specific?"

He gave her another 100-watt smile. "My firm was conceived in sin, you might say. Our founders were Reagan campaign hands who then leveraged their connections with the new administration to lure and service high-powered clients, including corporations, foreign organizations, and foreign heads of state, largely despots. A couple of the original plank owners are still around, with their names on the masthead." He shrugged. "Pete Vankov fit right in. So much so that he eventually torpedoed the partner who'd brought him in, to get his own name on the masthead."

He paused, like a comedian waiting for a laugh.

She said nothing, also waiting.

"So why did I sign on in the first place?" He shrugged again. "Part of the answer is simple enough: I'd become good at what I do. I'd helped win elections and change policy. Even if many of those outcomes, certainly in retrospect, weren't so good for the world." He waved his hand toward his front door. "And I like driving that Jag."

"And all that changed because . . . ?"

"I believed in a Republican Party that I no longer recognize." He eyed her and poked a finger toward her recorder. She hit the Stop button.

"We've both been married and divorced, seen the world," he said. "So I hope you won't be offended if I put it bluntly: I realized I was unsatisfied by the screwings I was getting and repulsed by the screwings I was giving. I want to make amends and I want to stave off a catastrophe, as in preventing a President Thomas Venable Hess. Does that give you enough to assess me as a source?"

She slid her recorder into her bag. "No good deed goes unpunished. By doling out your gouge in snippets, you know, you're going to have to deal with me, maybe on an ongoing basis."

They both smiled.

12
BRAINS

Ven Hess stared at the Time magazine article, at Pete Vankov's grinning face above the "Hess's Brain" headline. He let the image heat his brain and sear his ear canals, the way he used to when a hitter beat him in a long count or hotdogged around the bases after homering. So he'd remember the next time they met.

Hess hadn't read the whole Time piece, those newsweekly features were so windy, but he'd read enough to get the gist. He shoved the magazine into a tray on his desk.

He was about to buzz his assistant to ask what was keeping Vankov, when his maestro knocked on Hess's office door and sauntered in, not bothering to slow to be beckoned, like buzzing through a stop sign. As though Vankov were doing Hess a favor, interrupting his busy schedule to indulge his newbie candidate. The same way Hess's father acted as though he were suffering and indulging his wayward boy. Well, the Hessian didn't take snark anymore, and certainly not from the help.

"You wanted to see me, Mr. President," Vankov said. But Hess could tell Vankov used the airy greeting as a private joke, thought the title hung on Hess like a tuxedo on a chimpanzee.

And what was Vankov wearing? That yellow-striped thing looked like a zoot suit that should have come with eight-foot-long pants, so you could wear it with stilts in a circus tent.

"Have a seat, Re-Pete," Hess said. He'd given Vankov the nickname, Re-Pete, because Pete Vankov said the same thing again and again, always on message. As though Hess were too dim to get it the first time.

Vankov eyed him.

"What's the matter, Re-Pete? You don't like your new nickname?"

"Whatever floats your boat."

"That 'Dark Angel' thing is a little too haughty, don't you think, kid? I mean, the Dark Angel is basically Satan, who was God's number two until he tried to take over, then wound up in hell, a constant pain in God's ass.

"Now, you take my nickname, 'the Hessian.' That started in Double-A. After I racked up enough brushbacks, knockdowns, and hit batters, they began calling me 'Hess the Hessian,' then just 'the Hessian.' I've got some German in me, but mostly English and French; my father's stuck-up side of the family was British nobility going back to knights on horseback. But the thing is, that's not what being a Hessian—in in my case, the Hessian—is about. A Hessian was a professional soldier—fearless and efficient, and brutal when he had to be. And smart, and loyal to his team. They never gave the Hessians credit for those qualities, just wrote them off as savage mercenaries." He knew a lot about the Hessians; he'd Googled them and read a bunch of history pages.

Hess grinned. "Don't you feel better now, with a nickname that fits?"

Vankov, without speaking, eased into a chair in front of Hess's desk, careful maybe not to crease his outfit. As his campaign manager waited, Hess pulled a fresh stick of Wrigley's Double Mint from a pack, slid off the paper sleeve, carefully peeled back the tinfoil, and slid the stick into his mouth, bending it against his teeth and enjoying that first pungent bite.

Hess squinted at Vankov as he chewed. "What the hell are you wearing?"

Vankov cocked his head. "I don't think we have enough time for me to explain style to you."

"I understand fashion," Hess said. "I just don't understand the stuff you wear."

"I'm talking about taste and style, which are innate, though acquirable," Vankov said. "Not fashion, which comes and goes."

"Yeah, I got a crash course in taste and style from your predecessor, Bobby, from an 'image consultant' he brought in. I sent the guy packing, along with Bobby." The consultant had made Hess shave his sideburns, which he'd worn to the bottom of his ears, told Hess they made him look like a 1970s hustler.

Hess stood, looking down on the smaller man. "I'll tell you what's also 'innate,' but not 'acquirable'—and just as prominent as the clothes you wear: Breeding. What stock you come from. Not PC to mention it these days, but since we're on the subject. . ." That much his father had drilled into him, with the old man's British-pedigree pride. This grifter from New Jersey couldn't erase that edge, no matter how wild his costume."

He eyed Vankov's suit again. "Where do you buy a getup like that?"

"You don't 'buy' it anywhere. You have it custom-made. I haven't bought off the rack in thirty years."

Hess smiled. "Glad your paycheck's going to good use, kid."

From the tray on his desk, Hess plucked the copy of Time, paper-clipped at the "Hess's Brain" story and sailed it across the desk into Vankov's gut. Quick, no warning, like a pickoff move to first.

"Look," Hess said, trying for a reasonable, philosophical tone. "I know it's all about branding. All you freelance politicos do it—burnish your own brand on the boss's nickel. But it's a problem when you do it at my expense, promoting yourself by putting me down."

Vankov leaned forward and Hess raised his hand, settling him back like a dog.

"When Karl Rove was advising George W. Bush, Rove used to get the same kind of press you're getting: the man behind the curtain, the guy in charge, that kind of thing. Bush must have figured he was ahead, net, because Rove was so off-the-charts smart, so he let Rove have his headlines. Though he did call him 'Turd Blossom.' Good nickname." He grinned. "You're getting off easy with 'Re-Pete.'"

Vankov leaned forward again, and this time Hess let him speak.

"I didn't go looking for that Time story, and I didn't know it was coming, not like that. But we can't exactly demand a correction." He met Hess's glare with his own. "You want to argue I'm not your brain? The anger out there in the country—about immigration, urban unrest, racial preferences—who's making everyone understand that you're the answer? In two months, you may have the nomination sewn up. What more do you want from me?"

Hess shook his head. "You need to cut back on your press interviews. You want to do the dirty work, piss on someone who takes my name in vain, that's fine, kid. But we hook a big fish like *Time*, I'll do the talking. I got some experience with public speaking, in case you didn't know."

The heat seared his head again. "And I know a little about branding, too. Especially on my own brand. And not just from studying marketing textbooks in that mid-career MBA program at NYU. I've lived branding. And part of doing it right is not always hitting the other guy over the head with it, the way you do."

Vankov's neck tendons strained. "Airtime is my oxygen."

"You need to cut back. If you're going to play on my team."

Vankov seemed to think it over, then rose in the chair. "Is that all?"

"No." Hess settled again in his desk chair. "I've been getting calls about you."

"Yeah, who from?"

"I don't like your tone, Re-Pete, and I don't like the way you're looking at me."

Vankov shook his head. "You don't like my tone, you don't like my clothes, you don't like the way I look at you."

"You're glaring at me like you're some stud slugger. That's my game, kid—Intimidation. That's a tool I used for ten years to make a living. When the Hessian was on the mound, most batters wouldn't meet my eyes, didn't want to see the menace, the lack of fear or respect. A staring contest on a baseball diamond is as primal as it gets, a man with a rock versus a man with a stick. You really want to glare at me when I've got a rock in my hand, arm cocked—so to speak?"

Vankov crossed his arms, forming perpendicular lines in his zoot suit.

"A *New York Globe* reporter is calling up friends of mine, asking about you. Some woman. My friends are calling me, wondering what's going on."

Vankov shrugged. "Comes with the territory."

"You don't understand, Re-Pete. These calls I'm getting—You're being looked at. Not for a profile on how you're one of America's top political operatives, how you're my brain, how lucky I am to have you. You're being investigated on some real bombshells." Hess forced a blank expression. "They're going to say you're the devil himself, kid. The real Dark Angel."

Vankov sat there shifting his mouth, as though searching for words that Hess could understand and that wouldn't further steam him.

"This *New York Globe* piece that's coming, is this news to you?" Hess scratched his head. "Doesn't seem like you have any good answers. You say you don't know about the *Globe* investigation, you look like an amateur, which is a big sin to you. If you do know and you've been holding out on me, doesn't make you look like much of a team player. Which is it?"

Finally, the stud spoke.

"You know who I am. You knew who I was when you called me and begged me to come save your campaign. It comes with the territory."

"Did you know about this *New York Globe* investigation?"

A second inning of glaring.

"No good answer, is there?" Hess asked. "But no answer at all is even worse. As long as we're airing it all out, though, you hit the right words there a minute ago: 'My campaign.' Couple of days ago, I gave one of my people an assignment: put out a statement calling to raise tariffs on the Chinese, bunch of spies and thieves. No statement arrived on my desk." Hess lifted his hands as though seeking a divine explanation for a mystery. "When I asked about it, my guy said you told him to forget it. Said you told him, 'You need to understand, you don't work for Hess, you work for me.'" Hess stood and glared down again. "Let me help you understand something, maestro: That guy does work for me, and so do you. Who do you think is paying for your pimp suits?"

Vankov yawned. "Do you want to be president or not? You know who I am. Do you want to be president? If the answer is yes, then let me get back to my job. If the answer is no, I'll pack my things."

His fist tightened. He wanted to slug the guy right where he sat, send him reeling, chair and all.

He pressed the intercom button on his phone. "That bunch still here from Iowa, from the 4-H?" he asked. "The tourists in the blue corduroy jackets?"

"They're just leaving," his assistant's voice squawked through the intercom.

"Well, have them hold on." He turned to Vankov. "Take a walk with me. Meet the kind of people who are going to put me over the top more than those tiki-torch neo-nazis you're sucking off."

He placed a hand on the back of that zoot suit and steered Vankov toward the door. Vankov had to pick up his pace and fight the urge to resist as he was nearly into the hallway.

When they stepped into the reception area, the 4-Hers beamed wholesome Midwest smiles at him under their new green "America First" Hess hats. Three teenage boys, one of them Black, a girl, and a den mother, all of them riveted on him, the woman near orgasm. He floated in the adulation. That was a vibe radio and TV couldn't deliver—the fans' grins and swoons. You could hear it their voices sometimes, but it wasn't the same as seeing it, like now. Which was part of the reason Hess did so many rallies.

"Folks," he said, "I want you to meet Peter Vankov, my campaign manager. Pete keeps the trains running on time."

One of the boys put out his hand, and Vankov extended his own arm fully to shake, as though trying to avoid contagion.

"I was just telling Pete here that a lot of people who are for us—a lot of great Americans on our team—don't have college degrees and have pretty thin wallets these days, with Wall Street shipping most of our jobs overseas and trying to replace the rest of us with robots." Hess felt himself sliding into his radio groove. "My people grew up in households where one breadwinner provided a pretty good middle-class family life, but now even two can't seem to keep up." He looked at the den mother. "You know people like that, don't you, Carol?"

"That pretty well describes me." She glowed from twinkle eyes in her eyes toward the man she now practically worshiped.

Hess nodded. "What do you do, Carol—when you're not leading tours of Washington, DC?"

She laughed. "I'm an assistant manager at a Kroger's in Cedar Rapids."

"Love their broccoli. I don't usually admit to that—politicians aren't supposed to like broccoli, but I do."

Carol laughed again.

Hess went through the 4-Hers, getting brief bios, until he found a chubby boy whose father had once worked in a farm-equipment factory that moved to Mexico.

"I'll bet nobody asked families like yours if your dad's job should be given away. And nobody asked families like yours if they were okay with having their sons and daughters—who, let's face it, enlisted in armed forces as a last resort, not only for Uncle Sam—also shipped overseas to fight, and sometimes not come back, or not in one piece. In wars planned and ordered by America's 'elite'—which means guys in fancy suits with fancy degrees, whose kids were safe at home eating veggie burgers." He glanced at Vankov, long enough for one of the boys to get it and chuckle. "Wars that same ay-lete haven't figured out how to win for fifty years now."

Hess shook his head. "You've held your own, economically, families like yours, if you had two breadwinners and maybe more than two jobs between you. Your husband works, too, I'll bet. Right, Carol?"

"He's chief mechanic for the biggest Ford dealership in Cedar Rapids." She raised her chin.

Hess nodded. "The ay-letes and the lefties are always talking about equality. Equality. Which to them means handouts to people who aren't doing the work to get ahead. To me, equality is when everyone gets a chance to make what they can of themselves. Equality is when people rise or fall on what they do, not on who they are, not on what groups they were born into. You sure as hell don't owe anybody what you've worked hard for—what little you've got left of it—because you were 'privileged' by being white, straight and cis, whatever that even means." He glanced at the Black kid, like checking a runner at first.

He waited for the nods and silent "Amens." Even got a nod from the Black kid.

"For years now," he went on, "lefties brunching on kale salad and avocado toast that you can't afford—hell, that I can't afford—have been telling you that you've caused other people's poverty, and you felt pretty bad about it, and then you watched some of those people looting and burning stores, and the brunch crowd called it 'peaceful protests,' 'legitimate First-Amendment expression.'"

More vigorous nods. He turned to Vankov, who gave him a grudging half-smile.

Hess shook his head again. "And your children come home from school—schools you pay for with your taxes—and tell you that every president carved into Mount Rushmore is a monster, that people who take a knee during the National Anthem or burn the flag are patriots, but people who salute the flag are Neanderthals, that most cops are jackbooted thugs who hunt and murder Black men for sport, and that the Girl Scouts need to be renamed 'The Persons-who-Identify-as-Female Scouts,' and on and on. And God knows what they say about the 4-H."

A chorus of laughs. He chucked the Black kid on the shoulder and adjusted the bill of Carol's cap. "Got to go back now and help get America back on track. To the way it was meant to be."

He led Vankov back down the corridor.

"The media libs are calling me a racist and saying all my supporters are your tiki-torch nazis. If the pundits ever talk to people like Carol, they'll get straightened out. I'll take the Nazis' votes, but that won't get me to 1600 Pennsylvania Avenue. I also need all the Carols. You tell our press people, if some lib reporter says I'm dog-whistling about Black looters, they should say, 'No, he's talking about all of them, starting with the white morons in Portland, Oregon, smashing through storefronts and 'occupying' half the town because the Dem mayor's such a pussy.'" He locked on Vankov's eyes. "It's our ideas that are going to win this thing, not the color of voters' skins."

He went on as they rounded a corner. "Even the Black kid was nodding about the looting. He's going to be a working guy; he doesn't have time for that crap." After a beat, he added, "The Blacks love me."

Vankov's eyebrows rose.

"No white guy is more popular with the Blacks than I am," he insisted. "Besides, what the hell have they got to lose?"

"I talked to America—with America—for years, on the radio. And then on the TV. Sports, public affairs, politics. Local, regional, network, satellite, across the country. You really think you know America better than I do? Do your job, kid, your Dark Angel thing, and I'll lead a movement. Together, we're unstoppable."

Vankov didn't say anything, but his half-smile filled out.

Hess went on. "Americans like to complain, and they're always comparing themselves to people who have more and can do more in life than they can. That's why bankers in Manhattan making half a million bucks a year think of themselves as working stiffs. The American middle class is actually doing fine. Just check out the parking lot at the Red Lobster on a Friday night. They haven't 'collapsed,' no matter what both parties have been telling them. But families like Carol's feel held down and put down by the 'elites.'" He said the word straight this time, without the exaggerated l, and fake, Huey Long inflection.

"So now folks like Carol and her mechanic husband are flipping off the country and its establishment leadership and looking to make a statement. And that statement is going to be a vote for us. A vote for the Hessian, for me."

He studied Re-Pete. Vankov allowed a nod.

"All right," Hess said, faux friendly. "I'll see you on the tarmac at seven."

Vankov gave him a blank look.

"Crissakes, is the candidate the only one around here who knows the schedule? We got that TV forum in Manchester, New Hampshire, with the other wannabees for the nomination. It's probably going to be a bitch. Those other jerks are finally waking up, now that we're pulling ahead in the early innings, figuring maybe they should take me a little more seriously. Well, consider yourself lucky, kid; you learned that lesson before it was too late."

13

OPPO

When Alec Maynard stepped into the utility conference room at his campaign headquarters, the oppo was already sitting at the Formica table, working on a Diet Coke with two other cans waiting. A hard pack of Marlboro Lights sat near the sodas, maybe waiting for a break. His campaign manager was sitting beside her, studying papers.

She listed to the side as she stood, like a ship that was taking water, then righted herself. Probably her weight. She was a big woman, close to six feet, nearly Maynard's height, and an easy two hundred pounds. She reminded him of a schoolteacher or a lefty activist, with her printed blouse in a bold geometric pattern, her heavy turquoise necklace, and lots of metal rings on her fingers, wrists, and ears. Her stringy mouse-brown hair was tied in a loose bun over sharp blue eyes.

She introduced herself as "Joanne, one word." Her handshake was firm and strong and dry.

Maynard settled onto a chair upholstered in thin vinyl across the table from her.

"You have a fascinating background, Senator," Joanne told him. "A Caribbean from San Francisco, via London, who went to Andover and Annapolis and MIT, then decades in the Navy. You'd be a tough subject to investigate."

Maynard nodded. "Well, happily, that's not what we're after. Jeff briefed you, I understand." He glanced at his campaign manager. "On the situation, and what we are after."

"The outlines, yes."

He looked to Jeff, who nodded.

"This is a short-fuse situation; we need to stop this nonsense soonest. Jeff tells me you're ready to devote the time required. I know you're working other campaigns this cycle."

"Not a problem. If we begin promptly."

"Okay, good. We've deduced that the 'Sistas for Sistas' money is coming from the other side, from conservatives. Engineered by Peter Vankov, Ven Hess's campaign manager. We need to find out who these racists are that Vankov's tied into, who might love the judo of it. Jeff assures me that if a trail from Sistas for Sistas to Peter Vankov can be found, you can find it."

She sipped her Diet Coke, waited for him to continue.

"Let me fill in some context and specifics." He unbuttoned his suitcoat, a heavy gray chalk stripe. "Vankov took a chance by meeting with Laronda Tibbs, exposing himself like that. Probably for the pleasure of humiliating her without her knowing it. That's how we knew Vankov was involved, when Tibbs told me they'd met. Vankov is probably also behind the other PACs sniping at us. He's like a serial killer taking ears or noses as trophies. A guy like that must love being on the knife's edge, must pull stunts partly for sport; Catch me if you can. Which makes him dangerous. And vulnerable."

Joanne took another swig of soda, emptied the can. "Why don't you just work through Laronda Tibbs? She could expose the Sistas PAC and Vankov, which should put them out of business. Or maybe she could stay at the PAC and get Vankov to reveal their funding source. Then you'd have all of them."

Maynard shook his head. "Wish we could. I tried, that very approach.

No go. When Senator Tibbs and I had our joint epiphany about Vankov, at the CBC convention, she was on fire. About to erupt. I thought I had a real ally. Then her fire faded. Her furor gave way to shame and fear. You could practically read her thoughts as they flashed across her eyes. 'I'm a fool, I've been used and I'm going to look like a fool when this gets out.'

"And there I was asking her to make Vankov's scam public, telling her she was the obvious choice, as spokeswoman for Sistas for Sistas. In the end, Tibbs chose escape. She resigned from the Sistas PAC and returned to hawking causes."

"Too bad." Joanne cracked the tab on a fresh Diet Coke.

"Well, we got something out of it. Senator Tibbs is still pushing Fahringer for president, but she's no longer savaging me. Now, when she's asked about me, she says, 'Voters in the Democratic primary can make their own decisions. I have my own opinion, but let the voters decide.'" Maynard laughed.

He leaned across the table, toward Joanne. "We've got to find where the Sistas money is coming from. That's the key. Tibbs won't help, and I can't enlist the Federal Election Commission because PAC money is secret. We have to trace Sistas to its inception: who did Vankov talk to and meet with who might have put out this kind of scratch? That kind of financial autopsy is beyond the reach of this campaign. We need an expert, a pro. Will you take this on?"

Joanne took a long sip of Diet Coke from her second can and peered at Maynard over the lid.

"Figure out how to get video surveillance of whoever opened up that PAC bank account—or however you can find out," he told her. "I won't presume to tell you your job. But find out."

She wiped her lips with the back of her wrist and nodded.

14
CORNER TABLE

Vankov scowled at his office phone inside his sheetrock cube at Hess headquarters. "You think the ad is too hard?"

"Well, I mean, you said you want to start with a soft bio spot," the media consultant said. "And you said you want to unite the party and the country behind Mr. Hess. But this ad is going to kind of magnify cynicism and tribalism."

"Watch a classic western, see what happens to a gunslinger who gets soft and hesitates on the draw. Go with it, the full buy." He hung up.

A moment later, his direct line rang.

"Mr. Vankov?" That flat Midwest voice with the throaty rumble that tickled his ear. He'd know who it was even without the "*New York Globe*" caller ID.

"Ms. Berglund. How can I help you?"

"Well, first, thanks again for the tip about Senator Maynard's financial disclosures. I assume you saw the story."

"Nearly made me puke. Not your story—Maynard's response. 'Administrative error by staff.' Never blame the staff. Maybe that's what admirals do in the Navy, blame some poor swabbie or lieutenant junior grade, but that doesn't wash in Washington. He probably fired a couple of his finance geeks, poor bastards, after he had to give back the dough."

"What do you think Senator Maynard should have done?"

"Hey, when you're explaining, you're losing. He went off-message, justifying a fiasco—and he still looks bad; he took money from bad guys—instead of talking about saving the whales or whatever lib crap he wanted to push. Best thing in a situation like that, get done with it quick and move on. You can pass that on to the good senator, no charge."

That got a titter out of her. He slid his hand into his pants.

"I'd like to run some stuff by you, for a different story. In person." The tickle was gone from her tone. "Would you have a few minutes today or tomorrow? I think you'll want to comment."

"What does this 'stuff' involve?"

"Some of your accounts, outside the Hess campaign. I'll give you all the details when we meet."

His brain whirred, considering possibilities. Nothing good, clearly. How much more leash did he have with Hess, after *Time*'s "Hess's Brain" piece?

"I'll be glad to swing by Hess's headquarters, on North Capitol, if that makes it easier," she said.

I bet you would. Sure, come in, look around, cultivate some sources and snitches among the staff, let Hess and the underlings watch a *Globe* reporter grill me.

When he didn't answer, she said, "Or you can swing by the *Globe* (Washington) bureau."

Nearly as bad. Like a perp walk.

He considered suggesting they meet at a gentleman's club, either downtown on L Street or on Wisconsin Avenue north of Georgetown, whichever she found more convenient. The talent would be rehearsing midday, grinding on the poles, sweat-streaking the floor.

"How about lunch at 1789?" he finally said. "Restaurant in Georgetown, good food. You know it?"

"I'll find it."

"They don't have a big vegan selection, if that's your thing, and I'm not sure their veggies are organic."

"I grew up in Nebraska. I'll be fine."

Vankov settled into a corner table at 1789, his back to a wall. Even midday, the place was dark under a coffered wood ceiling, the walls lined with oils, antiques, and equestrian prints. A balding waiter in a tux swept by and took his martini order. Vankov checked his pocket watch, which had once belonged to a German bank president. Ten minutes early.

The place was beginning to fill with K Street types in pricey suits, or what they considered pricey, off-the-rack at Brooks Brothers or J. Press, or maybe made-to-measure.

He pulled a letter from his pocket, some cease-and-desist threat from a hack Palm Beach real estate lawyer, Vankov had better stop excavating to expand his backyard swimming pool or else. Even the boilerplate was overheated. The guy sounded like a night school grad wannabe-tough guy who spent half his time paying off health and building inspectors on behalf of slumlords.

Vankov unfolded the letter, turned it over, flattened it, pulled a charcoal pencil from a case in his pocket, and began sketching. He outlined a woman's figure, extrapolating from a waif waitress posting by the bar, nailing the siting and proportion, then making the woman taller and fuller.

He poised his pencil and sighed. Not what he needed now, this Berglund on his neck. He had enough trouble with Hess already. Didn't help, that little rat bastard staffer squealing to Hess about Vankov's "You work for me" line.

He sipped his martini—a bit too dry, but not worth sending back—and went back to his sketch. A few lines and curves and the woman was straining her blouse, her nipples poking through. Vankov extended his arm to retract his shirt cuff, keep it out of the charcoal. He'd dressed heavy gangster today, a navy three-piece suit with broad off-white pinstripes. A salmon tie and gold pocket kerchief. On his sleeves, silver cufflinks framing circles of a baseball used in some big game, a welcome-aboard gift from Hess. Berglund was supposed to be a jockette, a basketball player back in Podunk, Nebraska, and might appreciate the sports motif.

Vankov wondered again, was Maynard behind this press investigation of him? Had Maynard sicced Berglund on him as payback for Vankov's campaign-donations stunt? Maybe Vankov should have given that donations tip to a friendlier news outlet. Reporters were like dogs, and new reporters were like strays; you pet them, you risk getting bitten.

On the page, the woman's face had morphed into Olga's. With lips parted in ecstasy. Jesus, that had been nice, that session on the conference room couch.

Vankov pulled out his pocket comb and checked the small mirror inside the leather scabbard. He seemed to have aged a decade in the last couple of weeks. His fair face, aided by the sun and too many martinis, had wrinkled, lined, puffed, and sprouted age spots. He rotated his neck to loosen the pressure on his pinched nerve.

A shadow crossed the table and Vankov looked up to see Jane Berglund giving him that smile that had made him ache, even on video. But her lips seemed about to pull back to bare fangs.

She was dressed suitably, though barely, in a gray pants ensemble over a burgundy blouse. Didn't matter, she'd look great in almost anything. Or in nothing. Her smile retreated into a scowl, and Vankov saw she was staring at his drawing.

He folded the page, no doubt smearing the charcoal—a shame—and slid it into his jacket pocket. "A study from a picture I saw in a museum," he said, the first thing that came to him. "Appreciate your flexibility, coming here."

She nodded and looked at her watch. She pulled out a voice recorder, sat, and set the machine in front of her, just so, ignoring the menu.

"No small talk first? Even a condemned man gets some last words."

She forced a smile.

The waiter scurried over, plump middle-aged eagerness, and asked if she'd like a drink.

"Just water," Berglund said. "Filtered if you have it. If not, bottled is fine."

"Another martini, sir?"

"A Coke, with lemon."

"Small talk," she said. "You're really quite a talented artist, though I can't say I admire all your subject matter." She angled her head at his jacket, where he'd stashed the charcoal drawing.

"Sometimes I think I should have focused on painting, played that out." He shook his head. "Thing is, I wound up a glorified graphic designer for hire, a philistine. My nature. I figured, if you're going to go for the bucks, go big." He glanced at his pin-striped sleeve and the howling-wolf ring.

She nodded. "On that tip about the finances, I got the sense it's personal, your feelings about Senator Maynard."

"It's always personal about the enemy, and never personal."

"You don't like him? Senator Maynard?"

"Hey, 'Thank you for your service,' and all that. The guy made a career out of second-guessing his bosses, denouncing the 2003 invasion of Iraq while he was still in uniform. Now he wants it both ways—big military hero, but also man of conscience."

She glanced at her recorder, which was still off. "Just to set the record straight—not to defend Senator Maynard—his antiwar activism didn't make his military career, it ended it."

"You're going to split hairs? Made his political career. Which is what he was from the start, a politician. The guy walks around spewing this holier-than-thou, officer-and-a-gentleman, Navy submarine hero hokum. Picked up a bunch of medals in Gulf War One lobbing missiles into Iraq from way out at sea—how dangerous was that?

"He's like a lot of Dem saints, running a 'do as I say, not as I do' operation. He's already selling out his vaunted centrist principles, making concessions to the Wokesters. Promising freebies on health care, college tuition, and student loans he knows he can never deliver. Free ponies for everybody."

He felt a pulse pounding in his neck. "Tell you a story. "When I was fresh out of the University of Florida, I did stint as an NRCC field rep, and they assigned me to this Kansas congressman who got named co-chair of the House Ethics Committee, which was the only House committee a minority-party member could co-chair. But this guy refused to make any noise about it, wouldn't even put out a news release. Everybody has skeletons, he told me, and 'trumpeting yourself as a moral paragon just invites scrutiny.'" Vankov shrugged. "That Kansas rep may have been wrong, short-term—he barely won his re-elect—but he was a hundred percent right if you're playing a long game. Our Mr. Maynard—Admiral Maynard, Senator Maynard—missed that lesson. His whole campaign is a long press release about how righteous he is. Which will eventually bite him in the ass, and it's part of the reason I told you about his financial monkey business."

She nodded and pointed at her recorder. "You don't mind, do you?"

He shrugged. "Small talk's over?"

The waiter swept by with their drinks, set them on the table, and dashed off.

She pulled a notebook from her jacket pocket and flipped some pages.

"I was a Dem like you once," he said. "I assume you're a big Dem; you were married to one. I know your ex, by the way." He held up his hands. "Hey, I'm not suggesting any impropriety or conflict of interest. I'm sure you had a Chinese wall, you didn't tell him what you were investigating, he didn't ask you to run puff pieces on his clients."

She gave him a hard look.

"Yeah, I started as a Dem," he said. "From a family of Dems. I caught the political bug at thirteen when my father took me to an event for a local House candidate in New Jersey, a Dem tight with my father's union. I wound up doing some grunt work for the guy's campaign—planting lawn signs, door hangers, that kind of thing—and stayed close after he got elected to Congress, even chauffeured him around the district one summer after I got my driver's license. That congressman became my first political rabbi."

"So your reverence for propriety and fair play comes from the Democrats?" She kept a poker face.

Vankov glanced at the red light on her recorder. "Nah, that was already ingrained. I pulled my first political dirty trick in eighth grade. Our school had this mock presidential election, Ford versus Carter, and I told my classmates that Ford wanted to run school year-round." He grinned.

She turned back to her notes. Damn, she had beautiful eyes. He inched closer, to give her a blast of his Maison Francis Kurkdjian cologne, which cost more per ounce than a 1789 martini. The stuff boasted an aroma "too enticing to refuse."

Berglund caught his motion, or maybe the scent, and looked over. He flashed capped, freshly whitened teeth. She squinted, then scowled again and turned back to her notebook.

After a few moments, he scooched back. He took a sip of the Coke, enjoyed that blast of carbonation burning the fuzz from the back of his mouth.

"We've got a story that says you did work for the president of Argentina," Berglund said. "And that the work included representing Argentina's interests in this country with federal officials, investors, and members of the media."

He looked down to take another sip of Coke.

"Yet you failed to register with the State Department as a foreign agent, as required by US law. Which is a felony." She locked her cobalt eyes on him, breaking once to glance at her recorder.

"Doesn't sound right. Any work I do, especially foreign work, I always make sure to cross the Ts and dot the Is."

"That's not what we're told."

Who had ratted him out? There were only three possibilities. Well, some Argentinians might have gotten wise to Vankov's moves, loyalists to the opposition leader, but that seemed a stretch. No, only three possible suspects. The Mossad man, Yair, didn't do it. Wouldn't do it. That left Gruber and Olga.

Berglund hadn't mentioned her source, hadn't boasted about high officials tipping her, which meant she probably had rats hiding in the dark who'd poked their heads up to squeal but wouldn't let her use their names.

Which sounded like Gruber and Olga.

"Where are you getting this from?" He kept his tone neutral.

"Come on. You know I can't give you that."

"This is America, where people have a right to confront their accusers." She threw another scowl at him.

"You're going with a story like this based on an unnamed source? Somebody with some ax to grind spewing bilge in your ear. Even when I'm telling you there's nothing to it?"

"We have multiple independent sources."

"Meaning anonymous sources." He chanted his mantra silently: Attack, attack, attack. Never defend. Deny everything, counter-attack.

"You're not here to give me a chance to comment. You want to trick me into confirming your hearsay. Well, I deny it. I deny it. You say I did work for Argentina. Paid work? You have the contract?" He waited a couple of beats, but she kept her gaze steady.

"And I have right to confront my accusers," he said, softer but still with an edge. "In the court of public opinion as much as in a court of law. You people printing this garbage with unnamed sources, you're abusing your First Amendment protections, perverting one of the bedrocks of this country."

She sighed. "I'm giving you a chance to tell your side."

He laughed. "Appreciate your fairness."

She was probably levelling about multiple sources, though. Which probably meant both Gruber and Olga.

She was so establishment for a reporter. Berglund. Her people had probably arrived amid boatloads of Swedes a century and a half ago but had gotten a warmer reception than other "wretched refuse from teeming shores," like Vankov's Bulgarian and Irish forebears. By World War I, those Scandinavians had lost their accents and their fish breath and deemed themselves real Americans, "settlers," superior to the "immigrants" floating and crawling over, like Vankov's people.

"Well, here's my side, for the record," he said. "I've done nothing improper, and this story, based on anonymous sources, is a disgrace."

She scribbled on her pad, as though writing his epitaph.

An hour later, Vankov was back at the Hall of the States Building, standing in front of Ven Hess's desk. Behind Hess, out the window, the afternoon was turning gray, and wind was whipping some bare trees. Hess was eyeing Vankov's outfit as though he'd bitten into a turd.

Vankov ran a finger up his tie until it found the reassuring firmness of his collar pin, made of pure silver. A timeless touch. "Wanted to give you a heads-up. That *Globe* story is coming soon, their look at me. It might be a gnat bite, maybe a mosquito bite, nothing worse. I'll take care of it."

Hess nodded. "Comes with the territory. Right, Re-Pete?"

"Nobody has ever been criminally prosecuted under this statute, failing to file as a foreign agent. I checked with my lawyers."

"You're behind in the count, kid."

Around 3 a.m., Vankov tired of tossing in bed, jumped up, grabbed a sketch pad, a box of pastels, and a charcoal pencil, and set up at his dining room table. A Persian Nain rug massaged his toes and seascapes by Turner and Wyeth soothed his pounding temples. He'd kept his dining room upbeat, a respite. Sunny seascapes and landscapes in his living room had given way to Robert Riggs prints of psychiatric wards, bludgeoned boxers, and circus grotesques; and Thomas Eakins boxing tableaus. Vankov had even hung Goya's hellscape of Saturn eating his son, a later variation.

He let his fingers float, drew red demons with horns and pointed tails swarming like cockroaches over a massive commode. Then he added a window frame around the image and a brick border, as though looking through an apartment window from outside, and filled the bottom of the window with a blue wash, as though the house were filling with water, drowning the red fiends.

By the time he'd finished, he felt tired enough to try sleeping again, and crawled back to bed.

By seven, he was up again, for good. He padded into his kitchen as his cell phone shook and beeped and his voicemail filled and his email clogged. He scrolled through the messages. Friends seemed amused, clients alarmed. Then he opened Berglund's story.

"Top Hess Campaign Aide Implicated in Illicit Foreign Lobbying," the *Globe* headline blared. They hadn't used his name in the head; they'd used Hess's name instead. That was going to cost him. He felt his limbs loosen, though. The story was a mosquito bite.

The piece ran on page twelve of the print edition, still the front section but buried, and hadn't triggered a separate "news alert," though it did make at least one *Globe* email news digest and various political hot sheets.

Berglund had Argentina's payments to Vankov, rounded off. She also had Vankov's pressing some congressmen to restore US military aid to Argentina. But she'd missed the most damning elements of Operation Cabot. She didn't have Vankov signing the contract with the Argentine secret intelligence service, which would have essentially proven that he'd dodged registering as a foreign agent. Which meant she didn't have the actual contract. She merely had his failure to file. Which he could dismiss as an oversight, getting snared in red tape. She also didn't have Olga and Yair. Maybe that was part of her deal with her snitches.

He made a quick cup of instant coffee, guzzled it, and headed for his dressing closet. The suit he wanted, a solid navy with wide lapels, was in storage, he remembered. He owned more than a hundred bespoke suits and had to put dozens in storage, even with the closet space in his five homes. His size kept changing with variations in his bodybuilding and steroids, and he'd shrunk since the pinched nerve had limited his lifting. He found a charcoal gray flannel and matched it with one of his fifty silver-colored ties.

By mid-morning, Vankov was in front of Hess's desk in his gray armor. Outside the window, the morning was bright and clear, the sky a rich azure.

Hess tapped a folded copy of the *Globe* against his thigh, his lip curled.

"It's nothing," Vankov said. "They have squat."

Hess glanced at the *Globe* and then back at Vankov. "It's a felony, the paper says."

"This failure-to-file thing? It's candy-ass, red-tape crap. They even write that I was talking to congressmen, for Crissakes; it's not like I was hiding what I was doing."

Hess kept slapping the paper against his thigh and giving Vankov that sour puss.

Vankov sighed. "My lawyer is drafting the paperwork to retroactively register me as a foreign agent. The lawyer says that should take care of it. No criminal charges, probably won't even be a fine."

He gave Hess an assured smile. "Freedom and prosperity." He strutted out of Hess's office. In the hallway, he felt himself wilt. Berglund was working on more; he could smell it.

15
SNORKELING

Alec Maynard swiveled in his chair in his Senate office, away from his aides, to glance at the clock on his credenza, an old Chelsea 24-hour dial on a wooden stand. The clock had once hung in the control room of a World War II submarine, back in the days before nuclear power and manufactured air and water, when boats had to surface every few days to "snorkel," to run their diesel engines and recharge their batteries, when submarines stank of the three Fs: Fuel, fish, and farts.

The old clock looked out of place in the Hart Senate Building, a modern marble-and-glass colossus so lacking in charm that when it was unveiled in 1981, iconic New York Senator Daniel Patrick Moynihan introduced a resolution to put the building's plastic cover back on. The old Chelsea's minute hand had crept only a smidgeon since the last time Maynard checked. In just under an hour, he would meet with Joanne, the ace oppo researcher, and learn what she'd found.

Outside his window, bare trees swayed as the wind gusted. Winter was coming.

"Can we tell the Majority Leader you're a 'Yes,' Senator?" Maynard's legislative director asked. When he didn't answer, she said, "The leader's giving passes on this one only for conscience, not convenience. The vote's expected to be close."

He swiveled back to see his legislative director fold her arms across her glen plaid suit jacket, a picture of blonde resolution, and frustration. Beside her, Maynard's legislative assistant for education, a twenty-something kid out of a lefty Midwest college, stared at his hands.

"No chance of this vote getting put off?" he asked.

His LD shook her head. "The leader wants to pass some key measures and leave town for mid-December recess."

He smiled. "'State work period,' it's called now. Not 'recess.'" Whatever you called it, in an election year, recess meant campaigning.

"Why are you so eager for me to vote for these giveaways?" he asked. "Forgive billions in student debt and forego billons more in tuition at public colleges. Noble idea, if you can get past the personal-responsibility aspect. But it's a budget buster."

"Sir, we laid out the rationale in the briefing memo. And in the vote-justification letter." The LA, asserting himself on his issue. Like a young officer of the deck defending his watch against a department head overseeing him.

"So you expect some blowback? From the fiscal-restraint crowd?"

"At these funding levels, yessir." His LD.

"I don't see the primary rationale in your memo or your letter. Or who's pushing it. But it's clear enough."

His LD met his eyes while his LA looked down.

"You know how you can tell an accountant's personality?" he asked the kid. "An introverted accountant stares at his own shoes, while an extroverted accountant stares at the other guy's shoes."

The kid looked up and met his eyes.

"My chief of staff told you I need to vote for the education bill, right? Because Fahringer's nipping at us, and we need to cotton to progressives. And because a pass would cost me with the majority leader, and we don't need to rack up more debt with him." He was going to need the leader for all sorts of favors as the presidential campaign wore on: scheduling Senate votes at convenient times, not putting some legislation awkward for Maynard on the calendar, promptly moving on other bills, and so on.

Neither of them said anything.

"Well, I'm inclined to vote 'aye,' but for the reasons you laid out in your memos, not for presidential politics. Not that I'm opposed to politics on principle; I just like to know why my staff is advising a given vote. When Abe Lincoln was in the House, he said he voted his conscience ninety percent of the time. Someone asked him, What about the other ten percent? Lincoln replied, 'That's so I can stick around to vote my conscience ninety percent of the time.'" What was Maynard's quotient now?

"You're getting to think more like a politico and less like a policy wonk," he told his LD. "I guess that's what happens when you split your time and paycheck between Senate and campaign. They don't let you do that in the House, maybe a rare case where they have one up on us, ethically.

"A few months from now, if we get the nomination, you'll probably be a fiscal hawk, hollering about deficits and debt, shoving me toward the center for the general."

He glanced at the Navy clock again. The big hand had crept two minutes.

He checked the "Aye" box on the briefing memo, initialed it, and slid it across his desk to his LD. "It'll look like another concession to the Shiites. Another step away from those lofty centrist ideals on our glossy brochures and our glitzy website."

His LD shifted and her lips began to move. Then she clamped her jaw. "Anything else?"

"No, sir." She and his LA padded out of his office.

He punched his chief of staff's number on his intercom. His Administrative Assistant, or AA.

"Any way we can get that oppo over here now? Is there somewhere kosher we can meet her?"

"Not in the Hart Building, and for sure not in your office," his AA said.

"We can't bring a political hitwoman into your Senate sanctum."

"Staff can split their time between campaign and Senate, which lets them keep their Senate parking spots, health insurance, and time toward a federal pension. They can do all kinds of campaign work in Senate spaces and call it 'de minimus.' But I can't meet with a political operative in my office. Makes as much sense as anything in Washington."

"Sir, the meeting is scheduled in forty-five minutes from now. Which should be right after the education vote."

"Why is she playing coy?"

"She's not. She just wants us to wait for her presentation."

"Before telling us anything—even whether she succeeded or failed?"

"Less than an hour, Senator."

"This 'master sleuth' of yours better deliver."

"If a trail can be found, she'll find it."

"The woman carries herself like a jaded combat vet who's done too many tours. In her case, probably too many political campaigns, too many years living on fast-food takeout out of fleabag hotels, spending her days combing through statehouse and courthouse records and interviewing political marks' ex-wives, disgruntled business partners, and estranged relatives. Juicing on Diet Coke and Marlboro Lights."

"Sam Spade and Easy Rawlins had some mileage and wear, too," his AA offered.

"Joanne probably woke up one morning in a Motel 6 in Des Moines or Phoenix or Boise and realized she was forty, her youth was gone, and it was too late for a family or even much of a life."

His AA didn't say anything. Static snapped over the line.

"This isn't where I expected to devote my efforts and energy, on a presidential campaign. On this crap. But I suppose that's the idea. Vankov's strategy."

He closed his eyes and leaned back in his desk chair. "I'd hoped we could present our campaign as a Democratic Eisenhower. Position me as not merely as a transcendent figure, but as a transformational figure, not so much overcoming race as overshadowing it, incarnating the American ideal for an increasingly divided, diverse nation. The country and the world need that, a leader like that.

"That's not hubris. Not in context. How can anyone run for President of the United States who doesn't think that way, that he or she is ideally—perhaps uniquely—qualified to lead the nation and the free world?

"But are we doing the Big Think? No, we're fending off attacks from 'Sistas for Sistas' about my dating white women and marrying one. Both my parents were mixed-race, part-white. But that doesn't count to Laronda Tibbs; to her, I'm just another Tom."

He could tell from the light on his phone and the static that his chief of staff was still on the line.

"Well, this campaign will serve as a litmus test for American progress. Will a decisive voting bloc balk at putting another Black man in the White House? In that sense, my candidacy is also a verdict on Obama's election: A barrier-busting revolution or merely a well-timed pass?

"If I win, America really has defeated the demon of racism. That doesn't mean no racism, but it means society has moved on. But if I lose, it means we're still mired in a racist dystopia of police stops for Driving-While-Black and store clerks shadowing Black shoppers. If I lose, America's not there yet, and I'm not the transformational figure to complete her evolution.

"Today, I'll vote for the education bill, take another step into the moral morass. But I'll be damned if I'm going to mortgage my principles, and my soul, only to be cheated out of the prize—by some psychopath hitman for a bush-league ballplayer turned huckster. This Joanne better come through."

A bell blared above Maynard's head and the official clock high on his wall flashed, signaling a vote. The vote.

"End of sermon." He hung up the phone. He stood, slipped on his suitcoat, and steeled for the trip to the Capitol. The movements took him back to Norfolk on a December day like this decades earlier, bundling into an exposure suit and climbing a rung ladder inside a fast-attack's conning tower to the sub's exposed bridge, and chaining himself to the railing. Then he'd driven the behemoth out of Navy Station Norfolk, through the Chesapeake Channel, and into the open waters of the Atlantic. And into the depths where the boat lived. Where he'd lived. In a windowless steel tube under the ocean for six months, 140 men crammed into the space of a two-bedroom home, cut off from the rest of the world in a self-contained universe that made its own electricity, oxygen, and potable water. A perilous world where a fire, a steam leak, or a flood could all prove fatal in minutes. Where one misstep, one oversight, one momentary lapse in attention could spell peril for all aboard. Where you went to sleep knowing you were placing your life in your shipmates' hands. Where you did your job right because you knew your life and your shipmates' lives depended on it. A world that also provided an absolute, complete belonging Maynard had never found anywhere else.

He'd placed that level of trust, with his political life, in his staff and in this oppo Joanne. Would they come through?

When he reached his anteroom, his staffers were waiting and fell silently in step behind him. They strode an open Hart Building hallway, their footfalls silent on the carpet, a towering black metal Calder mobile and stabile dominating the nine-story atrium. Maynard kept a quick pace and an intense gaze, radiating purpose and urgency, to ward off any tourists or gadflies looking for a selfie or a chat. At the elevator landing, he pushed the hidden button for the "Senators Only" car.

When the elevator door opened, Maynard found himself facing a pudgy Georgia Democrat, a two-term pecan farmer who hadn't yet endorsed in the presidential.

As the door closed behind Maynard and his aides, he asked, "How's your race look, Ed?" Handicappers were calling the Georgian's reelection a toss-up.

"It's a tough fight. Guy's coming at me from the left, and you know how that is these days." In other words, Can you spare a few bucks from your bulging presidential campaign kitty to help keep a fellow centrist Democrat in the Senate?

"Well, I'd like to help," Maynard said. "But I have my own troubles in Georgia." That is, endorse me, and soon, if we're such kindred spirits. Don't wait for the early primaries to make sure I'm a good bet for the nomination. Take sides while your endorsement means something. If you lose some Fahringer voters in the process, that's the price.

The Georgian nodded. When the doors opened in the Hart basement, they headed to separate areas on the platform for the Capitol tram.

A minute later, Maynard and his aides squeezed into a middle tram car. Maynard watched the Dirksen Building basement as it passed outside the tram's windows. He'd miss the Senate, some parts of it, anyway. He was the senior senator from the nation's largest state, which by one metric made him the biggest fish in the congressional pond. He'd been ecstatic winning that first election. And his two re-elections. His first job in which he hadn't been appointed or selected but chosen by his neighbors.

The tram docked in the Capitol basement and Maynard followed his LD—ladies first, especially in public—onto the landing. He headed to the escalators, aides trialing, for an elevator beyond that would take him to the second floor, just outside the Senate chamber. In the corner of his eye, he caught a form moving toward him, and spun.

A *Washington Post* political reporter. An older guy with ferocious white eyebrows, snaggled bottom teeth, and a worn brown corduroy sportscoat. Maynard had bumbled into a press ambush point, the crowd slowing to funnel to the escalators. Did these press guys study military tactics, or were they just natural predators or parasites?

"How are you going to vote on the education bill, Senator?" The guy whipped a notepad from a stretched patch pocket of his jacket.

He stepped to the side, in front of a stone staircase adjacent the escalator, resigned to forfeit two minutes of his life to this guy. His aides watched him, maybe as eager for his answer on the vote as the reporter.

Maynard forced a smile. "You'll know in four minutes." He turned to his young LD. "Never reveal your plans on a close vote. You lose leverage, and measures can get pulled at the last minute, and you've gone on record for nothing." He angled back toward the escalator.

The reporter slid in front of him, cutting off his aides, nearly clipping his LD. Maynard considered calling the guy a rude bastard. But the guy was onto his next question, and Maynard saw he hadn't expected an answer on the education vote, didn't care about it, it wasn't even his beat.

"Senator, your campaign slogan is about restoring honor to the White House," the guy was saying. "Yet sources tell us you've got lobbyists drafting campaign white papers; and you've got staffers quitting, complaining about backstabbing cliques and lack of due process and biased punishment. If that's how you run your campaign, is it an indication of how you'd run the country?"

Maynard's couldn't help starting to sweat. Even his ears felt hot. "We run our campaign precisely along the lines of our slogan. If we fall short in any particular, in the heat of battle, we do after-actions and we make adjustments. That's what the American people can expect from us in this campaign, and that's what they can expect from us in the White House. Beyond that, I'm not going to comment on internal process." He raised a hand. "But I will say it's a striking question, about protocol and propriety, from a man who shoves a woman out of the way to ask it."

Fifteen minutes later, Maynard stepped out of the Capitol into a crisp breeze and climbed into the back of his waiting Lincoln Town Car. An aide weaved through a block of Constitution Avenue, turned onto First Street, and whisked Maynard half a mile, to his campaign headquarters across from Union Station.

When Maynard stepped into the windowless conference room, his campaign manager and the oppo researcher were waiting for him. Joanne was wearing a shiny, medium-blue, double-knit suit and sucking on a can of Diet Coke. An accordion file sat beside her on the Formica table, bulging. The room smelled of Joanne's cigarettes, even if she hadn't lit up here. Third-hand smoke was wafting from her.

Joanne put down her soda and stood. Courtesy and deference, or a reminder that she was nearly Maynard's size?

"I was thinking, Senator, that your parents were both in the same line of work: Your father was a banker and your mother was an anesthesiologist. They both put people to sleep."

He looked at her with more confusion than amusement. She said, "You'd laugh if you met some of the bankers I've had to deal with."

He smiled and slid into a chair at the head of the table. "Very thorough, Joanne. Have you had as much success with our research project?"

She straightened and pulled in her own chair. "The financing for the Sistas for Sistas PAC came from a man named Stockton in Charleston, South Carolina." She'd adopted a good command voice, strong and fluid. "He's local gentry, think *Gone with the Wind*. Vankov calls him 'Colonel Sanders.'" She paused, maybe for applause.

Maynard cocked his head. "How do you know this?"

"Sources. And following the money. After Stockton's name came up a few times, it seemed worthwhile to take a trip down to Charleston and do some digging. And I found that Stockton talks too much. In circles where he feels secure."

Maynard turned to his campaign manager, asking tacitly whether Joanne's intel was worth her airline, hotel, and fried-chicken, burger, and donut bills they were going to have to cover.

Jeff gave him a "you'll-see" nod.

"Stockton talked at his golf club, mainly," Joanne said. "Thinking nobody in the room had a different opinion."

Maynard smiled. "And he was wrong." Maybe the world was advancing, if a cracker couldn't even trust members of his own country club with his racist secrets.

"Well, not the way you might think," Joanne said. "Nobody at that country club—no members—would say a contrary word about Stockton. And none of them could recall ever hearing him mention the Sistas PAC, when I talked to them."

Maynard eyed her, waiting for the punchline.

"But Stockton did discuss the Sistas for Sistas PAC with his friends at his club. And they all thought the Sistas thing was funny as a barrel of monkeys—their term." Joanne took a swig of Diet Coke. "Somebody else in the room didn't find it so funny, though. Think Mitt Romney's '47 percent' fiasco during the 2012 campaign. You know, when Romney went to a fundraiser in Boca Raton said 47 percent of people don't pay income taxes and think they're victims and that the government has to take care of them. Which was recorded by an event staffer."

"Joanne, with all due respect, I'm getting tired of squeezing out information I've already bought. So who didn't find Mr. Stockton's idea that funny?"

Her grin faded. "Well, Stockton and his friends are pretty far out—think *Birth of a Nation*—and so is their country club. The members are all white, the staff is mostly Black, there's a grinning Black lawn jockey outside the front door, that kind of thing." Joanne sipped Diet Coke. "So I figured the Black staff might have something to say about Colonel Sanders."

Maynard nodded. "Go on."

"A Black woman working as a waitress at the country club overheard Stockton and his pals laughing about the PAC. She didn't like the idea of a Black sisterhood being played with by these crackers, as she put it."

Maynard nodded again. A Rodeo Drive shopping excursion came back to him from a couple of years earlier, when a clerk at a boutique had watched him as he flipped through some leather jackets, and Maynard could tell the punk wasn't ogling his state's senior senator, but was surveilling a potential thief.

"That's good, Joanne. But it's only the word of a waitress who overheard part of a conversation among some local big wheels. Did you find any documentation?" He glanced at her accordion folder.

Joanne took another swig of Diet Coke, lifted her wrist to her lips, and let out a belch that was only partly muffled.

Maynard rose in his chair. Jeff rose beside him, his face blanching.

"I told you, Senator, think Romney's '47 percent.'" Joanne put down her soda. "This waitress was thinking, 'All I have to do is turn on my phone in my pocket and record this.'"

Maynard nodded. "And did she?"

Joanne lifted the Diet Coke again, tilted it, and drained it. She slapped the can on the table. "She did. But she's not a political activist, not a player at all, and she didn't want to lose her job at the country club. So she sat on it."

Maynard's head thrummed. Was this a shakedown? If a recording did exist, did the waitress want to be paid for it? Or, more likely, did Joanne want to be paid for delivering it, probably taking a big markup on whatever the waitress was asking? Was Maynard going to have to pay serious coin for a tape he hadn't heard, which could be worthless? If there was any tape at all. "This is beginning to sound less promising."

Joanne pulled a Zippo lighter from her purse, rubbed it, fingered the trigger. "The waitress told me, 'I was scared, I didn't know what to do with it, but since you're here on my doorstep, here it is.'" Joanne reached into her accordion folder and pulled out a clear plastic case with a single flash drive inside. She slid the case across the Formica table.

The case was labeled with the name of a Charleston country club and a date. Maynard laughed. And then again, feeling the day's tension float away.

An hour later, Maynard stepped away from a laptop computer after listening to Joanne's recording a second time.

"Make copies of this," he told Jeff. "Give one copy to a reporter, make sure she understands it's an exclusive. The one at the *New York Globe* who wrote that piece a few days ago on Vankov and Argentina. Also did that pain-in-the-ass piece on our fundraising. She's a pit bull. But make her our pit bull. Berglund is her name. Jane Berglund."

16
A THING OF VALUE

Vankov sipped his vodka martini, felt the alcohol loosen him. Pretty good martini for a strip club, dry, not too much ice. Good T-bone, too. He'd always liked this place, this "gentleman's club" on Wisconsin Avenue north of Georgetown. He should have lured that reporter Jane Berglund here for their meeting, that would have shaken her. He'd been longing for a visit since then and had seized this chance today. Even on a weekday afternoon, though, the place stank of beer and funk. Didn't they mop the floor?

He turned to Yair, the former Mossad man, beside him at the table in the back of the dark room. Yair knew how to wear a suit, Vankov would give him that. Yair's gray flannel was supple, snug, and nicely cut for the guy's hard, lean frame. Looked like Savile Row work. Vankov would have gone with a cutaway collar instead of a semi-spread, but at least it wasn't button-down. Now the guy only had to lose that clamped-sphincter, righteous vibe, and he could pass for normal.

Vankov drained his martini, his second. "Don't worry about Argentina. That *Globe* story was a mosquito bite. A gnat bite. A gnat. G—N—A—T. It's a tiny insect, flutters around, gets in your ears, annoying as hell but doesn't have much bite to it. Anyway, they did us a favor, showed us who we can trust—and who we can't."

Yair stirred his club soda with lemon with a swizzle stick.

"You were in the army. You should appreciate what we're doing; it's like a military operation. Grand scale, lots of moving parts, like the Battle of the Bulge or Midway. A lot more complex than Entebbe. You've read Sun Tzu, right, *The Art of War*?"

Yair gave a slight nod.

"Well, that's what we're doing in this presidential race. Attack your opponent on multiple fronts, make him feel besieged. Distract him, fluster him, confuse him, make him spend precious resources trying to answer your blows that come like so many jabs, crosses, and hooks. We've got these PACs firing at Maynard like mortars and RPGs, .50 cals. And now I'm setting up a Big Bertha. Hell, a nuke. I'm calling this next assault 'Operation Loose Fly.' I need your help with it."

Yair sipped his club soda.

"We've been working together what, seven, eight years? We've got a rhythm, like gears meshing in a Swiss watch. You're not going to let a fart in the wind like Argentina ruin that, are you?"

"You told me once I was merely a horse in your stable. You said you are in the 'people business,' that you have a collection of people, like horses, that you use and lend out for various chores. People to run errands, people to operate PACs, people to topple foreign governments. Well, find another horse."

"I'm a little thin on foreign agents right now. And it's not the kind of job I want to start interviewing people for."

Yair shrugged as though to say, "Not my problem." Then he scrunched his eyebrows in mock confusion. "But you have a whole campaign staff to command now. Like a general. Like a field marshal." He cocked his head. "Though perhaps you do not want those 'weenies' to know about your 'Operation Loose Fly.'"

Vankov angled his head at a buxom brunette gyrating on a pole on the stage. "Would you like to meet her in the back, after her set? I can arrange it."

"Some other time."

Vankov shook his head. "I live by Gore Vidal's maxim, 'Never turn down a chance to have sex or appear on television.' You have discipline, my friend. Or maybe you got your balls fried off in a tank battle when you were in the Israeli army."

Yair shot him a glare and sipped his soda.

Vankov shot his cuffs. He'd chosen today's outfit to convey casual control: a double-breasted blue blazer with brass buttons, paisley pocket square, tattersall waistcoat, white shirt, woven blue silk tie, gray flannels, and brown capped-toes. Now, upon reflection, the blazer bothered him; it had derived from Alec Maynard's old uniform, Navy dress blues. Too bad; a blue blazer was a staple of any gentleman's wardrobe. He'd shift to single-breasted blazers until the campaign ended, until he buried Maynard, then don this one again like a trophy. He flagged a waitress in fishnets and pointed to his empty glass.

"Look, the *New York Globe* piece on Argentina: They're a bunch of hyenas running a lefty propaganda factory. They didn't mention—the progressive pygmies never mention—that I work only for pro-Western nations and clients. I'm a patriot, like you. A practicing patriot—in a world where talk is cheap."

Yair took another sip of club soda.

"You see the *Batman* movie where Heath Ledger plays the Joker?" Vankov asked.

The Israeli squinted at him.

"It'd take too long to explain. The Joker, this arch villain, says, 'Introduce a little anarchy. Upset the established order, and everything becomes chaos. I'm an agent of chaos. And you know the thing about chaos? It's fair!'" Vankov leaned toward the Israeli. "That's us. And for a noble cause. A patriotic cause."

Yair nodded.

The fishnet waitress sashayed by and swapped Vankov's empty glass for a fresh martini. Had Vankov had her? He vaguely recalled a boozy winter night. He met her eyes, nodded his thanks, and got nothing back, no recognition, no spark. Her eyes weren't dead, exactly, just neutral, emitting a faint light, aware of being studied but uninterested, immune to shame or desire. She'd make a great artist's model, could probably hold even the most revealing pose, just sliding into herself. He might have to ask her, later. He slid his chair closer to Yair.

Yair looked at his watch.

"Hey, buddy, you can drop that 'find-another-horse,' 'I'm too cool to bother' bit. You meant that, you wouldn't still be sitting here. Now listen to what I'm going to tell you." He waited as Yair scowled but met his eyes.

"I got a tip from a woman I know," Vankov continued. "She runs an upscale house in Dubai—you know, a cathouse—and she got it from one of her escorts."

Yair sighed.

"Hey, this madam runs a string of thirty upscale brothels in moneyed playgrounds around the globe—Tokyo, Shanghai, Sao Paolo, Cape Town. The kind of source your Mossad pals would cream over."

Yair looked at him.

"I visited her London house recently." He felt a smile play. "The place was furnished in a Victorian motif, marble and velvet, ultra-high end. I expected one or two babes in an upstairs bedroom, not a full-out orgy in the salon. Most of the others were middle-aged, moneyed Brits. You've got to see these upright patrician chicks walking around naked with their tits bouncing; it's almost too much. Anyway, it was like a smorgasbord, walk over to any woman I fancied, cup her breast or nuzzle her neck, and I was in. At one point, I was recharging in a corner—need more refractory time these days, not as young as I used to be—and I'd gotten only partly stiff when this shapely brunette walks over, probably some big corporate VP—does an about-face, sits on me, and guides me in." He grinned at the memory.

Yair raised his eyebrows and sighed again.

"Anyway, after a couple of hours, I find myself on a chaise lounge nibbling grapes like some Roman emperor. I'm spent, but I'm still not satisfied. That's me. Like Johnny Rocco, Edward G. Robinson's gangster in *Key Largo*—'Yeah, that's it—More. I want more'... 'Will you ever get enough?' 'Well, I never have.'"

Pretty good Bogie and Robinson impressions, but all it got the commando was a sullen glare.

"This madam sits beside me on the chaise and helps me finish the grapes. She's Eastern European by background, maybe Hungarian, but you can't tell, after top schools and a decade in London. As we ate the grapes, she gave me the intel. Second-hand, but I knew it was reliable. She wouldn't have given it to me otherwise. We're essentially business partners; I send her a steady flow of clients, on top of my own patronage."

Vankov's eye caught motion and he saw that Yair was pushing his club soda aside. Good. Now focus on what I'm telling you, asshole.

"The intel from this woman," Vankov continued, "it's really more of a nugget we need to track down, pin down. The tip is that our friend Mr. Maynard, when he was with the Navy in Bahrain, was diddling—was having an affair—with a woman under his command. He was an admiral, she was a lieutenant commander. You were a military guy, you understand this. It was adultery because he was married. But it was also a very serious military breach because this female officer was in Maynard's chain of command."

He stopped, seeing Yair's eyes light. No need to tell Yair where the tip about Maynard's affair had originated, from a Navy officer who gave it to a Dubai hooker because he didn't like Maynard, didn't believe a Black guy should have commanded a submarine, much less an entire fleet, or been a deputy commander, whatever. A Jew like Yair might not like the idea of discrimination, but some Jews didn't like Blacks. Why complicate things?

"Okay," Vankov said. "We've got this tip, and we need to run it down. And the people who are going to have the evidence are in the United Arab Emirates government, because the UAE spies on our people over there, they're as bad as the Chinese like that, no way they wouldn't have been watching a big-wheel admiral. Those guys feed off dirt, they make a living on blackmail."

Yair laughed, a quick chortle. "The UAE intel service would know about Maynard's affair even if they had not spied him in the act. Your madam would tell them back when it was happening. A foreign, high-end madam in Dubai would stay close to the UAE intel service because her tourist visa does not authorize her to run whores, and the spies could kick her out anytime. And if she did not volunteer the information, the UAE would ask. If a madam wanted to live in a ninety-story condo tower on the Dubai waterfront and not freeze in Chechnya, then when a UAE spy knocked on her door and said, 'I want to know everything you know,' she would tell him."

Vankov shrugged. "Whatever. The point is, the UAE knows."

Yair nodded slowly. "Did he beat her, force her to do things against her will? The admiral?"

"No, nothing like that. It was consensual. No harassment, no retribution; that's not what we're after here. But you know how those things are, though—how consensual can it be when he's giving her orders and writing her fitness reports, or whatever they call them, and then he's bending her over a desk? Either way, it's a major violation."

"Okay."

"Okay, what? Okay, you're in?"

"Okay, what do you want me to do, and I will tell you if I am in."

Vankov pictured a thirty-second spot they'd cut, maybe open with some grainy bedroom footage, two figures cavorting under the sheets, then cut to Maynard in his dress blues. If the press coverage alone didn't blow Maynard out of the water first. Voters remembered everything in an attack ad, even when they said negative campaigning offended them. They'd sure remember this.

"You need to talk to the UAE intelligence guys," Vankov said. "See what they have on this."

Yair spread his arms. "I am an Israeli. A Jew. Things have thawed between Israel and the Gulf States but there's still no trust."

"This has nothing to do with trust. Meet them in Geneva, or Oslo. Someplace neutral. You work a quid pro quo. You tell them—these spooks from UAE or Bahrain, or both—you tell them, 'My guy is connected to this Republican candidate who's likely to be the next President of the United States. If your government helps us to do this, we'll be very favorably disposed to your policy agenda.' Like that."

Another slow nod.

The club's soundtrack shifted to an old Blondie song, "Call Me," with shrill howls and a beat that rocked Vankov's guts. On the stage, a bleach blonde was working the pole, swinging like a gymnast. Firm, lithe calves and thighs. Defined abs. Only medium height but she looked as though she could crush your kidneys if she wrapped those legs around you. Vankov felt himself stir.

"So you're on board?"

"I don't know," Yair said.

Vankov turned from the stage to glare at the former Mossad man. He clamped his jaw until a pain shot through the hinge and dissolved his alcohol haze. "You don't know. You just like being difficult. You've always been difficult. I don't know why I put up with it. Nobody else does. Usually, you don't leave the Mossad unless you're dead or missing a limb or two. You found another way. You kept ignoring orders until they kicked you out. Nothing so flamboyant as shooting the wrong mullah or bombing a hospital. You were just too much of a lone wolf. They told you to go left down the street, you went right."

Vankov took a long sip from his new martini. Flat, watery. He'd waited too long, let too much ice melt. "What don't you know, lone wolf?"

Yair studied him. "Lone wolf, yes, with you and your stable," the commando finally said. "I will tell you one thing, If I am going to do this, I am doing it alone, after what happened last time."

"That could happen on any operation."

Yair shook his head. "Argentina blew up because Olga was ultimately not trustworthy." He waved his hands, as though shooing any objections Vankov's might lodge. "It is between you and her as to why. But the fact remains, she turned on you."

"'As to why?!' You're blaming me because she turned rat? You're siding with her? You boink her over there in Buenos Aires? You must have tried; how could you not?"

Yair scrunched his face as though he'd spotted a cockroach crawling along the bar. "I also need more. Call it hazard pay. You are hazardous." He angled his head at Vankov's third or fourth martini. "Fifty percent more than for the last job."

"So that's what it's about, money. Why didn't you say so upfront and spare us all the time and BS?"

They stared at each other for what felt like at least a minute. Finally, Vankov shrugged. "You want to work alone? Lone-wolf Yair. Fine. I figured Operation Loose Fly as a two-person job, but I'll redraw it for one. That adds risks, which'll justify your 'hazard' pay." In a way, Yair was doing him a favor. Vankov should come out ahead, paying Yair a fifty percent bump instead of paying two guys. And it reduced another problem: Hess would eventually find out about the payments, which would spark a tough conversation. A cheaper one-man job made that conversation easier.

Vankov slid his martini aside. "Any other conditions? Are you done squeezing me?"

"I do not particularly love making deals with Arabs," Yair said, as though Vankov cared about the guy's politics. "On the other hand, we Israelis and the gulf Arabs and Saudis have come closer together because we have a common enemy, Iran. If Iran gets nuclear weapons, Hitler gets the last laugh." Yair nodded, as though resolving an internal debate. "I want your man to win, because your man will be tough on Iran, the opposite of that pussy admiral. I am on board with this mission, under the terms we have agreed on. For Israel."

Vankov raised his glass. "For Israel. Freedom and prosperity."

Whatever it took.

17

ROUGH RIDERS

Jane Berglund followed the dirt path on Theodore Roosevelt Island as it wound up a rise and opened onto the expansive memorial, as into Elysium. A massive bronze TR was waving to her from the far end, beckoning, and she stepped onto the stone plaza. She scanned the stone benches flanking the statue for David Gruber.

If Gruber were excited to see her, he'd have shown early. Well, she was five minutes early, but he would have arrived even sooner. She laughed at her folly and cautioned herself against mixing personal and professional with a source.

Roosevelt, seventeen feet tall in patinated bronze, faced her with his legs spread in an almost martial pose, his frock coat open, immune to the autumn chill. The copse around the memorial, even with the trees bare, blocked the wind but also blocked the afternoon sun. Berglund raised the collar of her suede jacket, a favorite that she saved for special occasions.

She had discovered Roosevelt Island some months earlier, a fifteen-minute drive from her apartment at the edge of Old Town, Alexandria, a straight shot up the George Washington Parkway. She liked to come here sometimes to hike, read, or think.

As she waited, she scanned the granite tablets engraved with TR's wisdom. She reread one of her favorites, titled "Manhood":

. . . All daring and courage, all iron endurance of misfortune make for a finer, nobler type of manhood. Only those are fit to live who do not fear to die and none are fit to die who have shrunk from the joy of life and the duty of life.

Something in Roosevelt's hokey, dated words spoke to her, about the kind of man she was after. A Paula Cole ballad floated into her head, "Where Have All the Cowboys Gone?" The song had come out when she was working her first newspaper job, and she'd turned up her car or kitchen radio whenever it played. She sang the keening chorus about an old-fashioned, rural-rooted man to herself.

The song, which pointed to conventional gender roles at once appalled and appealed.

She didn't want domestic 1950s *Leave it to Beaver* masculinity in her man, which would force her into a 1950s house frau, she'd decided. She didn't want reactionary John Wayne either, exactly, but the spirit of John Wayne, an essence of traditional masculinity.

TR glared down at her. He looked ready to jump on his steed and charge up San Juan Hill. Where have all the cowboys gone?

A form strolled onto the monument grounds, and she lurched. Gruber? No, a fortyish man in a ski parka, sunglasses, and a ball cap. The guy walked to the far end, away from her, and sat on a stone bench. Something about him looked familiar, but she couldn't place it.

She checked her watch. A minute to three. Was Gruber going to be late? Was he going to show at all? If he still hadn't shown by five past, she'd text him.

The man on the far bench was reading a magazine. Now she realized what was familiar about him. His nose was bent to one side, mostly the bulb, which gave him an odd, almost cubist aspect. The deformity looked even more pronounced with his sunglasses, which hid the bridge. She'd seen him the other day at the Pret a Manger, at 16th and I Streets, when she'd dashed out of the office to grab a sandwich. It was the same man, she was sure. She remembered his nose because she'd studied it, wondered why he didn't fix it, and decided that it wasn't the nose so much as the shape of his head that was uneven. She also remembered that he'd bought only a cup of soup, hadn't even taken the complementary roll that came with it, and nursed the soup for the whole ten or fifteen minutes that she'd been there. She also remembered his nose because it had made her think about her own face and her own best feature, her cobalt eyes, and her regret that her eyes were too small. She didn't want cow eyes or even doe eyes, exactly, but hers, despite their vibrant color, seemed stunted.

"Hey."

She snapped around. Gruber.

He was smiling. And right on time. A tweed sportscoat over a sweater vest. Dark suede oxfords with black rubber soles. Big-wheel Washington jaunty. He even smelled nice; his understated cologne brought back the afternoon on the Chesapeake.

He set a small nylon cooler on the bench beside her bag and sat, leaving the bags between them. He pulled out two bottles of raspberry Izze sparkling juice from the cooler, carbonated fruit drinks that the rich called refreshers instead of soda.

He offered her one of the bottles. "Won't compromise your journalistic integrity, will it?"

She took the bottle with a smile, anticipating the fruit tang. Then wondered whether she was starting down a slippery slope.

In the corner of her eye, she saw the man with the crooked nose shift on his bench, and she turned. He had put down his magazine, but quickly picked it up. Too much of a coincidence. Should she text 911, or the park police, or whoever patrolled the island? And tell them what, that a man she'd seen in Washington was now here?

"Thanks for making time," she said, curt, turning back to Gruber. She buttoned the raised collar of her suede jacket.

"You going to be warm enough in that thing? I probably should have brought coffee, or more hot cider."

"It's forty-five degrees. In Omaha when I was growing up, it rarely got above zero in January. My senior year in high school, the thermometer hit seven degrees, and I was so thrilled that I took my old beater Chevelle to a do-it-yourself car wash. I got home fifteen minutes later, and was shocked to find gray ice covering the car in slicks, like malignant growths. When the temperature hit nine degrees—nearly double digits—one night that same January, I opened my coat and took off my gloves. But now, after a few years in the East, I've grown soft, my father would say." She opened the button on her jacket collar.

She inched away from him on the bench. Now she wished she hadn't worn the suede jacket. Or pulled her hair back in a chignon or put on blush. Gruber was a source, and she strived to avoid any impression that she used her looks to cajole sources.

She twisted the cap off her Izze and took a swig. The sparkling juice was wonderful, rich raspberry with a charge of carbonation.

"You talk about your father a lot."

The soda soured in her mouth. "All girls are attracted to their fathers, right? The Electra thing." She shrugged. "My father was an agribusiness exec, a Knight of Ak-Sar-Ben, which is Nebraska spelled backwards; backwater civic royalty. A Swedish Lutheran who ran his home with all the joy and frivolity and open-mindedness you'd expect from that clan."

He was watching, listening, so she went on. "It all erupted my senior year in high school. My father expected me to advance to what he considered the apotheosis of higher education, the University of Nebraska at Lincoln. He was aghast when I told him I was going to the University of Pennsylvania, especially when he learned that Penn was Ivy League, which he considered a decadent eastern cult."

They sipped their sodas—their "pops," her father would say—silently for a time.

"Any pushback from Pete Vankov on your Argentina story?" Gruber asked.

Is this why he'd agreed so readily to meet, because he was worried about himself, worried that she'd reveal him as her source if Vankov challenged her story? She noticed that Gruber's sideburns were cut sharp, clean and even, precise, the way they'd been that Sunday at his beach house. Obsessively precise. She shook her head. Stop, she told herself. Stop trying to tear down Gruber, to make him unappealing, to spare yourself the dilemma of wanting him.

"No pushback," she said. "Not after it ran. Mr. Vankov did end our interview by expressing a lack of enthusiasm for anonymous sources and saying that the story—which I hadn't even written at that point—was a 'disgrace.'"

"You got one of his PG versions. Maybe even G-rated."

"When I first met Peter Vankov, I thought maybe he wasn't as bad as his reputation, or no worse than so many others in a scummy game. Like my ex. No offense. Maybe like that Sam Spade line from *The Maltese Falcon*, which happens to be one of my father's favorite books and films: 'Don't be so sure I'm as crooked as I'm supposed to be. That sort of reputation might be good business.'" She shrugged. "I don't doubt that Vankov is crooked. Or Hess. But I wonder if they're the gang that couldn't shoot straight."

Gruber raised a finger, nearly wagged it. "Don't underestimate Pete Vankov, and what he's capable of. And don't underestimate Ven Hess."

She felt her face pucker; Gruber was telling her again how to do her job.

He spread the palm of his raised hand. "Everybody underestimates Ven Hess, and he counts on that. I just don't want you to get sucked into that trap. Hess comes across as an empty suit, or in his case, an empty jersey. But Ven Hess has a has an organic feel for politics. Yes, Hess.

"And Vankov knows the secret sauce that might get Hess the win: Hess can appeal to the largest voter group there is, whites without a college degree. In a way no one has since the Democratic social justice warriors scratched that group from their identity-politics bingo card of those with legitimate grievances. First, Hess is trying to ride those people to the nomination, now that the Republican 'establishment' has sacrificed its own 'Reagan Democrat' base on the altar of globalization. Vankov knows how to sharpen that appeal, turn dog whistles of discontent into a white nationalist movement.

"Vankov has the strategy and Hess has the tactics. Hess knows how to connect with people. Specifically—and this is key—with the masses that the political establishment is ignoring. That's what he did on the radio all those years, on TV. He's honed his pitch to the point he makes it look easy, like there's nothing to it. Smooth like Johnny Carson. All Carson did was sit at a desk and chat, right? Anybody can do that. Sure."

Her head lit, as though catching Gruber's intellectual fire, and she understood why firefighters said flames "communicated." Why hadn't she found that spark with her ex? Why hadn't she learned from, grown from, and grown with his purposeful mind? Maybe because he was a serial cheater, and she soon wanted nothing from him, not even him. She studied Gruber's face, noticed his crows' feet were deeper than she'd remembered.

"My own sister," Gruber said, locking on her eyes, "is going to vote for Hess. She doesn't have a hating bone in her body, but she's drawn to him by the notion of an outsider who cares about people like her, people without college degrees and without economic security in the globalized, fourth-industrial-revolution gobbledygook twenty-first century. And even if she doesn't think Hess can win—she also underestimates him—she wants, in her nice, polite way, to give the middle finger to the establishment."

Berglund nodded. "Okay, I got the point. You've seen I'm serious about reporting this out. Now how about telling me more about our Mr. Vankov, for a 'Peter Vankov's greatest-hits piece."

She caught motion and glanced at the far bench. The guy with the nose was still there, with his face still in the same magazine. Fifteen minutes on a cup of soup, at least that long on a journal.

She turned back to Gruber. "You want to barter? I've got some new intel you might find interesting."

"Yeah, what's that?" Gruber sipped his Izze.

"Why should I always show you mine first?"

"Because I'm able to confirm yours. I doubt you can confirm mine."

At least he hadn't made some sophomoric joke about hers and his. "I got a voice recording this week involving Sistas for Sistas." She watched Gruber's reaction to the PAC's name. Nothing, a poker face.

She took a deep breath and summarized the recording of the Charleston country club chat that Maynard's chief of staff had given her, without naming Maynard's campaign as the source.

"So, basically," he said, "all you have is audio of unidentified voices from a source you won't name. And an assurance from this source that those voices belong to conspirators in Vankov's orbit."

"I'm going to Charleston in a few days," she said. "To talk to the waitress and try to talk to Stockton. 'Colonel Sanders.'"

"Let me save you the airfare. We're on background, right?"

"Yes." She pulled out her pocket recorder and placed it on the bench beside her bag, at its reassuring bright red light.

Gruber stared at the device for a few seconds, then seemed to regain his rhythm. "Vankov is behind Sistas for Sistas. I got that from the lawyer who drafted the papers to form the PAC. Pros like that, as a rule, don't talk. But he told me because he felt guilty. Because it stank."

She nodded. "I've still got to go to South Carolina, but this helps. Thanks."

She glanced again at the far bench. The man seemed to be eyeing her over his magazine. Was she getting paranoid?

"Do you have to play this like Deep Throat, confirming what I find, expanding a little, maybe steering me, but not providing any new intel?"

He shifted on the bench and gazed up. "I wasn't much of an athlete as a kid. Sort of a stereotypical American Jewish nerd. Never played a team sport and sat out high school gym with a note from a doctor friend of my parents about a curved spine. But one lesson from sixth grade basketball stuck with me. The coach asked us how fast we should run while dribbling the ball. Then he answered his own question: You run as fast as you can and still maintain control. I've been working that way ever since, and that's what I'm doing here. Or trying to do."

"Your coach was basically right. But sometimes, like when the clock's ticking down and you're behind, you've got to go all out."

He sipped his Izze.

"Have you always been so self-assured? Bordering on cocky? Or are you just playing John Wayne with me?"

He smiled. "I've always had lofty aspirations and, as I got older, some confidence I could realize them. Another bit from my youth: When I was a scrawny eighth grader in the throes of puberty, a female teacher sensed my lament and one day she whispered to me, 'I know it's super hard for you with the girls now, but I promise you that at thirty you'll be fighting them off with sticks.'"

"Was she right?"

He shrugged. "I did okay. Once I figured out that wit, charm, and confidence in one's lofty aspirations are as hot to many young women as their looks were to me." He met her eyes.

They looked at each other for a few beats and both laughed.

"I have to move soon on this story about Sistas for Sistas," she said. "Which should make a nice hook for the larger Vankov's greatest-hits story. Sources abandon you after a while if you didn't use what they give you."

"Maynard's still moving up in the world, building a lead, but he hasn't cinched the Democratic nomination, so he's focusing on that. I'm assuming that Maynard is your source for the tape."

She tried to affect her own poker face.

"But, yes," Gruber continued, "Maynard must also be looking ahead to the fall and to Hess and Vankov, and he'd no doubt love to preemptively blow them out the water. Especially since he knows they're already sniping at him, Sistas and the other PACs. But Maynard isn't going to fixate on it and begin phoning you every morning to ask when your piece is going to run. So you should have a little time."

Now she knew what bothered her about Gruber's sideburns: Her ex used to keep his sideburns sharp, too, before he became a shaggy lefty. He'd flick out the retractable blade on his Norelco and hold it by his ear, just so. Well, fastidious grooming was hardly unusual among beltway politicos.

"You're still partners with Peter Vankov. He's the Dark Angel and all that, but does it bother you to betray him like this? Not that I don't appreciate the information."

"Betrayal bothers me, as a general principle. And I don't look for a crooked way to do something when I can do it straight. I went after Vankov head-on, tried to boot him from the firm. Didn't work out. Then you approached me; I didn't approach you. And my calculus at the time, weighing all the variables, was that the best way forward was to cooperate with you. On a Utilitarian basis, the greatest good for the greatest number."

"And that's still your calculus?"

"Clearly."

"And that's your only calculus?"

He studied her, then patted her thigh and smiled. "What other calculus could there be?"

She studied his sideburns again and his crows' feet.

He took a deep breath and closed his eyes a moment, as though gathering himself. "My partnership with Vankov at this point is only a technicality. There's no professional relationship anymore. I'm on my own island in the firm, and he's on leave of absence to run Hess's campaign. What happens after the election, that's up in the air. But it's not going back to the way it was." He scratched his chin. "And we've had no personal relationship for years. Except like a snake and a mongoose."

She laughed, feeling herself loosen. "Reporters shouldn't get involved with sources."

"Works the same in my business. There's a leak, the first one you look at is the guy who's screw—who's involved with a journalist. But where do you draw the line? Don't get involved with anybody with whom you have any professional ties whatsoever? If you're working eighty hours a week, as I suspect we both do too often, who else are you supposed to meet?" He shrugged. "There are ways to navigate these conflicts, make it work. You must know that; you were married to a politico."

Yeah, she and her ex had made it work. He liked their professional wall when she asked about matters that touched his practice. He didn't feel so encumbered when he asked her to run stories that helped his clients and causes.

"At a certain age, your chances begin to dry up," he said.

Yeah, and it got tiresome building a new social network every time she moved somewhere—New York, Trenton, Washington.

He looked up, as though sifting his mind. Then began reciting something:

Had we but world enough and time,

This coyness, lady, were no crime. . .

But at my back I always hear

Time's wingèd chariot hurrying near;

And yonder all before us lie

Deserts of vast eternity.

She squinted. "I've read that. In college. Give me a minute."

"Probably freshman lit. Andrew Marvell, 'To His Coy Mistress.'"

She smiled at the memory. "Well, Mr. Gruber, there are a lot of 'variables' to consider. Maybe there's a cathedral in there somewhere, but right now I can't see it through the scaffolding."

Gruber's face shifted, as though he were concentrating or had to relieve himself.

"It occurs to me we actually have been on a 'Mr. Gruber' and 'Ms. Berglund' basis. Proper nineteenth-century stuff. I go by Dave, or David. May I call you Jane or Esmerelda or Bathsheba, or whatever you go by?"

"My current crowd calls me Jane or occasionally Berglund. But good friends call me Janey."

Gruber seemed to be trying out her nickname in his head when she caught motion again and turned to see the man on the far bench putting down his magazine. He gazed at one of the Roosevelt tablets, on Nature. Another of her favorites. "There is a delight in the hardy life of the open."

"Something wrong?"

She snapped around. Gruber was eyeing her.

"No, it's nothing. Just . . ."

"Just what?"

"That guy over there—Don't look!"

Gruber squinted at her.

"I think he's been following me."

"Why do you think that?"

"Because I keep seeing him, here and there, and he keeps looking at me. You don't have to be an ace investigative reporter to figure that one out, do you?" She took a deep breath. "I saw him at a lunch place in Washington a few days ago. And now he's here." She gave Gruber the details.

Gruber stood and adjusted his tweed coat, straightened the sleeves, turning casually toward the far bench as he did.

"You think I'm nuts, right?" she asked.

He shrugged. "Is there anybody you've written a tough piece about recently, maybe using unnamed sources? Some schemer who might want to know who you're talking to?"

She angled her head at him. "Come on. You don't really think he'd . . ."

Gruber shrugged again. "I've known him for years, and he still surprises me." He shook out his arms, as though preparing for a boxing match. "You want me to handle this?"

"My John Wayne." She shook her head. "He's my pest now."

She began walking across the memorial toward the man on the bench. Her heart thudded against her ribcage. Each step on the stone plaza vibrated through her. What if he had a gun or a knife? Her heartbeats pounded in her ears.

About twenty feet away, the man with the nose looked up, and she met his eyes and glared. She should have wielded her cell phone and begun recording; that's how a lot of would-be victims foiled and even helped catch their attackers. Too late now. Maybe Gruber was recording. At least he was watching, witnessing.

When she got about ten feet away, the man stood. She'd never seen him standing before, or not next to anybody for context, and hadn't realized how big he was. Six-two, at least, and solid. She noticed now that his cheeks were pitted and his hair was thin below his ball cap. He was balding in an unfortunate way, that would leave him one day with a head of loose thatch.

She halted a few feet from him. He squared to face her, saying nothing. Daring her to speak or move.

"Tell Vankov that he's his own worst enemy." Her voice sounded strong and even, if a tad high.

The man gave her a quizzical look.

"You heard me."

She turned and strode back toward Gruber, her heartbeats now pinging her ears. Probably unwise to turn her back on a potential assailant, but she didn't think she could hold her facade much longer. The twenty paces felt like miles. Cold sweat trickled down her sides.

Gruber stepped forward to meet her, closing the distance.

"Whatever you did seemed to work."

She spun around. The man on the bench was sliding his rolled magazine into a jacket pocket. He straightened his ballcap and trudged off toward the footbridge and the parking lot beyond. A glow lit her head and warmed her body. Then a pang shot through her middle—What if he was going to sabotage her car?

When she turned back to Gruber, he was still grinning at her.

She grabbed the shoulders of his tweed coat, pulled him toward her, and gave him a deep, long kiss.

18
ALBUQUERQUE

Pete Vankov's cell phone blared, echoing off the stucco living room walls of his Albuquerque split-level. He bolted upright and tossed his sketchpad onto the coffee table, narrowing his eyes against a shard of morning sun that hit him through the blinds. Was this the call?

Suddenly, he felt a fierce need to urinate, after crossing his legs for half an hour against an urge to go as he worked on the charcoal drawing. The project had begun an hour earlier as a whimsical diversion, but now seemed somehow important, vital, urgent. On the matte paper, a squad of musclebound blue demons with pink Mohawks was ravishing some buxom nymphs, one with hair like Medusa, all of them on a timber raft floating toward the edge of the Earth. Hieronymus Bosch meets Bob Kane.

"Come on, Yair," Vankov pleaded aloud as he snatched his ringing phone. The former Mossad man should be meeting in Geneva now with spooks from Bahrain and the United Arab Emirates. Had the commando nailed intel, evidence about then-Admiral Maynard's dalliance with a subordinate? He better have something, especially after Vankov had paid half of Yair's inflated fee up front, along with his travel. Come on, bro.

Vankov read his iPhone screen. "Shit." Hess again. The guy was crunching in Iowa before the caucuses at the end of the month, mired in media hits, fundraisers, and meetings. He'd figured the SOB would be too busy to bother him, but Hess had been texting and phoning him all morning.

Vankov took a deep breath and clicked the green button. "Yes, sir." He couldn't toss in his usual blithe "Mr. President."

"You got answers for me, Re-Pete?"

"Answers to what?"

"Answers to the questions I asked you about your self-promotions. Don't you read your messages? I sent you two this morning. We also talked on the phone an hour ago. In one ear and out the other?"

"My self-promotions?"

A sigh rattled into his ear. "Let's go through it, since you don't do your homework. I texted you at six this morning—five Central, where I am—to ask why my bio spot campaign ad includes a shot of you."

Actually, the ad had two shots of Vankov: One of him pumping a fist when Hess won the Iowa Straw Poll, and another of him being swarmed by reporters and cameras shortly after becoming campaign manager. Why? Because, you dolt, the world needs to know that the Dark Angel is running your campaign. That I am your brain.

"Color, flavor," Vankov said into the phone. "The ad has a montage that projects the vibe and brio and energy of your campaign, and that shot you're talking about seemed to capture that vibe."

Dead air. Vankov was about to ask whether Hess was still there, when Hess said, "Next: Why are you listed as a 'host' on invitations to my fundraisers? On one of them, in shiny, raised, embossed print. You're not a host, kid. You're an employee; the help."

Vankov closed his eyes and breathed. "Standard practice. It's understood to mean the employee who helps arrange the event."

More dead air, then another breath rattling into his ear.

"Next: Why is my campaign buying a quarter million dollars of Facebook ads through your personal Facebook fan page? With links to your personal page at your consulting firm?"

Vankov shook his head. "Again, standard practice."

"Maybe your standard practice, kid. Not my standard practice."

"Look," Vankov said, with more of an edge than he intended, "I'm not making a dime off those ads. We're also placing Facebook ads through other staff and surrogates' pages." Which Vankov had arranged as cover, anticipating a call like this one. He cringed at lumping himself among "staff and surrogates."

"Well, stop it."

"Yessir. Never again, sir. Anything else, sir?"

"Yeah, Mr. Campaign Manager. Why aren't you here in Iowa with the candidate? I'm busting my tail out here, and you could be useful."

Vankov felt his arms thrum. He admired the subtle sheen of his cashmere sweater. "I don't do Iowa."

The line went dead.

Vankov studied his phone, then set it on the coffee table and picked up his sketchpad and charcoal. So much for the exquisite Albuquerque respite he'd planned. He had hoped to set the mood with a triumphant call or text from Yair by eight or nine a.m.—Switzerland was eight hours ahead of New Mexico—and then spend the rest of the morning strolling through Old Town Albuquerque.

His cell pinged again, a message from one of Hess's lackeys about scheduling. He ignored it. Then a call from a direct-mail house, the woman probably jonesing about unpaid invoices for a batch of Hess's "the only thing between you and the woke apocalypse is me" letters. Vankov let the call go to voicemail.

He shifted on the sofa and opened the fly of his jeans to ease the pressure on his package. He was still sore from the night before, which was strange since he hadn't joined in much of the action. Two pros from a local high-end service had come over around 9 p.m., but by the time they arrived he'd found he'd lost most of his appetite. Mostly, he'd watched as the pros did a long, slow 69 on his king-sized bed, sliding their lips and tongues down each other's bodies, moaning and writhing, until their mouths finally met. He felt himself stiffen and shifted on the sofa to ease the pressure.

His current wife didn't like this contemporary split-level in Northwest Albuquerque that he'd bought before they married, which left the place more his than any of his other homes. That was reason enough to come here. But January was the coldest month in Albuquerque, so no vegging on the deck catching rays this trip. He picked up his sketch pad. Maybe he'd frame the demons-and-nymphs orgy and hang it in the study.

His cell phone pinged.

Vankov steeled himself. What did Hess want to bitch about now? He reached for his device. An encrypted message from Yair through the Adeya app. Finally! He opened the email, nearly jamming his thumb through the screen. The subject line was "Update and request for guidance." Come on, Yair, come through, bro.

As he read, Vankov nodded and offered color commentary. "Good, good, Yes!" and then, "Okay, okay, all right, nothing we can't handle." Then, "Uh-oh." He reread the message.

The Arabs had evidence on Alec Maynard, a fifteen-year-old audio recording of the admiral in a Dubai hotel room with his paramour, a female Navy officer under his command. Excellent. No, better than excellent, Outstanding. Wasn't that the highest swabbie-jarhead praise, their version of an A-plus? Outstanding, Bravo Zulu.

Yair suspected the Arabs had broken into Maynard's cell phone and used it as a microphone. Vankov chuckled. Dumb weasel. Maynard had been a top US official in a hostile region; hadn't he expected the towelheads to watch him at the hotel, and everywhere else he went? And you're going to "restore honor to the White House," huh, buddy?

Now the tough part, at the end of Yair's email. The Gulf emirs wanted more than Vankov had authorized Yair to offer. What a shocker. Specifically, though, in exchange for corroborating and documenting the dirt on Maynard, the emirs wanted a pledge from Hess not to join any new or renegotiated nuclear deal with their arch enemy, Iran, and to slap stiffer economic sanctions on Iran. Essentially, the emirs wanted to control US Middle East policy and guarantee US military protection for their regimes.

Vankov scrolled through his contacts list on his phone and poised his thumb over Hess's name. How would he explain not calling "the Hessian" on this one? He pressed Hess's name and the number came up, along with a green dial icon.

A molten spike shot down his left arm. The pain sometimes hit without warning, especially when he was tense. He realized he'd forgotten his physical therapy exercises last night, amid all the action.

He circled his thumb around the dial icon in a slow orbit. First, Hess would need a ten-minute primer on the Middle East. Then he'd just gum things up or want to take over and take credit. Or even worse, chicken out. The guy was turning into such a weenie lately. Besides, who was better equipped to negotiate future US foreign policy, Vankov or some bush-league spitball pitcher turned snake oil salesman?

And on the merits, who liked the Iranians, anyway? Generations of geopolitical geniuses had gotten nowhere on the Middle East. For seventy years, the Gulf Arabs and Israelis had been feuding, twisting the United States into a miserable bind: Honor consensus support for Israel, but also maintain good relations with countries that supplied most of the world's oil. Maybe Vankov could do better, applying some hardball realpolitik. If he could put Israel and the Gulf Arabs on the same side, US policy would suddenly become much easier. Vankov could put Hess in the White House by pursuing the policy path Hess ought to take, anyway.

This might be Nobel Peace Prize territory, if Vankov could pull off this alchemy, put the Arabs, Israelis, and Americans in a quasi-alliance against Iran. Hess, of course, would get the invite to Stockholm, which somebody would have to show him on a map.

Vankov shifted back to Yair's email, scanned it again, and typed a one-sentence reply: "Agree to all their demands." He reread the sentence a couple of times and then hit Send.

Vankov washed his face in the downstairs john and noticed that a putty-colored gob from last night's antics was clinging to his hair. He pulled it off and flushed it. He decided to walk to Old Town for lunch, salvage the afternoon, grab a bite at a brasserie near the historic KiMo theater. But his iPhone kept pinging and ringing.

He made a ham sandwich instead, grabbed a bottle of beer, and settled in the living room with the demons-and-nymphs sketch. As he reached for a white highlighting pencil, he caught movement outside the window. Two roadrunners prancing around his deck. He watched them dart and sprint on their long, skinny legs. He flipped his sketchbook to a pristine page, began to outline one of the birds' long torsos, then decided to watch them instead.

Magnificent creatures with their white bellies and black-streaked, pink-spotted brown bodies. With attitude way beyond the "Beep Beep" *Bugs Bunny* cartoon version. Vankov had never seen what looked like a mating pair. Maybe they'd go at it right on his deck, like two Navy officers in heat. He grabbed a double-breasted black leather topcoat, worthy of the High Command, threw it on over his sweater and jeans, and dashed outside.

He eased along the outside of his house, settled against his chimney, and watched. Nature had always fascinated him in all its raw, feral, primitive beauty and glory. Eat or be eaten, no remorse, no thought that the creature you're slaughtering to feed your young might also have young.

Vankov watched the roadrunners a while, waiting for one of them—hard to tell which was the male—to mount the other and lock cloacae. He anticipated their blissful squawks.

One of them was turning and got a leg caught in the lattice of his fence, somehow poked a foot through one of the holes and couldn't pull it out. The bird began smashing its foot against the wood, squawking, and fluttering its wings. The other bird looked on, useless.

Vankov walked over. "Okay, okay," he cooed and squatted by the fence, expecting to get pecked. "You ought to run for president," he told the panicking bird. "You're dumb enough, and you've got the personality for it: you go apeshit when anything goes wrong."

He took hold of the bird's trapped leg with one hand, which set off more squawking and feather fluttering. He clamped his grip, reducing the bird's motion, and gently turned the foot to pull it through the fence hole.

Freed, the bird danced back a few steps, as though testing its limb. The roadrunner met Vankov's gaze for an instant, and he hoped for a glint of warmth or thanks. His iPhone blared again, and the birds dashed off in a blaze of feathers.

Vankov walked back into his living room and looked at his phone. Another Adeya encrypted message, this one from Frank, a former Baltimore cop Vankov had hired to shadow that *New York Globe* reporter, Jane Berglund. With two attachments. He clicked to open the message. The text was a report, larded with weaselly defensive phrases, saying essentially that Berglund had made Frank after two days of surveillance, preventing him from competing the five-day assignment. Amateur. Jesus. At Theodore Roosevelt Island, Frank wrote, Berglund had accosted him and told him, "Tell Vankov he's his own worst enemy." Je-sus.

Vankov dropped the phone onto his lap and sighed. He picked up his sketchpad and highlighted a nymph's breast with the white pencil, filling and flaring the side, and then picked up his iPhone and read Frank's final paragraph: Berglund was with a middle-aged white male at Theodore Roosevelt Island, identity unknown. The two seemed chummy, so Frank doubled back after Berglund thought she had chased him off. See attached photos.

Vankov clicked open Frank's first photo. Looked like he'd shot through bushes, with a couple of blurry leaves at the bottom of the picture. The rest of the zoomed image was sharp, though. The photo showed a man and a woman with their lips locked, sucking face. Berglund was facing the camera, her eyes closed in ecstasy. The man looked about six feet tall, wearing a tweed sportscoat, his hair graying. Looked like he belonged in a cognac ad. Vankov clicked on the second attachment, another photo. The same couple, probably a minute later, now a foot apart gazing at each other with what looked like postcoital bliss. Holy Jesus. Berglund and David Gruber.

"Allahu Akbar!" Vankov shouted, this new triumph dancing with the Mideast coup in his head. Juicy ammo on sexual escapades by three of his enemies, and all in the same day.

After a couple of minutes, Vankov's glee faded, and envy and ire prickled his face and neck. He'd written off Berglund as an ice princess after she snubbed him at lunch at 1789. He hadn't thought her capable of the passion in that second photo. And of all people to lavish it on, to lock those lush lips on, to press those tight, firm breasts against, Dave Gruber? Gruber? Je-sus Christ.

Vankov saved Frank's second photo, the one showing the faces, to his photos file. He searched the contacts list on his phone for a buddy at an alt-right patriots' website. The guy had a gazillion followers. All Vankov had to do now was email his friend and attach the image. He pictured the cutline on the website, something like, "*New York Globe* investigative reporter does deep probe." Or simply, "*NY Globe* reporter digs deep."

He'd savor Berglund's public humiliation. Even if she somehow stayed on at the *Globe*, she'd have to spend half her time on defense. I'm not a whore or a slut. He pictured her going on CNN's "Reliable Sources" to discuss this latest failure in journalism.

Vankov sighed again. No, a public ruin could backfire, make Berglund a sympathetic figure. The great unwashed might recoil at a public shaming of a sweet blonde lass, and her editors might even protect her instead of punishing her, in a spirit of "I can hit my sister, but you can't."

Besides, Vankov remembered now that the last time he fed something to his buddy with the patriots website, the guy gave him a lecture and a warning. The gist was that living the extravagant lifestyle Vankov craved clashed with the loud media profile he thrived on, inviting scrutiny that would eventually bring him down. "You're like a bug drawn to the flame," the guy told him. Tell me something I don't know.

Too bad; he would have savored the spectacle of pinning a scarlet letter onto Jane Berglund. But better to be strategic. Best to start small; he could always escalate later if he had to. He Googled some top *New York Globe* editors, clicked and pasted a couple of their addresses onto a fresh email, and attached Frank's money-shot photo. Then he typed the body of the message:

A friend who was outraged by what he understandably deemed a malicious and unfair article about me in your newspaper some days ago by reporter Jane Berglund happened on this scene and took the attached photo. It shows Ms. Berglund with one of her anonymous sources for that story, my disgruntled business partner David Gruber. I trust the *New York Globe* does not tolerate fraternization with sources by its reporters, especially when it involves such a blatant conflict of interest, and such high stakes.

Sincerely,
Peter Vankov
Campaign Manager, Hess for President

19
LEAKS

David Gruber shifted in the beanbag chair, trying to ease a spike in his lower back, and gazed at Jane Berglund across her small home office as she typed. He admired her sunflower hair, her form-fitting burgundy blouse sliding into her jeans, and he wanted to touch her, to hug her, to hold her.

Her face was partly obscured by a Felix the Cat plushie on her desk. He hadn't expected the intrepid scribe to live in such a femme redoubt, filled with dolls, folk prints, and a fleet of white furniture on a sea of pastel carpet. The small Alexandria apartment itself was a modern box of white sheetrock walls, low ceilings and generic off-white carpet.

Each peck on her laptop looked like a tantrum, and Gruber decided to let her alone for now. He realized he was studying her with a politico's eye and chided himself. He'd grown inured to assessing beautiful women as prizes, to be shown off at firm mixers and displayed in photos of them together on yachts, on ski slopes, and at soirees.

Don't screw up another one, he told himself. On his first trip to the altar, Gruber had married his high school girlfriend a week after college graduation.

He was scrambling to report in a few months to Penn Law School, always in a hurry to be like his grownup brother. After law school, he joined one of Philly's fast-growing corporate firms, and he and his wife became caricatures of the newly named "Yuppies." The marriage lasted through the Poppy Bush years but broke in the era of Clinton parsing the meaning of sex.

On his second go, Gruber married a beauty ten years his junior whom he'd met during one of his campaign-manager stints when she was working as an assistant's assistant. They had an affair, not his first, but this one felt much more important, way beyond "campaign sex," and he realized that his first wife had been a starter marriage rather than a love connection.

Marriage two ended despite maintaining much of the whirlwind-romance vibe in which the relationship had illicitly begun. As his wife put it, the scope and pace of Gruber's ambition to "rule the world" left her always a passenger in the racecar of his life.

Berglund smacked her keyboard rapid-fire.

"Any developments?" he called across the small room. He congratulated himself on his word choice, avoiding the term "news" because she was the one, after all, who was supposed to break news.

She shook her head.

"If it's any solace, Maynard got it a lot worse than you did."

She snapped toward him, gave him a look that said she couldn't believe he'd just said what he had.

"The photos of us at Theodore Roosevelt Island are embarrassing, but we're single, consenting adults. Maynard was married when they made that audio of him cavorting in the Dubai hotel with a subordinate."

She didn't say anything, didn't even look at him, so he went on.

"Your editor was probably steamed mostly at Vankov for spying on you, on his reporter. He didn't fire you, didn't suspend you, didn't even really chastise you—not that I imagine your talk with him was pleasant. He just gave you a lateral move, maybe even a step up. Your tough story on Maynard's finances gave him cover to reassign you to Maynard from Hess."

She snapped toward him and shot him another incredulous glare.

"Granted, it might have been a step up for two days, until the Dubai audio hit."

They sat in silence for what felt like an hour, punctuated by her occasional keyboard clicks.

Finally, she said, "I wonder what the record is for shortest time on a beat. At the *Globe*, anyway."

"Look, I can give you perspective from at least a little distance. Well, not much. Not any, judging by that photo." He laughed.

She didn't join in, didn't look up from her laptop.

"Your editor seems like a decent guy, all considered." He held his breath. When she only moved her head, he went on. "He must have said to himself, 'I don't care whom she sees'"—he nearly said "sleeps with"—"I know she's a good reporter. What I care about is, are the facts she gives me real? Can I count on them?' He figured, yes. In a way, it's a vote of confidence, a commendation."

She kept silent, so he continued. "He had to do something. The stakes became perception, the newspaper's reputation, and he can't have those compromised. So he moves you over, but keeps you on the political team. On its face, it looks like he's taken a significant step. And he's protected the paper. Maynard and Hess are in separate silos, competing for separate nominations, never mind the larger whole of the race. Maybe one of them, or even both, don't get nominated, and they never face each other in the general. Or if they do, a 'decent interval' has passed that you can keep covering the race. Or your editor can revisit it then."

She sighed.

"He's sending a signal to the world that you're still a top political reporter. Partly because as your editor, he wants to be the guy who prints your 'Vankov's greatest-hits' story. He's with you, for you."

"Thank you," she said, arching her back but still not looking at him. "But I don't need you to tell me about my relationship with my editor."

His mind ran back two decades, when he'd tried to placate his eldest daughter, who'd also been moody. He shook his head to clear his thoughts; he didn't need a reminder that Berglund was nearly young enough to be his daughter. He hoisted himself out of her beanbag chair and padded over to her.

She turned as he neared her. "You paint yourself as a fellow victim of Vankov's spying. A fellow 'injured party,' as you lawyers might say. But with the strength of character to be objective. And philosophical. And reasonable. And so wise. But there's an element you've elided in your treatise on journalism. Actually, a couple of elements.

"First, I got a blast of shrapnel and you got a paper cut. Unless you forgot to mention you also had a Come-to-Jesus meeting with your boss. Second, you seem to be counting on me to paint Vankov as the sole bad guy in the Argentina scam, and maybe in some other . . . depredations. Even though other people—including you, my philosophical friend—were involved. Maybe you figure you're entitled to that. After all, you're the one who confirmed what I had. Might not be any story without you. That's the Washington Tango: 'If you're not the source, you're the subject.' Notice I didn't say 'Washington Hustle.'"

Berglund shifted on her chair to face him without turning her neck. "I agreed to your demand—to your condition, let's be polite—to speak only on background, not-for-attribution. That's a big concession, which I rarely make. I was essentially promising to go to jail rather than publicly reveal you as my source, if it ever came to that. And with these photos out, it might.

"If I honor that pledge, protect my source, and get held in contempt, I'm golden as a reporter—if I survive. If I break that confidentiality promise, I'm ruined, no source will ever trust me again. And I'll look like a cliché lefty journalist who threw a right-winger under the bus." She raised her hand. "Excuse me. Not a right-winger; a brave, reasonable, decent, pragmatic, philosophical old-school moderate Republican who happened to find himself in league with right-wing devils. That's a fair description of you, isn't it?"

She raised her index finger to signal that she wasn't done. "If I did give you up, though, I might still have a place in journalism. It might not cost me with the *Globe*. Like that exchange in the movie *The Wild Bunch*. Another of my father's favorites; a western about a bunch of train robbers. William Holden defends their former compadre Robert Ryan for coming after them, under pressure from the railroad. Ryan had no choice, Holden tells Ernest Borgnine. "He gave his word." Borgnine hollers, 'That ain't what counts! It's who you give it to.' And that's how the journalism world would react if I threw you under."

She stared at him, maybe waiting for him to say something. Eventually, she shrugged. "I won't do it, but just so you appreciate the dynamics here."

She turned back to her keyboard and began pulling up more images. He began to reach his hand out, to put it on her shoulder, then retreated a step. He searched for the right words but couldn't find them. Finally, he asked, "What's the latest on Maynard?"

She didn't move for a moment, then rocked back and forth with a deep breath. "Nothing. He's still hunkering down in his house in San Francisco." She clicked her mouse a couple of times, and her laptop screen showed what at first looked like a lawn party at a tony colonial, until Gruber saw it was a horde of reporters and cameras camped outside the house, some trying to peer through drawn curtains of downstairs windows.

She laughed, cold and dry. "Two days on the Maynard beat, and I'm already on his death vigil. At least I don't have to fly out there for that circus."

Gruber studied Maynard's lawn. It looked as though a pack of jackals had descended, smelling rotting flesh.

"You think he can survive?" she asked.

Gruber warmed at the question, at her bow to his expertise and savvy.

"I've handled candidates whose campaigns became unwinnable and urged them to fold rather than spend further into debt and embarrass themselves, which would foreclose future runs and opportunities. I could have bled them for a few more weeks, but my own reputation would have suffered as their campaigns sank. Apart from any moral concerns, which I did have; I'm not a complete antichrist. If I were handling Maynard, I would not give him that advice—yet.

"Can he survive? Hard to say. The public has limited interest in sexual peccadilloes. Clinton and Lewinsky proved that, and every tabloid has run stories about Hess treating women like blowup dolls. But this is a higher order of magnitude. The woman was in Maynard's chain of command, and she was working on much bigger stuff than a White House intern's portfolio. This is national security, integrity of operations, and a clear violation of basic, explicit military codes, which the public does care about." He shrugged. "On the other hand, it was fifteen years ago, and Maynard and the woman are both long out of the service. The Navy's not going to do anything; why would they wade into that cesspool? And the Senate's not going to censure him; not their jurisdiction."

"Do you have to call her 'the woman'? Like she's the help?"

Gruber felt acid rise from his stomach. "The female Navy lieutenant commander." He paused, took what he hoped would be a deep, calming breath, but fury percolated in his chest. "Still, even if Maynard somehow survives and keeps his Senate seat and even salvages his campaign, he's a toss-up at best for the Democratic nomination. Which does stick you with a devalued beat. To that extent, Vankov and Hess have scored a two-for."

Another silence. He tried again to fathom Berglund's pain. Reporting to her office yesterday must have felt like a walk of shame, or to the gallows, her coworkers sniggering—these things never stayed secret—and signaling that she was branded a sexual climber.

Finally, he said, "I would gently remind you that images of my face and lips are also making the rounds, along with yours. To channel Bill Clinton, I do feel your pain. Though maybe not quite to the same degree. But I certainly know that I'm no detached observer."

She waved a hand, brushing away the subject. "Okay. Fine. But, you know, you're doing the same thing with Maynard—what you would advise him if he were your client. As though it's equal, the same amount of skin in the game. It's different for a candidate than for a consultant. My ex had clients who went through crises, and he slept fine." She sighed and added, "It's still another level of remove for a reporter, a watcher."

"I've been a candidate," he said.

"Yeah. But no offense, darling, this is the presidency we're talking about."

"I was a candidate for federal office. I stepped into the arena, put myself out there. And took fire." He had taken a shot at elective office before settling into a career behind the thrones, a run for Congress from Maryland against a ten-year incumbent in a district that had been reliably Democratic for decades. At the time, he was bored as a Philadelphia lawyer and ready to break into real politics. He knew he'd lose but also that he'd make connections to launch a Hill career and whatever that led to in Washington. He hadn't counted on some of the incoming, though.

She nodded, as though humoring a child. He was about to speak when she laughed, for the first time that evening.

She pushed back from her computer screen. "Talk about calm under fire."

He stepped over and she clicked to restart a video. On her laptop, a middle-aged Black woman in a blue floral dress wagged a finger at Maynard and chanted, "Repent and resign!" Probably one of the Sistas for Sistas minions. The PAC had stepped up its vitriol recently, after replacing Laronda Tibbs with an even more militant mouthpiece. The group had been working overtime since learning that Maynard's Navy paramour had been white. "Repent and Resign!" the woman shouted at Maynard.

Maynard waited for the woman to pause and asked, "Wouldn't one or the other suffice?"

Gruber laughed, also a first for him that evening.

Berglund clicked to an image of Maynard's news conference the day before, the admiral standing nearly at attention in a charcoal suit, an American flag behind him, his wife beside him.

"I want to puke every time I see a political wife do that burlesque," Berglund said. "It's literally sickening to watch Claudia Maynard do a Tammy Wynette, stand by her man. 'We've had issues in our marriage, like many couples, and we've worked through them, blah blah. We ask our fellow Americans for privacy and understanding as we heal. Blah, blah, blah.'"

Gruber put his hand on her shoulder, and she flinched, then settled, then rested her hand on top of his. He gave a gentle squeeze, then knelt on the carpet and settled with his back against a leg of her glossy white desk.

Their heads were now a few feet apart.

"The only way Vankov could have gotten that tape," he said, and waited for her to turn toward him. "That audio of Maynard and . . . that female Navy officer in the Dubai hotel, is from the UAE."

She swiveled her chair to face him. "Why are you so sure Vankov's behind the tape? He doesn't have a monopoly on scummy. Or on dislike of Maynard."

"I recognize his signature."

Her face said she wasn't going to settle for empty assurances.

"The audio went out through StormSpill, which is just how Vankov would release a tape he shouldn't possess, in this case from a foreign intelligence service. StormSpill is technically an international nonprofit, but it's in the business of publishing news leaks and classified material supplied by anonymous sources. They release their material to the world unanalyzed, unedited, and uncommented on. The head of StormSpill, this shadowy guy who's dodging international arrest warrants, is one of Vankov's pals." He shrugged. "Some consider StormSpill an intelligence operation of a hostile foreign power, others hail it as a champion of free speech and transparency. Either way, their document dumps are always big news. They've become the nuclear option for releasing intel. And Vankov these days has been going nuclear."

She was looking at him, waiting for more.

"Vankov could have sent his StormSpill pal one encrypted email with the audio and said, 'Look what I've got.' The audio would go out, Vankov wouldn't be named, nobody would know he was behind it. I'm not suggesting you go to print with that, I'm just saying it's our starting point."

He thought she might balk at the word "our," but she locked on his eyes and nodded.

"Come here," he said, and took her hand. He tugged to guide her out of her chair and onto the carpet beside him.

She stiffened. "This didn't work out too well last time."

He laughed again and stopped tugging but kept hold of her hand. "My brother was a grunt in Vietnam. He told me a story, maybe it's apocryphal, about a guy in his unit who smoked a lot of weed. Another grunt warned the guy he was breaking the rules, and the pothead said, 'What are they going to do, send me to Vietnam'?"

He gave her arm a gentle tug. "The worst has already happened. And we've already taken the consequences. Yes, you more than me, but both of us."

He gave her a gentle pull, and this time she went with it. She slid down beside him and settled with her back against his shoulder. The contact was electric. Nearly as exciting as that kiss at Theodore Roosevelt Island, when her tongue had sent so much current through him that he'd thought his brain might short-circuit.

"Okay." He draped his arm around her and reached for her hand.

She arched her wrist to let him interlace their fingers.

"Okay," he said again. "You've got to understand how Pete Vankov works, and then you'll recognize his signature. Pete has a code. He doesn't concoct dirt, doesn't frame his marks. He always begins with a nugget of truth, a seed of sin. Like here, with Maynard. He was just exploiting his enemy's failings. Just as he did with us in the park."

He felt her stiffen and shift.

"That's Vankov's M.O. The Dark Angel doesn't even tempt his marks into sin, like the original Prince of Darkness. He just capitalizes on sins they've already committed. He boasts that he can always find something on anybody; he just has to look hard enough. He quotes Willie Stark from his favorite novel, Robert Penn Warren's *All The King's Men*: 'Man is conceived in sin and born in corruption and he passeth from the stink of the didie to the stench of the shroud. There is always something.'"

She shifted back toward him.

"So Vankov finds out about Maynard's affair with his subordinate. Now he has to get evidence. So he goes to the UAE intel service, which is obviously going to tape an American admiral in a hotel room there. But how did Pete Vankov get something so valuable from the intelligence service of this fine country?"

Her laugh vibrated through him.

"There's got to be a deal between the Hess campaign and this foreign government for this audio. There's a key phrase in federal campaign finance law that prohibits political campaigns from taking anything of value from foreigners, from taking what the law calls 'a thing of value.' So the key question here, the legal question, is: What is a 'thing of value?' Did UAE spooks, by confirming Vankov's own intel, provide him a thing of value?"

Before she said anything, he went on. "By the way, Ven Hess is also culpable, even if he didn't know about Vankov's getting the tape, because it was done by his agent in his name, for his benefit. And if he is party to it, he's even worse than Vankov."

He unlaced his fingers and wrapped his arm around her middle, resting his wrist on the flare of her hip, where her silk blouse fed into her jeans. The bouquet of textures and scents jumbled his thoughts. She shifted farther toward him, easing the pressure on his arm, closing the angle between their faces.

"What could Vankov offer the UAE for the audio?" he asked, his voice weaker than before. "For a tape that would destroy his political opponent and change the election and the course of history? What did Vankov have that they'd value enough to trade with him?"

She angled her head up, studying him.

"It wasn't season tickets to the Des Moines Cubs," he said. "It has to involve US foreign policy. Foreign policy under a President Hess. Peter Vankov sold US policy to a foreign country to influence a US election. That's the biggest scandal in US history."

She leaned away, maybe for a better angle to study him. "It's only a crime if you get caught."

He laughed. "Spoken like a true cynic. And a true detective. But that's right." He stroked her thigh, savored the heat through her jeans.

"We're going to take down Pete Vankov," he said. "And not just because he's a slimeball. Not just because of what he did to us. Not just because he's ruining what's left of the Republican Party. But because he's selling out the country." He met her eyes. "You're going to get the biggest news story of this generation, and I'm going to get some mitigating circumstances on my sentencing report at the pearly gates."

"Sounds great. All we have to do is find a secret exchange with a foreign intelligence service, then prove it happened."

He snuggled tighter. "Yeah. And I know who I need to talk to first."

She leaned toward him until her two cobalt eyes merged into one big eye, and then she was on top of him, and he did feel his brain short-circuit, turning the screen in his head to snow. He stretched out on the floor and felt her weight settle on him.

20
CACTUS LAN

David Gruber settled into his leather swivel chair behind his mahogany desk at DNFV and did a few rounds of "The Breath of Fire," a yoga stress-relief technique a freshman-year dormmate at Columbia had taught him. He looked at his watch. Yair, Vankov's former Mossad agent, was due at 11 a.m., in ten minutes. Gruber rehearsed his pitch, yet again, then leaned back and took some slow breaths.

He tried to savor the trappings in this temple of power that used to electrify him, the view of K Street out his window, the throne, the matching leather nail head chairs in front of his desk, the rest of it. He recalled his first foray into DNFV's citadel, for a job interview with Ezra Fitch and some other partners, and how that onslaught of gravitas and power, capped by the photos of partners beside presidents, senators, governors, and kings, had struck him. Intimidated him—call it what it was—even after all his time on Capitol Hill. Sure, senators hung similar photos in their anterooms, but those congressional eight-by-tens, framed by the Senate's service in cheap, thin black or brown wood, showed mostly grip-and-grins during drop-by meetings. The photos at DNFV, shot mostly in the firm's conference room and enlarged to sometimes obscene proportion, then double-matted and framed by Georgetown galleries, showed masters of the universe beseeching these K Street wizards.

Gruber studied his silver cuff links and thought of Vankov. Have I taken so much from him that I've become him? Berglund wondered the same thing. He could tell from the way she sometimes looked at him and from some of the questions she asked, such as why he drove a $90,000 Jag.

"Janey." He liked calling her that.

Gruber looked at his watch again and noticed that his fingers had healed. Well, a few areas of taut new skin shined above the nails and a few cuticles were a bit discolored. But mere traces of the raw, red, and swollen mess of only weeks earlier. His hands looked healthy, for the first time in months, and he realized he'd stopped gnawing and picking at them when he met Berglund.

He gazed at a photo of himself with a former president, a former client. All this was going to end soon, he reminded himself. But not by his moving to a cushy gig at an educational streaming service. With a bang, not a whimper. One way or the other. He'd miss it, some of it.

He thought of the poem that featured that bang-but-whimper line, T. S. Eliot's "The Hollow Men," which had hit him like a gut punch in a college lit class. He still remembered snippets:

> We are the hollow men
> We are the stuffed men . . .
> This is the dead land
> This is cactus land
> Here the stone images
> Are raised, here they receive
> The supplication of a dead man's hand
> Under the twinkle of a fading star . . .

His intercom buzzed, and he jolted. He took a deep breath and told the receptionist to send Yair in.

A minute later, the Israeli strutted through his doorway, lean and fit in a charcoal suit and white shirt that highlighted his tanned face. His wavy hair, cut short and sharp, showed a few silver strands over his ears.

Gruber stood, big grin, and gestured at one of his leather nail head chairs. "Thanks for making the time."

Yair was studying him, maybe the way he'd been taught in some commando school to assess potential patrons. Or targets. Gruber had been in a room with Yair on Vankov's Argentine project and on an earlier Vankov special, but this was the first time they'd met alone. The Israeli wasn't that big physically, about Gruber's size, a lean six feet, but he radiated coiled strength. His eyes said he'd seen suffering and horror and might have inflicted some. Yair had what pulp novels described as brooding good looks, and he probably had his share of female attention, though something about him said he wasn't interested in romance, that his psyche was tuned to combat and conflict.

"Close the door?" Yair asked.

"No, that's all right." Gruber flashed another grin.

Yair settled onto a nail head chair, only a clenched hand betraying tension.

"Crazy weather, eh?" Gruber asked. "I feel for the airlines and the Florida tourism folks—What's the point of going down there when its seventy degrees in Washington? The Earth may be turning into a cinder, but at least winter's nice here, for now."

Yair gave a cautious nod.

A form walked past Gruber's open office door. Any partner would have done, but this was perfect.

"Bob!" Gruber rose in his chair. "Bob!"

Bob Snead stepped back into Gruber's doorway, looking as wary as Yair. Gruber hadn't had a substantive exchange with the junior partner in two months, since their standoff over Gruber's move to vote Vankov out of the firm.

Gruber swung around his desk and strode toward Snead.

"Excuse me," he told the commando. "Pressing issue." Then an afterthought,

"Bob, meet Yair. He's working with us on some projects."

Gruber considered throwing an arm around Yair, to stress their bond. It was a trick he'd learned from a grizzled old Philadelphia criminal defense lawyer. When the lawyer wanted to drive a wedge between conspirators who'd been caught, he'd throw an arm around one in the jailhouse while the other was watching, to make the other think his partner was ratting him out. But Yair gave off a vibe that said not to push too far.

Gruber's two visitors shook hands, like two tanned gym rats sizing each other up.

"Bob, I just wanted to make sure you saw my memo about the garage," Gruber said. "These breaks-in are getting absurd. I know you've got a nice ride, and they make juicy targets for these SOBs. At a minimum, you should make sure not to leave anything valuable in sight." He spread his arms in a world's-gone-crazy gesture. "Just trying to spare you some misery."

Snead nodded and eyed Gruber. "Thanks, Dave. I'll keep that in mind." He took a step before turning his back, then continued down the corridor.

Gruber wondered how long it would take Snead to tell Vankov about Gruber's meeting with Yair. Maybe even before the meeting ended.

"Sorry about that," Gruber told Yair, taking his chair again. "A partner's car got broken into last week, right in the garage in this building. You didn't drive here today . . ."

"No, I used Uber."

"Good." Gruber shook his head. "A brand new BMW 750i. They ripped out his infotainment system and took a pair of prescription sunglasses, of all things, but the damage was worse than the theft."

Yair scratched his chin. "You said on the phone you have a new mission on which I can be useful."

Gruber loosened. He'd won his gamble, that Yair didn't know the depths of Gruber's schism with Vankov. The commando probably assumed that since Vankov and Gruber were still partners, they were still collaborating, and dismissed their spat as routine friction among allies. From Yair's point of view, Gruber was talking about the next job, and that was enough.

"We'll get to that," Gruber said. "You can close the door now."

Yair eyed him but didn't move from the chair.

"Close the door, Yair. You don't want anybody hearing what I'm going to tell you next."

The commando seemed to think about it a moment, then stood and shouldered the door shut, keeping his eyes on Gruber.

Gruber waited until Yair sat again.

"First, understand that I'm not working with Pete Vankov. And you shouldn't be, either. It's not going to end well for him."

Yair cocked his head.

"I know what you did. To get the audio on Alec Maynard. And I can figure out why you did it."

Yair met his glare and crossed his arms over his lap. Only his wide eyes betrayed his fury, like a cornered animal.

"You think you helped Israel. But you didn't. Because once this is exposed—that an Israeli operative is involved in undermining US democracy and in letting these Arab countries drive American policy—you're screwed."

Yair's eyes narrowed.

"How do you think mainstream Democrats, who've been uniformly pro Israel since the '60s—Robert Kennedy took a bullet in the brain from Sirhan for supporting Israel—How do you think they'll react when your part comes out?"

Yair's jaw muscles flexed.

"You thought you were being a good entrepreneur and helping your country. To which you still feel allegiance, even after they kicked you out of the Mossad for insubordination."

Yair leaned forward in his chair and placed his hands on the seat cushion, as though preparing to lunge.

"You thought you were going to prove to them, your former bosses who threw you away, that you were the most valuable asset they had. You were going to deliver US foreign policy. But turns out it works only if it's a secret." Gruber met Yair's glare. "And I can blow that up."

Yair crossed his arms again.

"It'd be a shanda if this gets out. If you let it get out."

Yair finally spoke, in a voice that seemed to come from deep inside. "But you are my friend, David. And a landsman. You also do not want to hurt Israel. So you are going to help me, yes?" The sarcasm sliced through the air.

"That's right, Yair. We're pals. Landsmen. So I'm going to help you. I'm going to protect you, and protect Israel. I'm going to give you a way out."

Yair glared some more, then gestured for him to go on.

"You're going to get a call soon from a *New York Globe* reporter, the one who wrote that story a couple of weeks ago about Vankov and Argentina. Her name is Jane Berglund. She's going to call you about the Maynard hotel audio, and you're going to confirm everything, you're going to tell her everything."

Gruber raised a hand. "She won't use your name in the story or identify you as an Israeli. You don't matter, really; you were just Vankov's tool. I can't promise your name will never come out, but the odds are good it won't. Because this scheme, and every other scheme Pete Vankov's got going, will become moot when the story runs and blows him out of the water." Gruber leaned forward in his chair and locked his eyes with the commando. "But if you don't take Berglund's call, I can guarantee that your name will be on the front page of the *New York Globe* the next day."

Yair seemed to focus on a point above Gruber's head. Gruber could see him figuring possible escapes, calculating their risks and costs and odds. Yair might be thinking the way Vankov would think, that he could turn this into a bidding war. The Israeli had been spending time with the Dark Angel, and pets come to resemble their owners. Yair might be thinking that he could go to Vankov and say for enough money, he'd disappear, and the *New York Globe* could look for him under the mulch. He might ask Vankov, "What's the presidency worth to you?"

"Let me tell you a story, Yair. Might help crystalize your thinking. Around the time Vankov was setting up 'Operation Cabot'—that's a jackass name for the Argentine operation, by the way —he was also pressing some US senators to sponsor a bill to hold Austria, Germany, Poland, and some other

European nations directly accountable for their Holocaust crimes. For their atrocities. 'Make those rat-bastard, nazi-collaborator sons of bitches pay up,' as Pete put it. Sounds pretty noble, right?"

Yair shrugged, eyes still narrowed.

"What your friend Pete didn't tell the senators was that he was working for an insurance consortium that could save megabucks—big money—by letting Holocaust survivors die off while lawsuits against these countries bounced around the international courts." Gruber shrugged, mocking the commando's gesture. "Some friend of Israel, huh? That's who you've been helping. That's who you're protecting now."

Yair's jaw flexed again.

"Whatever else you are, Yair, you are an Israeli patriot. You've messed up, though, and it's going to backfire, and Israel is going to lose the US aid and support it's had for half a century. Unless you make this right. You going to talk to the reporter?"

Yair held his glare for several beats, and finally gave a short nod.

The next morning around eight, Gruber ambled across Washington Street in Old Town, Alexandria, toward a coffee shop near Jane Berglund's apartment house. His hair was still damp from a shower, and his scalp tightened in the winter chill. He was exuding a pink scent from Berglund's perfumed soap, which ordinarily would have annoyed him, but anything about Jane Berglund had come to excite and amuse him.

The coffee shop looked like a typical franchise, elevator music playing amid a symphony of stained wood and aluminum, with cheery displays of coffee beans, mugs, and grinders behind a long counter. The place was bustling with commuters, dog walkers, and joggers, while several lonely souls and teleworkers clacked laptops and nursed drinks at prime tables. Gruber ordered a Blonde Caffe Americano with honey, mostly because the name made him think of Berglund and Argentina and their impending triumph.

He found a small table toward the rear, set down the coffee, and went to the condiment station to fetch some extra napkins. When he turned around, a man was sitting at his table, his back to the wall, staring at him. Pete Vankov.

Gruber's head pulsed.

Vankov gave him a nod. Well, fine, Vankov must have gotten the message about Gruber's stunt yesterday with Yair. And now the Dark Angel was delivering a warning that he knew where Gruber went, what he did, who he saw. Or maybe Vankov had still been following Berglund, using a new thug they hadn't spotted, and had picked up Gruber again as a bonus. Strategically, Gruber had to figure that Vankov was tracking both of them.

Gruber had been watched before, probably, on a couple of Senate trips to Beijing. The Senate Security Office had told him he should expect to be under constant surveillance, warned him not to leave his laptop unattended, not to leave anything important in his hotel room, not to trust the hotel safe, to use the American embassy. Those trips had creeped him out, to use one of his younger daughter's phrases, and soured him further on China. Now Vankov was having the same effect.

Gruber stepped over and looked down at his partner. They were still partners.

"Sit down," Vankov said. "Your coffee's getting cold. I don't know how you can drink that swill, it's like a kid's drink with all that sugar, a woman's drink. I like a simple, straight espresso in the morning." He raised a hand. "No, no, please don't offer; I've already had one, back at my place."

Gruber pulled back the chair opposite Vankov and sat. He left the Caffe Americano cooling in the center of the table. He wasn't going to touch it after Vankov had been alone with it.

Vankov looked tired, dark sacs under his bloodshot eyes. He looked like October, before an election, and it was only January.

Vankov stood to take off his topcoat and drape it over his chairback, revealing one of his Al Capone double-breasted, striped suits. He shot his cuffs, but too hard, sending his suit sleeve up past his shirt cuff to the billowy white fabric. He quickly adjusted.

"That's you all over," Gruber said. "What you just did with your cuffs. Excessive force. You use an elephant gun when a fly swatter will do. Which shows your hand—in this case, your sleeve—and draws attention you don't want. But you can't help yourself. You've got a transmission with only one gear, high."

Vankov glanced at his cuffs and looked up, satisfied. "I know what your girlfriend is up to. And I know you're helping her."

"Is that supposed to be news, that you're watching us?"

Vankov shook his head. "I know everything that goes on. Through methods you don't know, and you could never imagine. I came to tell you that, and to warn you: Step away, stand down. It's futile, anyway. I've covered my tracks on anything you or that skank can come up with. Keep it up, and I'll send more than kissy photos next time."

Gruber felt his face heat, which he knew was what Vankov wanted. Vankov wanted him to make a scene, defend his lady's honor, hurl his designer coffee, take a swing, anything that would look unhinged, which meant Vankov probably had eyes on him now, some thug filming.

Gruber forced a smile. "That was beneath even you, those photos."

"Nothing is beneath me. To win, you have to do everything, be willing to do anything. Didn't you learn anything from me?"

Yeah, he'd learned a lot from Vankov. And he'd admired his teacher and mentor until he couldn't admire him any longer. "The ends justify means, and the end is winning. Winning isn't everything; it's the only thing. That it?"

"That's it. And, no, I don't lose sleep over the corrosive social effect. So spare me another lecture on the Tragedy of the Commons."

"No more lectures on civility, Pete. No more efforts to reach whatever humanity you may have left. We've passed that point. But I'll give you a warning, in the same spirit you just gave me one. For old time's sake."

Vankov leaned back and grinned. "I'm listening."

Gruber pushed his coffee cup aside, leaving an open channel between him and Vankov.

"First, some observations, for context: You thrive on recklessness, on gambles and stunts and on bulldozing your marks, even innocents. You'd rather do something crooked even when you could do it straight; a dollar stolen is sweeter than a dollar earned. You build your bank accounts and collect houses and paintings like a poker player admiring his stacks of chips. You should be discreet, but you can't hide behind a curtain; your ego and your narcissism won't allow it. You need the attention, the adulation. And that's your weakness."

Vankov shrugged. "The only thing worse than being talked about is not being talked about."

"Yeah. But you're like a dog who licks his balls. Why does he do it? Because he can."

"And you're different?"

"I get off on getting things done, not on power for its own sake. I like to think that my career is a net positive, even as a growing number of the candidates and causes we advance at the firm aren't advancing the world. While you're running a big net negative, especially if you factor in the lives and careers you've trampled. Not that you give a damn. That's the difference between us."

Gruber breathed and went on. "That's the substance. We may be closer on style. We both enjoy a good martini and a nice ride. Though I try to speak softly and carry a big stick." The old Rough Rider had been galloping through his thoughts since the Theodore Roosevelt Island afternoon. "After all, why bang heads for eighteen hours a day to make money that you're ashamed to spend?"

Vankov nodded. "You done?"

"Not quite. Oh, first, I nearly forgot, let me save you some trouble. After your stunt hacking my email about the Woodley Park condo, my accountant alerted the IRS to the situation, explaining that I'd only recently learned that there was a tax consideration, and he negotiated a settlement. The IRS sent me a closure letter a week ago."

"Well, that's fine, David. You're onto a new skank, I'm onto new 'stunts.'"

"They're not skanks, Pete. They're just more of your innocent victims."

Vankov grinned.

Gruber pushed his coffee aside. "We've been playing this Mutually Assured Destruction dance for a while, you and I. And just like the Cold

War between the US and the Soviets, there've been times when it looked like it was going to go hot, to escalate into the real thing. One side would go as far as they could go without pulling the trigger, and then the other side would back down."

Vankov covered his mouth to suppress a yawn.

"We've been playing like that so far, the way the US did with the Soviets. But the US has never really played that same dance with China. And the reason why is because early in the nuclear age, Mao basically told us that losing fifty to a hundred million people in China was okay. It wouldn't be a great day, but it was survivable. Mao told us they'd been there forever and they'd be there forever, and there were a whole lot of them. Whereas in America, if we lose ten or twenty or thirty million people, it's over, we're not America anymore."

Vankov raised his eyebrows, in mock horror.

"Mao and China scared the shit out of us," Gruber continued. "We accepted stalemate in Korea and Vietnam because we wouldn't risk escalating the nuclear ladder with China. We thought China was crazy, whereas Russia was at least rational."

Vankov sighed.

Gruber leaned across the table toward Vankov. "I'm Mao, I don't care what you do to me. Not anymore. I don't care what other stolen emails or taped conversations or spies' photos you have. You, Pete, even with all your nihilist threats, you're more like America, because of who you are and how you've decided to live and how you want to be treated by the world. Less damage ends you.

"I'm willing to be China, I'm willing to go all-in. So take your best shot. But understand what's coming."

Gruber shoved back his chair and walked out, feeling Vankov's glare heat the back of his head.

21
MOUNT VERNON

The next afternoon, Gruber found himself in a mid-level Baltimore hotel room with another middle-aged man, the curtains drawn. He wondered what the hotel staff would say, but reminded himself that they wouldn't say anything because they wouldn't know, because he and Paul Thompson had arrived separately.

The room was generic, matching beds with textured off-white spreads, pressed-wood furniture with worn veneers, bright landscapes in distressed frames, and a faint Lysol reek.

Thompson must have put on thirty pounds since Gruber had last seen him, maybe five years ago. His face was rounder, now moon-shaped, with a slick of sweat on his upper lip. His hair was thinner, though Gruber had no standing to criticize that.

"Feels like yesterday we were at that Capitol Hill bar doing scenes from *Double Indemnity*," Gruber said.

"'Every month, hundreds of claims come to this desk,'" Thompson said, sliding into the Edward G. Robinson part. "'Some of them are phonies. And I know which ones. How do I know? Because my little man tells me.'"

"'What little man?'" Gruber asked, playing the crooked truck driver.

"'The little man in here.'" Thompson pointed to his ample gut. "'Every time one of these phonies comes along, it ties knots in my stomach. I can't eat.'"

They both laughed. But the scene left Gruber with a tightness in his middle.

Gruber had known Thompson for more than twenty years, since Thompson was the contract officer for a Navy helicopter program and Gruber was lobbying for an aviation manufacturer, making sure the funds for his client's choppers were in the DOD budget that came out of Congress. Thompson had believed in the helicopter program, believed that the birds Gruber was hawking were top quality and that the money was better spent on them than on midnight basketball, or whatever the peacenik legislators were pushing. They had bonded over defense procurements and a shared love of classic films.

Vankov was also a classic film buff, but they'd never included him, and Gruber reassured himself that the Dark Angel didn't know Thompson, had never heard of him.

They took soft drinks from the refrigerator, a sparkling water for Gruber and a Coke for Thompson.

"So, Paul, how'd you like to be an actor, pretend you're committing a major federal crime, and risk prison?" He grinned.

Thompson squinted at him.

"I'm serious about the risk. Your part in my little scheme would violate the Hatch Act, which prohibits federal executive branch employees from engaging in political activities."

Thompson poured Coke into a glass.

"There's a lot of money involved here, a lot of cash that you're going to get hold of," Gruber said. "But you won't keep any of it. Sound appealing so far?"

Thompson took a long swallow of Coke. "Go on."

"I think you'll find it worthwhile. I hope you will. It's never been about money with you, and it's not really about money here. You're a genuine patriot,

Paul. You love our country, and you need to know that this . . . operation is for the greater good, just as your support for my client's helicopters served the greater good.

Thompson took another swig of Coke.

"You remind me of my brother, Paul. Who's also a brilliant guy. You've spent a career in the civil service, running your segment of the system but having to kowtow to an endlessly changing cast of political appointees, having to explain your programs and justify your position over and over again to the latest new hack who's made a campaign donation. For thirty years, you've had to deal with an endless stream of them, each one lasting no more than four or eight years, but you never got to be the decider. Well, now I'm giving you a shot at it.

Gruber outlined his plan. An hour later, as he finished a Dr. Pepper, Thompson said, "I'm in."

The next day, on a crisp, clear afternoon, Gruber and Jane Berglund ambled across the back lawn of George Washington's estate, Mount Vernon, after a guided tour. Grinning like tourists, they passed the dung repository, just up from the icehouse, and turned down the back lawn, toward the Potomac River.

Mount Vernon had struck Gruber as an inspired spot to meet to propose his latest—and biggest—gambit. Convenient for Berglund, just eight miles south on the George Washington Parkway from her apartment house. And tough for Vankov to surveil. Mount Vernon forced its visitors into a queue to enter and offered open spaces far enough from trees, Gruber hoped, to foil one of Vankov's henchmen from hiding to snap photos or aim a parabolic mic or read lips through binoculars, whatever device they used. He and Berglund had driven separately; why make it easier for the Dark Angel?

For years, Gruber had searched for the right setting for events, which he considered an art, like finding the right score for a film. The Lincoln Memorial had clearly nudged Ezra Fitch toward approving the oust-Vankov vote, even if that effort ultimately busted. Gruber had once arranged for a liberal Republican presidential candidate, back in the days when they existed, to hold a news conference outside the Jefferson Memorial to hail the separation of church and state. Which at least drew headlines, even if it didn't derail the GOP crusaders.

Gruber angled toward a small open boathouse that looked like a cross between a pagoda and a child's clubhouse. Extra security. He assumed Vankov was doing the full surveillance panoply, including phone bugs, internet surveillance, even dumpster diving. Gruber now regularly checked his office and home for bugs and sometimes covered his mouth when he spoke outdoors, like a mobster under FBI surveillance. At what point did caution become paranoia?

"Looks like Alec Maynard's going to survive." Berglund settled against a wooden beam. "Which should keep me employed, at least through Election Day."

He nodded. Election Day. It loomed like Armageddon. "Yeah. Probably Vankov's ideal outcome. Maynard's now damaged goods, which gives Hess a good shot at beating him in the general. Why kill your opponent and face a fresh adversary if you can cripple him instead?"

She shook her head. "The way you people think."

Gruber eased onto a bench. "Pete takes it all a tad further than I do. Further than most anybody does. Which gives us an edge. I know him better than he knows us."

He gestured for Berglund to sit beside him. She settled on the bench a couple of feet away.

He cupped his hand over his mouth, trying to look casual. "You spoke to Yair?" He'd given her the phone number two days ago.

"I'm going to call him tomorrow. There's an expert I need to talk to first. I'm going to get only one shot at your commando friend, and I need to be ready."

He chewed his lip and nodded. A couple of days shouldn't matter.

"I'll call him tomorrow." She patted his arm. "Thank you."

"Okay. Something even more pressing we need to discuss."

She focused those cobalt eyes on him, wide, bright. She was looking at him with the same admiration that his daughters used to project when they were kids, and he felt a twinge at working her.

"I've got a plan to take out Vankov," he said. "It's even more decisive than your piece on the Maynard Dubai audio, because Vankov is going to deny everything Yair tells you about that, and it might take time for it to all shake out."

She cocked her head.

"This new plan might require you to go a bit out of your comfort zone."

Her eyes narrowed. The awe was gone, replaced by wariness.

"Is there someone at your paper that you trust, who'd be willing to send you a bogus internal email? Ideally, a reporter or editor." He raised his hand, as though to ward off her objections. "This person's name would probably never come out, but I can't guarantee it."

He heard her breath hissing.

He went on. "This internal *New York Globe* email should say that a Department of Defense source approached the *Globe* to offer internal DOD documents. To sell them. Specifically, Navy documents that show that then-Admiral Maynard was indeed involved in an improper sexual relationship with a subordinate in Dubai, and that further, during the affair Maynard disclosed classified information to the—to his lover, beyond her security clearance."

He gave her a moment. When she didn't stop him, he went on. "You're now covering Maynard. If something like that happened, you'd get flagged, right?"

She nodded. "What documents?"

Gruber wanted to tell her that the less she knew, the better. But he could feel himself slipping into his smartest-guy-in-the-room groove, which often happened when he briefed, and could be fatal here. Best to lay out the whole scheme, right here in George and Martha's boathouse.

"Here's the layout: The Navy found out around 2001 that Maynard was involved with that female officer under his command. Maynard went to his mentor and protector, a top admiral, who got the Navy to bury the matter. The Navy didn't put up much of a fight; they didn't want to prosecute Maynard, anyway—They'd rather avoid a scandal, especially one involving a

Black admiral, and avoid disclosing classified information at trial.

"This top admiral had the woman reassigned—excuse me, the lieutenant commander. She was a junior officer, so there were plenty of jobs at her pay grade." Gruber shrugged. "They sent her to a good post somewhere far away where she wouldn't complain and wouldn't cause trouble. Then this top admiral told Maynard to keep his pants zipped and wrote a memo to the file on the episode, never expecting it to see the light of day. But somebody found that memo, saw its value, and kept it all these years. And now that person is offering the memo to the *Globe*." Gruber spread his arms, as though to say, Voila!

She scrunched her face. "That doesn't seem likely."

How would she know? Oh, yeah, she'd covered the military briefly for the *Globe*. She was an expert by the Washington definition, somebody who'd done something once before. He didn't like to think of her in Afghanistan with those soldiers in fatigues with their guns and battle grit on their faces. That was stiff competition.

He felt a pulse pound in his neck. "It doesn't have to be likely. It just has to be possible. Actually, it doesn't even have to be possible. It just has to strike Pete Vankov as possible, and he doesn't know squat about the military. In fact, he hates the military. He thinks the military stole his birthday; he was born on Veterans Day, and his big day always gets overshadowed. He bitches every time he sees a car dealer or an ice cream shop offering a military discount." He softened his tone. "Would you be willing to arrange this internal email?"

She shoved away from him another foot. "Your 'layout' doesn't work. That wouldn't happen, some secret memo from a top admiral. This was 2001, ten years after Tailhook—You know, the Navy aviators' convention where they groped and raped female officers. After that, the Navy was hyper-sensitive about even a whiff of sexual harassment. No admiral would write a memo like that."

Gruber took a deep breath. "The Navy and the military are consummate paper pushers. I get this from my brother, who's spent an entire career working with them, for them. They have a form for everything. They've got SITREPs and FITREPs and After-Action Reports. And they're masters at documenting to cover their asses. The first thing they teach newly minted ensigns is, 'Never be the highest-ranking officer with a secret.' This top admiral had nobody higher-ranking to tell about Maynard's secret, so he told himself, in a memo."

She smiled and shook her head.

He pushed himself off the bench and turned toward the Potomac. He watched the waves bob, studied a small motorboat in the distance that was leaving a tiny wake, and focused on slowing his breathing. He wanted to perform the Breath of Fire, but this wasn't the place. At least he didn't feel an urge to chew his hands.

"I'll tell you how it might work."

He spun around.

She was smiling. "Your brother's right about the military and its paper-pushing. You want to hear a better 'layout'?"

He gestured for her to talk.

"Make it a routine security update, some language included in the report."

He gave her a quizzical look.

"Everybody in the Navy with a security clearance —which means every officer, for starters —has to periodically renew their clearances, or sometimes upgrade their clearances. Maynard was an admiral, and he would have had a top secret clearance, so even a routine update investigation would be kind of involved.

"So, for your purposes, maybe the intel officers conducting the investigation got wind of Maynard's affair and his security breach. They could have heard about it from somebody they questioned about Maynard—'Do you have any reason to believe Admiral Maynard could be pressured to act against the interests of the United States?'—They ask those kinds of questions. It could have been one of Maynard's references, which is usually who these intel guys talk to. You never know what somebody's going to say about you, or who's an enemy. Which is why the investigators talk to those people in the first place."

She was waiting for his reaction. This was the first time he'd seen her in action, apart from her initial interview of him, and he liked her intensity and command. Her scenario shouldn't change his arrangement with Paul Thompson, or only a few details, if he went her way. "Go on."

"Well, these investigators would ask Maynard and his lover about the rumors, about both the affair and the security violations, and they would both deny everything. So the investigators would write on their form that they'd heard these rumors, checked them out, but couldn't confirm them. The Navy would ultimately approve Maynard's security clearance, but there'd be an official mention of this scandal—or alleged scandal, whatever—in Navy personnel records. Now, those records are never supposed to go public, but somebody inside could probably dig around, find that passage, and offer it to the *Globe*."

He laughed. "That's great."

"If you do it my way, I'm guessing you'll need a fictitious security clearance form on Maynard at some point." She shrugged. "That shouldn't be too difficult. I should be able to get you a blank form, the version they were using in 2001, and you can fill it out. Or I can."

He walked over and put a hand on her shoulder. He caressed her neck. "Great stuff. Okay, that security report is the document the DOD source is trying to peddle to the *New York Globe*. Absolutely, let's write that report. You want to hear the rest of the plan?"

She mimicked his "go ahead" gesture.

He laughed. "The email —the internal email from your colleague to you— should say that a *New York Globe* editor told the DOD source that the *Globe* doesn't do 'checkbook journalism'—That's the term you use, right?"

She nodded.

"Okay, no checkbook journalism. So the *Globe* editor told the DOD source to take a hike, stick his stolen security report you-know-where. The internal email you get should give some hints of who the source is: A Navy senior civilian official based at the Pentagon. And it should include a contact phone number for the guy. But no name. I'll get you the number."

"Whose number is it?"

"It'll be a burner cell phone. A friend's." He smiled at her. "You don't really need to know much about him. His part in the operation is going to begin after yours ends." He certainly wasn't going to reveal Paul Thompson to her until she'd committed to the plan.

She got up from the bench and walked back to her perch against the beam. "Let me make sure I understand the situation: You want me to expose myself and strain my hold at the *Globe*, which is already so tenuous after our little TR island scene that it makes 'walking on eggshells' solid by comparison. Further, you're going to use the improved script I gave you. But you won't even tell me the details of what I'm getting into, or rather, who I'm getting into it with. Is that basically the idea?"

Gruber sighed. "Our source on the document is a real Department of Defense official. There's no way anybody else could pull this off, the way Vankov's going to check him out."

She swished her mouth and looked at him, waiting for more.

"I've already told you more than I wanted to say. For everybody's benefit." He hadn't disclosed much; the Department of Defense employed more than three quarters of a million civilians, including Paul Thompson.

Berglund stood against the boathouse beam for what seemed like minutes. "If I can arrange this email," she finally said, "what do you want me to do with it once I get it?"

He smiled again. "The whole setup kind of stinks, don't you think? Which is why the editor told the DOD rat to go fish. Fictitiously, of course."

She shrugged, like a student telling a teacher, "I don't get it."

"When you get the email, you're offended by the offer to sell the classified documents, as the editor was. You print out the email. Then you crumple the printout, as though you're going to throw it away. Then you straighten it, flatten it, put it in its own folder. You mark that folder 'Maynard—Middle East' and you put it face-down on the backseat of your car, under some other folders, magazines, and such. And you leave that folder and those papers in your car like that. Even at night, when you park your car in the lot behind your building. You just leave it there."

Berglund's eyebrows scrunched.

Yes, someone is going to rifle your car. Come on, I need you to pull this off; we're partners. Now you're going to make news, not merely report it, which is what you said you wanted.

"You're asking me to cross a bright line. To violate a canon." She crossed her arms. "If this got out, it wouldn't just ruin my career, it would hurt reporters generally. Hurt the kind of classic, objective journalism I'm clinging to, which is already endangered. It's the same kind of damage you'd get if a CIA officer posed as a reporter, which is why that's prohibited."

"No damage if you don't get caught." He smiled. "You'd be like Superman. As long as nobody sees you in your cape, everybody figures you're just Clark Kent, mild-mannered reporter for a great metropolitan newspaper."

She swished her mouth again. "Let me think about it," she said in that crisp, authoritative voice she'd used when she first phoned him for an interview. "I'm not there yet."

A couple of hours later, as an orange and pink dusk flared, Gruber was waiting outside the Pentagon's main entrance for his brother. Military and civilian, in groups and alone, ambled and rushed before him. Servicemembers walking in opposite directions exchanged salutes, always initiated by the lower rank. Gruber noticed a technique that some subordinates used to avoid the exchanges, pretending not to notice their superiors, like elevator passengers failing to notice cries to hold the doors. Female brass, particularly, seemed to resent being ignored and denied their salutes.

Jake came out just after 5:30 p.m., which they probably called 1730 here. Gruber braced for a hearty handshake; Jake had been crushing his hand for forty years.

"I'm honored," Jake said as they walked toward California Pizza Kitchen in Pentagon City. "What have you gotten yourself into this time?"

Gruber laughed. "Nothing yet. I've got a project afoot, though. I'm not going to tell you the particulars; it's better that you don't know."

Jake trained those hard eyes on him, with the usual wilting effect. Part of Gruber was hoping his brother would talk him out of the document ploy, the way Jake had shot down his education-streaming job some months earlier.

They walked for a minute, the silence punctuated by Gruber's leather soles slapping the pavement.

"I can still remember watching our sister's thirteen-inch TV as the Senate voted to investigate Watergate," Gruber said, "and wondering what you were doing at that seismic moment in Vietnam."

"Keeping my ass down."

"It was your service in Vietnam that steered me to politics, government, world affairs."

"Patriotism is the last refuge of a scoundrel."

Gruber sighed to stifle a laugh. As they waited at a streetlight, he said, "I read recently about some Middle Eastern terrorists who separated their hostages into two groups: women, children, and men over fifty—all considered feeble—in one room, and younger men in another. It hit me, I'd be in the feeble group. It also hit me, more and more bucket list things are going to become 'now or never.' Not news to you, of course, at your advanced age."

They crossed the street.

"I realized a few years ago how much the battles were draining my soul," Gruber said. "Well, the political arms race to me, political crap to you. I realized, after two failed marriages that what I really wanted is true intimacy, to find the one. Yes, a bit late for that epiphany, you might say. I'd been so eager to meld with another soul that I went overboard, arranging the Woodley Park condo for that Smithsonian curator. I should have seen that romance wouldn't last, that we were too different." He shook his head.

"My vision was cloudier then," Gruber continued. "Now I'm fairly sure I've finally found 'the one.' But it's all tangled with this project that I need to tell you about."

"Jesus," Jake said. "Sounds like this is going to be a long dinner."

"Not necessarily." Gruber took a quick half step to regain Jake's infantry pace. "Question: Security clearances. I know how the vetting process works on the Hill, in the civilian world. But are they stickier about it in the military?"

Jake's mouth puckered. "I don't know how civilian investigators handle it, but I wouldn't think so. All these things are taken pretty seriously everywhere."

Jake stopped and waited for Gruber to meet his eyes. "If you're asking for my advice, it's this, as always: Don't do anything I wouldn't do. Which you regularly ignore."

22
FISH

Alec Maynard marched the Des Moines Hilton's corridor, his black oxfords silent against the thick patterned carpet, watching his wife's body shift in her taupe dress as she strode. Her beam had widened over the decades, but she still radiated the same intensity. He reminded himself of the sacrifices she'd made, abandoning her studies and her dreams of teaching college history to become a naval officer's wife, running their household during his deployments and charming his shipmates and superiors at officers' clubs. And now she'd had to listen as Laronda Tibbs and then Peter Vankov's other proxies called their union an abomination, a betrayal. And then that Dubai hotel business.

Claudia kept a few steps ahead, flanked by Maynard's press secretary. She seemed to relish this respite after standing by Maynard's side as they popped into a few caucuses earlier that evening, capping two days of bouncing around Iowa together. For at least a few minutes, she didn't have to plaster a grin, didn't have to talk to him, didn't even have to look at him.

Which, in a way, was okay with Maynard. Because everything Claudia had said to him since that Dubai audio release had a subtext of "How could you do this to me?" Now she was The Spurned Wife, she'd railed, and everyone who met her or saw her or saw a picture of her thought, "So this is the woman Maynard cheated on." Claudia was right; Maynard could also read those looks, including some that said, "She's not half bad, what's Maynard's gripe? Maybe she's a cold fish, like Jackie Kennedy."

He turned to Jeff, to his side and half a step back. "You have the latest Iowa numbers?"

His campaign manager drew his phone and began typing.

"Write them on a piece of paper and give it to me, will you? Before I speak."

"Yeah. They keep getting better. Bad day for Fahringer. If the governor from neighboring Minnesota can't win in Iowa, his prospects look bleak. Especially if he gets walloped by a Black immigrants' son from flakey California—no offense."

Maynard smiled and shook his head.

Jeff gave him a grin, the same grin he'd been flashing over the polls for months. Gen X or Z, whatever Jeff was, didn't care about affairs, or dalliances, or flings, or whatever the preferred term was these days. Fuck buddies is really what it had been in Dubai, at least to Maynard. Convenient release in a hostile posting. Close enough to "campaign sex" that Jeff and Maynard's other aides understood; they were veterans of the dalliances that sprang when a bunch of horny hard chargers were thrown together in a crucible.

He fell back a step, to stay out of Claudia's earshot. Jeff matched his pace, like a faithful hound.

"Turns out the party that loved Bill Clinton and Jack Kennedy doesn't care much about who their leaders slept with," Maynard told Jeff, barely above a whisper. "The voters were even willing to look past statutory harassment and violations of military protocol. The Dubai episode is meaningless." To everyone but Claudia.

As they turned onto the corridor that led to the hotel ballroom, a din hit Maynard's ears, distant shouts and cheers. Ahead, politicos on cellphones and canoodling couples saw him, peeled off the papered walls, and gave their best civilian versions of "Attention on Deck." He smiled back.

He closed the distance to Claudia, took her hand. She didn't resist, but it felt like gripping a dead fish. The din buffeted and roused him as he stepped into the hotel ballroom, an assault of sounds and colors and flashing lights. He scanned the windowless ecru barn, squinted at the spherical chandeliers hanging from a coffered ceiling and at the television screens on each wall. The place pulsed, a model of diversity. Burly union types in loud sportscoats milled with pin-striped bankers, shaggy tree huggers, and soup-stained academics. A few military types here and there, easy to spot by their haircuts, bearing, and sharp gig lines.

As the applause and the flashes ebbed, a sea of glistening, boozy faces beamed at him, the faithful ebullient at making the right bet, ecstatic that their work had paid off, hopeful for rewards. Along with some arrivistes swooping in to claim a share of the glory.

A big blond guy in a plaid tent of a jacket was at his side, an Iowa public employees union honcho, pointing a sausage-sized finger at the far wall. "The guys did a pretty good job on the bunting."

Maynard eyed the red, white, and blue streamers draped from the ceiling and from some tables. "Terrific."

The blond guy beamed. "If you need work done, call Labor."

Maynard felt a hand on his back and a "Congratulations!" drilled his ear. He turned to see a scrawny guy he vaguely recalled, a Sioux City schools honcho with big glasses in worn plastic frames.

"Congratulations all around," Maynard told him, giving him a friendly pat in his flat gut, mostly to angle the guy's hand off his back.

Maynard caught his own image on all the TVs around the ballroom, a stock headshot, with the Iowa caucuses tally in blue below his face, which gave a mugshot effect. With nearly all precincts reporting, he'd won 49 percent of the vote, Fahringer had 34 percent, and some second-tier players split the rest.

"Iowa was Fahringer's first stand, and maybe now his last," a banker with garlic breath told him. "I can't imagine what it must feel like to be as close to the presidency as you are now."

Maynard nodded and smiled. "The greatest job I ever had, and ever expect to have, was commanding a nuclear submarine, as an O5. More than overseeing a submarine fleet as an admiral, more than serving as a US senator. And probably more than serving as president, if we get there. At sea, a naval captain is a monarch. He's a techno-warrior who has to be equally comfortable fighting a $1 billion boat or grappling with advanced physics. I was at once ship's captain, nuclear power plant manager, and father figure to a family of officers and men. I just can't imagine anything as heady."

The banker gave him a confused smile and walked off.

Maynard tried to enjoy the din, the grins, the raised Champagne flutes, as he glided past a melting ice sculpture of an eagle. He wished his parents were here tonight. How proud they'd be.

He noticed a couple of bearded longhairs scarfing boiled shrimp and recalled his parents' scowls at some California events during his first run for the Senate. Maybe they wouldn't be so thrilled, after all, especially after they heard his stump speech, his new lefty stump speech. His parents had both been socially liberal, but with some traditional taboos from their British upbringings, such as drugs and gay sex. And they'd been hard-nosed fiscal conservatives. They also probably wouldn't be too keen on adultery, even if the voters could look past it.

The din ebbed, and Maynard exchanged more grins and waves with his flock. He stepped to a wooden dais with the hotel's seal in front. Why hadn't one of his people plastered a Maynard sign over the Hilton logo? He found Jeff, made eye contact, and glanced down, but his campaign manager's dopey grin suggested Jeff missed the message.

"I just got a call from Governor Fahringer," Maynard began, and the room hushed. "Congratulating us on our resounding victory."

Raucous clapping.

He let the words flow. He'd prepared a short speech in case he lost, some pabulum to spew amid the pain and fury, but he'd known he could wing it if he won. He let himself float in the moment.

"We've sent a message today, laid down a marker. You've come together from all across Iowa, from all ninety-nine counties, rural and urban, from all walks of life, young and old, from every corner of the Democratic coalition first built by FDR, to put unity over division, to take a stand against exclusion and extremism, to say that the American dream lives, that her best days lie ahead, and that together we can deliver that promise."

He tossed bits about a soybean farmer he'd met before dawn at a Denison diner and a vascular surgeon in a Cedar Rapids hospital, the full spectrum committed to their cause, all of them showing the discipline and desire and drive it was going to take in the months ahead, although it all sounded a bit tinny and hokey and backwoods to his ears, too much FDR and Hardy Boys can-do optimism. The applause kept coming, though, the red faces kept beaming, and he went on.

He ended by saying that the job was just beginning, warning that the political graveyard was filled with frontrunners who took too much for granted. But, together, they could march to victory.

When he finished, a media scrum enveloped him, lights flashing, cameras rolling, mics jabbing. Reporters jostled each other like jackals angling toward a kill, each eager for a bite, burly cameramen generally winning out. A tall blond woman gave him a nod. The *New York Globe* reporter now assigned to cover him, Jane Berglund. He had a few things to tell her that should wipe that grin off her face. Maybe later.

He gave the press a variation of his speech, obliquely said that Fahringer could never catch him now.

When he opened for questions, one scribe shouted, "Are you saying your victory today makes the Democratic nomination yours to lose?"

Damn right, Maynard wanted to say. "Today we won a key battle. You can feel the momentum, you can see it." He gestured at the crowd.

"An Iowa win lacks the definitive cachet it once had," another reporter shouted, clearly an out-of-stater. "In some recent cycles, the Iowa winner flamed out right after the caucuses. You downplayed it yourself, just a minute ago."

Maynard considered giving the guy a lesson on campaign logistics, that the candidates he was referring to couldn't raise money quickly enough from their Iowa win to give them the boosts they needed in New Hampshire. Which wasn't Maynard's problem because he was flush with cash. Instead, he said, "No one can argue that we appealed in the corn belt but might fritter in more diverse states, as some other Iowa winners did. Just the opposite. Like President Obama, if we can win here, we can win anywhere. From a strategic viewpoint, we're well positioned."

"Any battle plan is only good until you meet the enemy, right, Admiral?" another reporter shouted. "Ven Hess won the Republican caucuses here, and he's been pretty critical of you recently. That's only going to increase now that he's won Iowa. What's your plan to handle that?"

Yeah, Hess was now the presumptive Republican nominee, and Vankov would focus his filthy arsenal on Maynard, increase his firepower. If Vankov could increase his firepower after releasing that Dubai audio; not hard to see Vankov's greasy fingerprints on that StormSpill stunt.

"I saw a baseball game last season, the Giants," Maynard said. "The shortstop set beautifully to field a grounder, square in front of the ball, but he was so excited, he whipped the ball to first before he had a good grip on it, and it dribbled out of his hand. Mr. Hess should concentrate on the Republican nomination before he worries about the Democratic contenders."

He drew a few laughs.

A reporter in a blue blazer over a gold golf shirt asked him if he was going to tack back toward the center now. "Or are you worried about what they say, that the only things in the middle of the road are yellow lines and dead chickens?"

Maynard felt a spike run up his spinal cord. His father's face floated into his head, austere. He summoned one of his old stump speeches, from before he declared for president, like opening a musty file in his head. He gazed up and spewed.

"I belonged to a majority, I'd thought, committed to live and let live, but respectful of tradition. To a majority that wanted to empower the needy and underserved, but not bury them in entitlements that bred dependency and despair. A majority that wanted effective government but was wary of turning over broad aspects of life to those who ran the DMV.

"I believed in a society founded on the Enlightenment 'truth' that democracy is possible because reason will beat passion in a marketplace of ideas, and that when passion does enter politics it will come in in the form of hope and charity rather than fear and resentment, and not by armed mobs. Now I've seen both the Right and the Left choosing tribe over truth and twisting the English language past the breaking point in the service of advocacy. All these foundational American precepts now seemed under challenge and stress as extremists of both sides purged the public square.

"On the economic front, I knew that a handful of billionaires had greater wealth than the bottom half of all Americans, and that such inequality tore at the fabric of a nation dedicated to moral equality. But I'd seen what societies dedicated to redistribution looked like in the real world, and preferred strategic regulation of capitalism to the fever dreams of Marxist millennials." He looked into the reporter's eyes. "Does that answer your question?"

He drew some more laughs. He raised his hand in a wave, said, "Thanks, guys," and stepped away.

He saw Jeff, now with a concerned look, but turned away. He listened to the din and tried to savor the moment. Later, he'd think about Pete Vankov and about taking yet another progressive oath. For now, how sweet to swat Fahringer. He'd always enjoyed combat—two men go on the mat, one man comes off—as a test of character, a metric of success. He'd made what felt like an organic progression from schoolyard scraps to the fencing strip to submarines.

He'd perpetually surprised opponents, seeming so mild. Well, he was mild, off the strip and ashore. He dreaded and abhorred war because he knew its pain. But when war came, he was ready, he was home. He'd get on the 1MC, the ship-wide public address system, and tell the crew what they were going to do and how they were going to do it. How they were going to win. He'd felt a visceral thrill firing Tomahawks during the Gulf War, hearing and feeling the massive missiles rush off to destroy his enemies, America's enemies. He knew he'd killed scores, maybe hundreds. He'd had no regrets and no tough nights. He'd done the job that he'd been trained to do, that the nation had counted on him to do. Collateral casualties? Those were on the enemy. He sometimes felt bad that he didn't feel worse.

His minions cornered him by a tray of raw vegetables, a swarm of cell phone cameras clicking and flashing, a stream of Iowans lining up for more photos with him.

As he posed for the shots, he felt the old pride surging. In a corner of his vision, he caught an attractive blonde by a table laden with sesame chicken skewers and boiled shrimp. Stop. Haven't you gotten in enough trouble stepping out? Just admiring. No harm in that. Wait, it was Berglund, the *Globe* reporter. Like some trope from a horror film, a fantasy turning into a succubus. Well, she wasn't a succubus, but she'd proven a net negative. He needed to talk to her. No. Have Jeff do it.

Berglund had caught his glance. He nodded to her and turned to a hefty woman in a floral dress who knocked him back half a step as she nuzzled in for a joint photo.

As the photo line wound down, Berglund walked toward him. He looked around for Jeff. His top aide should be within sight, within reach. But he wasn't at his station. A court-martial offense.

Berglund neared, notepad out. "Congratulations," she said, neutral, without the passion of his minions. Objective. Blind.

He nodded. "Thank you."

"Were you surprised by the margin? Fourteen points way outperformed the polls."

He'd answered that to the scrum, but she must want an "exclusive interview," so she could say, "Maynard told the *Globe*," or "told me" or "told this reporter," whatever they used these days. He tried to formulate a glib but humble response, something fresh, but felt acid washing over his words. "You're doing a straight election story?"

She laughed, as though surprised by the question. "Well, it's pretty big news."

"Come over here." He led her to a corner, behind a table strewn with soiled plates and half-filled glasses. He turned his back to the room, a signal that even these half-drunk Midwest revelers should get, that this conversation was private.

She waited, pen poised over her pad, an expectant smile on her face. Which made him want to punch her.

"I understand that for weeks you've had exclusive possession of an audio tape that shows that the Sistas for Sistas PAC"—he couldn't help spitting out the words—"that has been attacking my campaign and me is a Republican setup, a front. Any story coming on that?"

She chewed her bottom lip, and her grin finally faded. Was she going to stonewall him, tell him that journalists, like lawmakers, didn't discuss internal deliberations, how they made the sausage? Her face tightened, her lips began forming words, as though she were eager to tell him something, and her eyes said it was something big, something he'd want to hear. Then her features relaxed into a resigned calm.

"I need to verify the audio, Senator," she finally said. "Which is going to require a trip to Charleston, which I need to find time to arrange." She gestured at the ballroom, as though signaling how busy she was. "The *Globe* can't just go with audio of unidentified people—unidentified in that they don't identify themselves on the tape. Especially when we get it from a campaign that wants us to use it to impugn their opponent."

"I see." He nodded, as though thanking her for enlightening him and commending her and her paper for their professionalism, thoroughness, and ethics.

He'd been counting on Berglund and the *Globe* to run a story on the Charleston audiotape with Colonel Sanders, hadn't expected a hard charger like Berglund to sit on it. If Berglund had promptly exposed the Sistas PAC and Vankov's dirty tricks, that Dubai audio—which also smelled of Vankov—might never have come out. And Maynard's marriage would be intact and his campaign numbers would be higher and his blood pressure would be lower. Had somebody gotten to her? No, that was campaign paranoia.

Maybe she wasn't such a hard charger after all.

He studied her, the way he might study a vaunted sailor who'd flubbed a promotion exam or cracked under pressure. "You didn't seem to have such qualms, or need such due diligence, when you ran that story on my campaign donations."

Her forehead scrunched and her head angled back, as though recoiling from a blow.

Go ahead, let's hear your argument, dig yourself in deeper. He waited a few beats, but he wasn't enjoying this as much as he'd hoped, and he needed to get back to his troops. And away from his parley with her in a corner.

"If you had checked out those contributions," he said, "as we did after your story ran, you would have found that they were setups. Those donors weren't my supporters. Not one of them had ever attended any of my events, had ever made another contribution to us, had ever said anything about us. I challenge you to find one time any of those people ever mentioned my name publicly, ever said or did anything to advance my candidacy, other than writing me that one check. They were strawmen, professional donors. Setups." He stroked his beard. "I wonder how you found out about them."

Her lips receded as though she were about to puke. Then her eyes angled up, as though searching for words, probably for another bureaucrat alibi.

"Write this down, for your story." He angled toward the ballroom swim. "We're thrilled by today's victory, but we know we've got a tough fight ahead against some clever and ruthless opponents. We intend to campaign on the issues, to give America a choice of visions. But let no one think we're going to roll over. As my father taught me long ago, when you're dealing with a nice guy, be a nice guy. When you're dealing with a sonofabitch, be a sonofabitch." He locked on her eyes until she looked away.

He spotted an aide, an eager kid from his Des Moines campaign office, and waved him over. He shifted to position the kid between himself and Berglund. She took the hint and walked off.

"Find Jeff for me," he told the kid. "Tell him I want to see him."

The kid scurried off. In two minutes, Maynard and his campaign manager were huddled in the same corner where he'd talked to Berglund. The stack of soiled plates had grown and was exuding a sour, fishy odor.

"First thing when you get back to the office," Maynard said, "I want you to give that Sistas for Sistas audio to StormSpill. They're fundamentally nonpartisan, they have no filter and no qualms, they'll take it and release it. You identify Colonel Sanders for them, but you make sure it goes out anonymously, with no mention that we had any part in getting it or giving it to them. They won't fight you."

Jeff nodded. "Yessir."

Maynard smiled. "In submarine warfare, the sweetest shot is from behind, firing a fish up an enemy sub's ass."

23
LAFAYETTE PARK

Jane Berglund shifted in Ogden's itchy chair and tried to read the *Globe* (Washington) bureau chief's face as he read her draft on Peter Vankov's greatest hits. The editor's small office, with the door closed, filled with a musty odor.

Ogden, at his desk, kept sweeping a long lock of graying hair back over his forehead, maybe training his nascent comb-over. He scowled a couple of times, which she hoped showed moral indignation over her revelations.

Berglund's story featured a detailed account of Vankov's bartering US Mideast policy to the UAE in exchange for the Dubai hotel audio of Maynard and his mistress. Thanks, Yair. She noted the trade was also a campaign finance felony, Hess's taking "a thing of value." Thanks, David. Her greatest-hits story would have been even stronger if Berglund hadn't lost a couple of elements, especially the Sistas for Sistas PAC as a Vankov setup. StormSpill had spoiled that scoop by dumping the country club audio. Berglund should have corroborated that audio as soon as she got it, made that Charleston trip, as Maynard had told her. Once she left the Hess beat, the trip became nearly impossible, though how could she have anticipated that?

After the *Globe* switched her beat, she'd considered pitching the Sistas for Sistas piece to her editors as a Maynard story, that Maynard was being sandbagged, rather than as a Hess story, that Vankov was doing the sandbagging. She could have claimed later to have discovered Vankov's role. Not her style, though, and she was already on double-secret probation. Oh, well.

Still, her Vankov's greatest-hits piece should be the biggest news story of this generation, as Gruber had hyped it. Maybe a Pulitzer. And enough to finish Pete Vankov. The country and the world would be better off without the Dark Angel. Without Pete Vankov, the louse who'd followed and photographed her and then sent those photos to her bosses like revenge porn. And probably had a big laugh over it, and added the episode to his war-story repertoire so he could boast about humiliating her for years to come at bars and brothels. When Berglund was covering the cops early in her career, a detective used a phrase whenever a "scumbag" got murdered: "a public-service killing." Vankov needed killing. The Dark Angel needed to be sent back to Hell. Figuratively, with a keyboard.

She pictured the newsroom ovation when Columbia University's Journalism School, which gave out the Pulitzers, announced her name. Her Vankov pieces were the kind of work Columbia J-School had taught her to produce, groomed her to produce.

She heard paper crackle and looked up. Ogden had flipped to what looked like her final page. Hard to read his expression, but his finger was tracking down the page, as though studying every word, savoring them.

She shifted in the chair again, which was grating her back. Who would upholster a chair with itchy, textured fabric? More to the point, why would the *New York Globe*, or anyone else, buy it? Didn't speak well the paper's judgment. Or of Ogden's.

Her greatest-hits piece might also restore Maynard's favor, not that she cared what Alec Maynard thought of her. Except that Maynard might be President of the United States in a year. He'd written her off. His giving the Charleston country club audio to StormSpill proved that. And she was sure that dump was Maynard's doing; after all, it was Maynard's man who'd given that audio to her. Maynard hadn't even given her a last chance, a deadline to run a story. He'd just dressed her down and furtively dumped the audio.

She couldn't get Maynard's frowning face out of her head. The StormSpill audio dump was only part of it. Maynard's critique of her earlier story, on his donations, gnawed even deeper. Partly because his complaint had shocked her. Maynard had never asked for a correction or retraction or a follow story, never mentioned the piece until he berated her at the Iowa caucuses. Geez, most pols bitched throughout a campaign. In the delirium of their sleep-deprived desperation, they saw reporters and media execs as part of some conspiracy to keep them from winning an election.

She should probably do a follow story on those bogus Maynard donors. Or add it to the Vankov's greatest-hits story, if she could nail a Vankov connection within a day or two; that would be smoothest.

She heard a noise and snapped toward Ogden. He had slapped her story face down on his desk.

"Your strongest stuff—or, let me be more precise, your biggest news—here is Peter Vankov's arrangement to buy the tape of Alec Maynard and his girlfriend in Dubai." Ogden pushed the pages aside. "But you've got only unnamed sources. And they're not independent; one corroborated the other. You don't even identify your primary source beyond 'veteran international intelligence operative.' That could be half the staff on Capitol Hill; they don't call themselves 'junketeers.'"

"I have the guy who actually brokered the deal," she said. "The guy who was in the room with the UAE operatives." Project calm and control. "The single best source there is."

"The single best source would be Peter Vankov, if he confirmed your account instead of denying it. As did the UAE."

She heard her own breathing, which sounded as though she'd just finished wind sprints.

"I have, on the record, the man who made the deal with the UAE. I have his assurance that he did so on direct, explicit instruction from Peter Vankov."

"Maybe so," Ogden said. "But you don't have proof, like emails between this guy and Vankov or anything else in writing."

"There's no written record. I asked. They spoke by phone."

Ogden sighed. "You don't name your international man of mystery or tell us much about him. Anything about him. Who is he?"

"I promised him confidentiality."

"I'm not asking you to put it in the story. I'm asking as your editor. Who is he?"

"Ogden, that's the agreement I made—to identify him only as a 'veteran international intelligence operative.' To anybody."

"Even Deep Throat, Ben Bradlee knew who he was."

"I can't."

He squinted at her, then turned to her printout and flipped pages. "Your corroborating source, please tell me this isn't the same guy who corroborated your Argentina story." He grimaced. "Tell me it's not the same guy with you in the photos Vankov sent us. Gruber."

She felt her head heat, then fizzle.

"Oh, Jesus." Ogden shoved the printout across his desk. "We can't go with this."

The fizz ran down her spine and settled in her guts. "It's solid, all of it. And it's major news."

Ogden shook his head, giving her that disappointed, "you-know-better" look that her father used to give her.

"Come on, Jane. You're asking too much of this paper and too much of me. Especially with your track record."

"My 'track record'?"

"That's a polite term for it. We took you off Hess and put you on Maynard after Peter Vankov sent us those photos, showing pretty close involvement—no pun intended—between you and Vankov's estranged partner, this Gruber. Who seems to have a hard-on for Vankov. Kind of impugns your objectivity. Some people around here are worried about a lawsuit over your first Vankov piece, about the Argentina deal—'Actual malice' and all that."

She concentrated on keeping her expression calm, neutral. "The governor of New Jersey accused me of bias and banned me from his office. He didn't care for me any more than Peter Vankov does now. The *Globe* stood by me then and kept me on the beat."

"Different situation. And I wouldn't bring up that Argentina story—friendly tip."

Her breaths came heavy again.

"Just so you know, I stood up for you when those photos came in." Ogden swept back his hair. "Some other editors wanted to fire you on the spot. You should be glad you still have a job here, and a good job covering a top presidential campaign. And that's what you should be writing about."

He lifted her printout and dropped it back onto on his desk, as though weighing it. "We can't run a story under your byline that relies on anonymous sources to blow up Peter Vankov—Sources that we know represent a conflict of interest, and that Vankov himself knows represent a conflict of interest, because he's the one who flagged us to them."

He gazed at the printout, wistfully now. "The entire story is tainted." He raised his hand again. "That's not to say I don't believe it. Or that it's not superb reporting, apart from that one small glitch." He chortled. "Maybe we can save this thing. Give me your source's contact info, the guy who brokered the UAE deal, and we can have another reporter re-interview him and write the story. Same confidentiality agreement—'veteran intelligence international,' whatever. Maybe we can find a way to give you some credit, maybe a contributor tagline—no promises. That's the best I can do under the circumstances."

She started to speak, but bile began to rise from her throat, and he cut her off with his hand again.

"You should have stuck to covering Maynard. Which is another reason I can't sell this at a page-one meeting. The first thing they're going to ask is why you're still writing about Vankov when you should be covering your beat, and why didn't we get the Sistas for Sistas story, instead of StormSpill?"

Her head felt clogged, then suddenly light, dizzy. She wanted to tell him she was working the Maynard beat and did get that Sistas audio, exclusively, weeks before StormSpill. But that would only set up his next punch.

She pushed herself out of the itchy chair on legs that felt weightless, nearly numb. She extended her hand toward him, palm up, since Ogden seemed big on hand gestures. She waited until he placed her printout in her hand, then walked out of his office.

A few minutes later, Jane Berglund tromped out of the *Globe* (Washington) bureau into a bustling downtown street. She needed to move, to walk, to burn off rage. She vaguely felt the frigid air scratch her face but didn't button her coat, didn't need to, didn't care. She strode Washington's sidewalks, storming past storefronts and awnings. She bulled past suits and tourists, brushing a few, drawing glares and cusses. At a stoplight, she shoved through a scrum of Ladies Who Do Lunch.

She pictured Ven Hess in the Oval Office, leaning back and grinning behind the Resolute Desk, beside an American flag, and Peter Vankov stepping into the room through the hidden doorway, leering, to hatch some new scam.

Five minutes or maybe half an hour later, Berglund found herself in Lafayette Park, near the White House. She stopped by an equestrian statue of President Andrew Jackson, his mount's front hooves raised. Jackson was notorious, among other traits, for vindictiveness, she recalled.

She'd discovered and documented Peter Vankov's crimes and sins for the *Globe* to print and for the world to read. Through proper journalistic process. But her editors had balked over appearances, protecting their own tails. They'd even suggested a workaround to give them the glory without the taint of her name.

That the people shall know. Joseph Pulitzer's lapidary words, carved not only into Columbia J-School's stone but into her psyche. Time to stop serving up facts and then hoping and waiting for others to act. Time to act herself. To be a player, not a watcher. Along with Gruber. And as his partner, not his lackey or acolyte. After all, she'd saved Gruber's plan, maybe saved his tail, given him the security reports approach.

She fished her cell phone from her jacket pocket and dialed Gruber's number. The hell with whoever might be watching or listening.

"Janey," he said, joy and expectation and anxiety all blending in the single syllable.

"I'm in. Let's get this bastard."

24

DRAKE

Pete Vankov lifted his ringing iPhone off the coffee table in his Manhattan condo and shook his head. The device showed "Nuke," for Nuke LaLoosh, the erratic and ungrateful bush-league pitcher in *Bull Durham* who veteran catcher Crash Davis molds into a star. Hess. Calling again.

Vankov squinted against shards of morning sun shooting through his living room windows. He'd concocted a meeting in New York with some casino magnates and caught an Acela to Penn Station to get away from Hess. But he was still talking to "the Hessian" as much as ever.

Vankov pulled out a pen and grabbed a magazine off the antique walnut coffee table, a stale issue of Architectural Digest. His wife thought the magazines classed up the place, but only cluttered it. The apartment was a pied a terre, a 900-square-foot one-bedroom off Central Park West good for occasional overnights, but she'd dressed it up like a nineteenth century cathouse. He'd stopped trying to educate her; what could you expect from a lingerie model turned flight attendant? He'd gone for brains on his first trip to the altar, a tough finance lawyer, and look at the misery that had got him.

His thumb hesitated over the red "message" icon, then hit the green "answer." "Sir."

"Your boy down in Charleston has a big mouth," Hess began. "Which has some long fingers pointing at you and me, kid."

"You're talking about Stockton and the 'Sistas for Sisters' tape?"

A pause, followed by what sounded like a sigh. "Yes."

"Yeah, frustrating. But bizarre, a one-in-a-million chance something like that happens, a tape like that going public."

'Frustrating?' That's what you call it when one of your turds blows up in your face? And mine? Goddamned disaster, is what it is." Another pause. "And all your turds together didn't cost Maynard a step. His margin in Iowa was as big as mine."

"We did cost Maynard more than a step—Look at his poll numbers before and after. We wanted Maynard to win Iowa." Vankov shoved some magazines off the coffee table. "Best case for us. He wins the nomination, but he's so crippled from the Dubai tape that we pick him off easily in November." Well, best case would have been taking out Maynard a month ago, but this was okay, too.

Hess ranted that Maynard didn't look too crippled to him. Vankov held the phone away from his ear and let "the Hessian" rant. Hess was a what-have-you-done-for-me-lately guy, no pleasing him for long.

When Hess ran down, Vankov said, "I may have a silver bullet. Give me a few hours and I'll let you know if it pans out."

"Jesus, another turd. This one better not land in our faces."

"I'll let you know as soon as I have something. Freedom and posterity."

The line went dead before Vankov could hang up.

Vankov engaged the Adeya app on his cell phone for a secure, encrypted call. Before he typed the number into his cell, he reread the *New York Globe* email one last time. Well, the scan of a crumpled *Globe* internal email printout. He would have preferred the actual email, the way he'd gotten Gruber's emails about his mistress in the Woodley Park condo. But this scan seemed reliable enough. Vankov trusted the team he'd been using for a couple of weeks to watch Berglund. Real pros, a world beyond Frank, the burned-out former Baltimore cop whom Berglund had made after two days on the job. These new guys charged like pros, but that was okay, they'd already earned out.

They'd begun by watching Berglund around the clock, finding patterns, routines, obstacles, vulnerabilities. The first two weeks, the team's highlights included a receipt for a Pilates class and a flyer for an upcoming Penn reunion. On their third week, they found the *Globe* email. Pros.

According to their report, when they checked Berglund's car in the middle of the night, they blocked the surveillance camera in her parking lot so they wouldn't get caught on tape. They worked fast enough that the security dweeb at the building's night desk wouldn't report a camera problem or, worse, go out to check. They used some gizmo, a twenty-first century Slim Jim, to find the frequency Berglund's VW used and electronically open her door. Then photographed or scanned anything that looked interesting. Neither Berglund nor anybody else would ever know they'd been there. Pros.

Vankov punched in the phone number from Berglund's *New York Globe* email. This looks almost too good to be true.

The line clicked on the second ring. "Yeah?" A male voice, gruff, curt.

"I understand you have some merchandise you're having trouble selling," Vankov said. "I might be willing to take it off your hands."

"Who is this?"

"Call me back at this number on a secure line." Vankov hung up.

Vankov checked his email and began returning messages. If the guy really were a Department of Defense apparatchik, as the *Globe* email described him, even if his phone were secure, he'd need time to move from his cubicle or cubbyhole office to somewhere he wouldn't be overheard or interrupted. If his offer to the *Globe* was legit and he had any balls, he'd find a way to call Vankov back within half an hour.

Vankov opened an email from Hess's field director about a Republican senator running against them, a weasel named Carmody, who was going to hold a picnic in San Diego that weekend with a former California governor as headliner. The way Carmody tossed around tax dollars, he should be running as a Democrat or a Communist, if there was any difference these days between the two. "Rent a loud propeller plane," Vankov wrote back, "and have it fly over the weasel's picnic pulling a huge banner, 'Carmody Means Higher Taxes.'"

Vankov's cell rang, showing an unidentified number. Good. He tapped the answer button.

"This line is secure," the gruff voice said. "Now, who is this?"

"My name is Peter Vankov. I'm campaign manager for Hess for President. I understand you have a document showing that our likely general-election opponent improperly revealed classified information. If he did that, it's important for the voters to know, for the public to know. And, speaking as a patriot, it might even be important for legal authorities to know." He deepened his voice. "Now, who are you?"

"How'd you get my number?"

Vankov laughed. "We're always attuned to any information floating around that might prove useful. Legitimate information." In other words, bro, don't mention stolen Navy documents, or this is going to be a short call.

"I'm going to call Ven Hess's campaign in two minutes," the voice said. "I'm going to tell them my name is Drake—as in Sir Francis Drake—and ask for you." He hung up.

Well, old Drake was careful, which was a plus. But he also seemed like a pain in the tail. Vankov called Hess's Washington headquarters and told the receptionist to transfer any calls from a Mr. Drake right to Vankov's cell.

Vankov stepped toward the window, toward a prize of his art collection, an early Antoine-Louis Barye bronze of a panther taking down a stag. One of the great cat's forepaws gouged his prey's flank and its other foreclaws gripped the stag's muzzle. The panther's jaw clamped on the stag's neck, sinewy arms braced on the stag's shoulder, making the dying beast bear his killer's weight. Vankov exhaled; literally breathtaking. Savage and pure. Though not for everybody; he had to drape a towel over the piece when his wife was around.

Vankov's cell rang, a transfer from Hess headquarters, and he was on the line again with the gruff voice.

"Okay," Drake said. "But you're not the customer I had in mind. I need to think about this."

"Fine," Vankov said. "I need to think about it, too. You know who I am. Now tell me who you are, because this conversation isn't going any further unless I know who I'm dealing with."

Long pause. Vankov braced for the line to go dead.

Finally, the guy spoke. "Paul Thompson. Naval Air Systems Command. Civilian."

Two days later, Vankov was sitting in his office at Hess's Washington headquarters gazing out his window at the winter's first real snow, his view whitening like a dying TV, and again waiting for Paul Thompson to call him back. Waiting for the bureaucrat apparatchik to find some haven in his Crystal City, Virginia, office park—the guy didn't even rate the Pentagon proper—where he could make a secure phone call. Vankov shook his head. That was a slow death, whiling away your days scratching out forms in a cubicle, checking out for lunch and to use the can. Why bother getting up in the morning?

Through the falling snow, Vankov made out some other slobs across the quad grinding away in their sheetrock cubes, in the Capitol's shadow—So close and yet so far.

Thompson was going to be a pain. Vankov had sensed it, and the report from his ace sleuths confirmed it. Thompson had been a disciplinary problem at the Department of Defense for thirty years, the kind of guy who'd get booted from anywhere but the federal bureaucracy. The civil service practiced "progressive discipline" in meting out "adverse actions," Vankov's sleuths had explained, on two separate tracks: Performance and conduct. Offenders like Thompson got a warning, a lecture, a formal warning, a Performance Improvement Plan, suspension, probation, a final chance, and ultimately termination. Except that the slugs rarely reached the stiffer penalties because they could wait out whatever political-appointee supervisor was administering their progressive discipline, and then their next boss would have to begin all over again with a warning.

Thompson had been up and down the disciplinary ladder half a dozen times in his three decades at DOD. His problem was more conduct than performance. He seemed sharp, even brilliant, Vankov's sleuths reported, and a whiz on procurement. But he was a miserable, ornery, insubordinate, know-it-all cuss. Some of his political bosses probably figured they were better off putting up with Thompson; he got the job done, which ultimately made them look good. The executive branch was a world, Vankov had found, where the politicals didn't know anything and the careerists didn't do anything.

A knock. Vankov turned and looked through the window of his office door. Hess's new press dweeb, another slimy suck-up climber. Vankov flailed his arms, like an air traffic controller waving off a plane. What part of "the door is closed, so fuck off" did this guy not understand?

Vankov's cell blared. A secure call.

He swiveled in his chair to put his back to his glass-paneled door. "Okay. Tell me exactly what you're offering."

"A Navy security-clearance assessment report from 2001 on then-Rear Admiral Alec Arthur Maynard," Thompson began. "The original, signed, not a copy."

Thompson read him an excerpt, a passage about reliable intel obtained in interviews from officers under Maynard's command that Maynard had divulged top secret information to his paramour, beyond her security clearance. Thompson, sounding like the know-it-all Vankov's sleuths had described, then recited a definition of top secret information: "'Top Secret' shall be applied to information, the unauthorized disclosure of which reasonably could be expected to cause exceptionally grave damage to the national security."

"Sounds heinous. Why didn't they drum him out?"

"Both Maynard and his lady friend denied the charges, and the Navy ultimately decided that the evidence wasn't tight enough to strip Maynard's security clearance or take other action against him." Thompson coughed. "But Maynard never got another promotion—This is an admiral who'd been promoted twice below the zone—and he left the Navy a couple of years later."

Maynard left the Navy, Vankov wanted to say, because he was on the outs after badmouthing the 2003 US invasion of Iraq, the pinko weenie. But diddling his subordinate in the Middle East couldn't have helped. Maybe Maynard had even pissed on the Iraq invasion as cover for quitting the military, a pretext that he then parlayed into a Senate seat. Lucky for Maynard, Iraq fizzled out, making him a savvy hero. And now that sanctimonious, stuffed-shirt, lefty mandarin was claiming the flag, masculinity, and patriotism. Vankov's arm twinged.

"Okay. Your price of fifty thousand dollars, is that firm?"

Thompson laughed, his cackle drilling Vankov's ear like a jackhammer. "That was the price to the *New York Globe*. That's not the price to you. I went to the *Globe* because I happen to subscribe to some antiquated notions of truth and transparency in American politics. If I give that report to you, I'm getting into the dirt of a political campaign."

Vankov grunted. Another patriot willing to sell out his country, for the right price.

"And with the *Globe*, I know they'll literally go to jail to protect my identity. So I can buy a nice RV and see America with the Mrs., no worries. With you, I've got no protection at all from the Espionage Act. Not the same situation. Not at all. No. And not the same price. Not even close."

"The *Globe* turned you down."

"Yeah, so I'll go to the Washington Post. Or USA Today. Or the Wall Street Journal. Hell, CNN or the other networks. Hey, the *New York Globe* would have been nice, but these days, the Internet Age, it doesn't matter, one newspaper's as good as the next, once something's out there. Stuff this good? Some editor's going to bite."

Vankov grunted again. The schmuck was talking himself out of a sale. Vankov could sit back and let Thompson peddle his goods to the press. As Thompson said, one news outlet was as good as another, once this dynamite got out.

No, Thompson might not make a sale to the press. He might run into an editor who'd rat him out to the FBI instead of simply turning him down, the way the *Globe* had. Or Thompson might get spooked and climb back into his hole. Or he might make a sale, but to some pinko publisher who'd bury the Navy report to prevent a story, "catch and kill." All these news weasels were creaming over Maynard and saw Hess as the antichrist. They'd call it public service.

"What difference does it make if some reporter goes to jail to protect your identity?" Vankov asked. "Your secret's already out. I know about you."

"Is that a threat?"

"Jesus, Paul, lighten up. No, it's an observation."

"Because, again, it's a different situation. Nothing's happened yet but talk. That's all you and I have been doing, Pete—talking. I haven't done anything to trigger any statute."

I knew this guy was going to be difficult. "Right. Okay. Let's keep our eye on the ball. What do you want for your merchandise?"

A pause. Scratching over the line. Vankov held the phone away from his ear, to prevent any pain if the call clicked off. He tried to figure his maximum bid, the way he did at art auctions, and his opening bid.

"Two million dollars."

Vankov scrunched his face. "Say again."

"Two million dollars. Cash. That's the price."

His chest tightened. Two million dollars, and suffering an asshole amateur. Vankov sighed. "I'll call you back. Freedom and prosperity."

Forty minutes later, Vankov was huddling with Ven Hess just inside the kitchen doors of a premier seafood restaurant on 14th and K Streets, in the heart of downtown Washington. Scents of basil and broiling fish wafted through the warm, heavy air. In the background, cookware clanged, dishes clacked, and chefs and under-chefs shouted orders.

Hess began bitching about abandoning some heavy hitters he was squeezing over lobster cannelloni and pan-roasted Arctic char. Although the Hessian probably would have preferred a filet-of-fish sandwich, fries, and a chocolate shake from Mickey-D's.

"What's so damned important?"

"We've got the magic bullet." Vankov huddled close enough to gaze up the taller man's nostrils. "We've just got to pay for it."

Hess scowled.

Hess had the money, Vankov knew, from all his enterprises, all his scams. The minor league baseball teams, the satellite radio show, the TV ads, the movie cameos, the investment fronts for his mobbed-up pals. Come on, what are you saving it for? Vankov might be able to raise the money from other sources, but he wanted it from Hess.

"I've arranged to get hold of a document, the original, of an incriminating Navy report on Maynard," Vankov said.

Hess scanned the kitchen, eyed a busboy stacking dishes until the kid moved to an industrial sink.

"Turns out Maynard was whispering top secret pillow talk to the skank he was banging in the Middle East. The Navy couldn't prove it enough to file formal charges, but that was basically the end of Maynard's military career. Not all his blather two years later about the Iraq invasion being 'ill-founded and ill-planned'— that was just cover so he could bail from the Navy without egg on his face."

Hess narrowed one eye.

"A Pentagon lifer got hold of the report." Vankov lowered his voice to a whisper. "A guy named Thompson."

"Do I need to hear all these details?"

"Yes, you do. On this, you do." Vankov was about to do something big-time criminal, worse on the jail-o-meter than getting the intel from the Arabs, and he wanted Hess to know the details and to understand the situation and the stakes. You need to put some skin in the game. They'd take the risk together. And that would cement their bond. Blood brothers, The Dark Angel and the Hessian.

A young busboy scooted past, a small Latino. The kid must know somebody Hess wanted to deport, maybe a relative, maybe his whole clan. Hess didn't look at the kid, just stood tall, focusing above the busboy's head.

"This is the magic bullet," Vankov repeated. He detailed his plan to Hess.

"Two million bucks?" Hess squinted at him.

"The magic bullet."

Hess expelled air and scratched the back of his head. He grimaced and gazed up, then finally turned back to Vankov. He nodded. "Okay, kid. Set it up."

Half an hour later, Vankov was back in his office at the Hall of the States Building and back on the phone with Thompson. At least it was easy to reach these civil service hacks; they just marinated in their cubicles all day long. How much better was the sheetrock cell in which Hess kept Vankov? Outside the window, the snow had ebbed and the world had gone from white to gray.

"We have to meet someplace that's as private as exists in the United States." Much of the brio had seeped from Thompson's voice, maybe as the bureaucrat realized that his theoretical risk, which he'd thumped as a bargaining tool, was becoming real. There was also a lilt, though, probably at the prospect of becoming an instant millionaire.

"It has to be in the US because I'm not getting a passport stamp," Thompson went on. "And it can't be a twenty-hour flight away, because I can't be gone for very long. It has to be a three- to four-hour flight, tops."

"Anything else?" Vankov scratched his chin.

"Yeah. Planes aren't really so great, even for a short flight. If I tell my boss I'm taking off a couple of days for a colonoscopy, then somebody finds my name on a Southwest Airlines passenger manifest for those days, it's big problem."

A thought hit Vankov, and he smiled. "I know the perfect place. And the perfect way to get there." He let a silence scratch, let Thompson wait. "I need the privacy you need. I have the same risk as you. Be at the Manassas Regional Airport at 11 a.m., tomorrow, General Aviation. A plane will be waiting—"

"Tomorrow won't work. Tomorrow's a problem. I could do Thursday."

For two million bucks, you'll get on a plane when I tell you. Vankov sighed. "Be at the Manassas airport at 11 a.m. on Thursday. A private plane will be waiting to take you to St. Thomas, in the US Virgin Islands. From there, a private boat will take you to a private island—a ten-minute trip. I'll meet you on the island, and we can conduct our business. No passport stamps, I know a TSA guy who can deal with the airplane manifest, and no record for the water taxi. Okay?"

Another pause. Thompson had to be swooning; this was James Bond stuff. The most exotic place the paper pusher had ever gone was probably Atlantic City or Phoenix for some fed-conference junket.

"Okay."

As soon as he hung up with Thompson, Vankov dialed another number from his contact list through his Adeya app. On the third ring, the rich southern voice answered.

"I need to use your island on Thursday afternoon," Vankov said. "For a couple of hours is all. Don't worry, I won't even go in the house."

"Pete, I'm not running a timeshare," Stockton said. "The reason I have that place—"

"Hey, you shot off your mouth and obliterated Sistas for Sistas, which was a gold mine that took me months to set up. You spend your days collecting moldy old maps and sipping Pappy Van Winkle bourbon, but you want to be a player. Well a player's first rule is, keep your mouth shut."

"Hey, Pete—"

"You owe me, and I'm collecting. Whoever's on that island, get them out of there by noon on Thursday. It'll be me and one other guy. Have somebody there to wipe our feet, treat us like conquistadores."

The old man's breath hissed over the line. "Well, Thursday's all right," Colonel Sanders said. "But this is a one-time thing, now, Pete—"

Vankov hung up.

25
ST. THOMAS

Pete Vankov sipped iced tea on Stockton's wraparound veranda and tilted his face into a Caribbean breeze. Paradise. From Colonel Sanders's stone mansion atop a hill, Vankov gazed at woods yielding to a lush lawn that fed into a rocky shore, with endless azure waters beyond. Squinting against the mid-day sun, he could make out shapes of a few nearby islands. A couple of sailboats and a mega-yacht floated through the vista.

Maybe he'd buy a boat like that after Hess's coronation. He'd work the playbook that some old salts at DNFV had pioneered with Reagan, leverage his connections with the new administration to lure big lobbying accounts, big bucks.

Vankov loosened his cutaway collar under his linen suit. Nearly eighty degrees, in February. Part of him wanted to shuck his clothes, pad through that soft grass, and plunge into that pristine sea. Maybe he'd buy one of those other islands, or buy this one off Stockton. Everything was for sale, for the right price. That seemed an exclamation point of success, owning a Caribbean island. How far he'd come from Hoboken.

His eye caught movement, and he turned to see the transfer he'd arranged from St. Thomas chugging toward Stockton's dock.

A pang hit. He was about to hand over two million dollars to a man he didn't know, had never met, had only spoken to a few times by phone. Was the guy real? Were his goods? Vankov's uber-sleuths had vetted Thompson, and they were pros. Tops. The odds seemed solid. Sometimes you had to rely on others.

In a minute, a portly figure was trudging up a flagstone path toward the house. Toward Vankov.

He studied Paul Thompson. Ironic, that people steeped in the most physically demanding and most health-conscious spheres, like sports and the military and medicine, were often the least fit and healthy. Go to a ballgame, world-class athletes competing on the field, and the bleachers filled with porkers stuffing their maws with chili dogs and beer. Go to a hospital, nurses and orderlies plodding around like they needed an ICU, or at least a fat farm. Here was Thompson, who spent his days supporting warriors, and he looked like a saggy blimp. Even more haggard than in the photos Vankov's sleuths had sent. Vankov felt a twinge of disappointment, as though finding himself facing an unworthy adversary, a bathetic challenge.

Thompson was wearing a blue blazer, open slate-blue shirt, and gray slacks. Not bad, conceptually, if a bit unimaginative. Vankov guessed Macy's or J.C. Penny, possibly Saks, surely not Savile Row. As Thomson neared, Vankov saw he was clutching a thin leather briefcase, more like a portfolio. Not big enough to hold two million in cash. Which meant Thompson expected Vankov to include a bag with the payment, maybe a matte silver case like the ones drug dealers used on late-night TV cop shows. Vankov should hand him the bills loose, just to see his reaction.

Vankov waved. Thompson took a deep breath and waved back. Now Volta could make out Thompson's small, dark eyes and small red nose in a round, sweaty face, stubble on his lip and under his chin. Chins. Ravages of the cubicle life. Glancing at the clock all afternoon, counting the minutes until Happy Hour. A patriot in our nation's service. A five o'clock hero.

Vankov sipped his tea in the veranda's shade as Thompson huffed up the path. He waited to stand until Thompson took the first flagstone step. Up close, Vankov could see broken capillaries on the red nose, white chest hairs poking the slate-blue collar.

Thompson's handshake was heavy, clammy. Vankov indicated a matching rattan chair opposite him, across a small table. Much like the setup on Stockton's Charleston porch, he recalled. If you've got multiple homes, you decorate them differently, with different vibes and styles. That's half the point. He'd have to tell Stockton that. And remind his own wife.

Thompson sat with his briefcase on his lap, hands folded over the bag.

"Trip was okay?" Vankov asked.

Thompson nodded. "Yeah, fine." He let his eyes sweep the scenery. "Not bad."

Vankov chucked. Yeah, beats the Atlantic City boardwalk.

A door opened and a housekeeper popped out, a small Black woman in a cream linen dress carrying a silver tray. Silently, she set a glass of iced tea in front of Thompson. She swapped Vankov's half-finished glass for a fresh iced tea.

Thompson eyed his drink, and a stricken look came over him.

"Pretty heady, huh, Paul?" Vankov smiled at the bureaucrat. "For a while, anyway. You cruise on adrenaline, get a little reckless, and pretty soon you find yourself in a galaxy far, far away, on the other guy's turf. And you start sweating." Vankov shrugged. "We can swap glasses, if that'll make you feel better." He slid his fresh iced tea toward the center of the table.

Thompson didn't say anything.

"What's the matter, Paul? You worried I'm going to take your briefcase, clonk you on the head, and throw you in ocean, save myself some dough?"

Vankov savored Thompson's fear, even as the cloying stink of it floated onto his tongue, spoiling his tea. He smiled again. "I don't do that. I don't have to. If I wanted to get over on you, I could have found something. There's always something. As Willie Stark said in *All The King's Men*—you should read that, if you haven't: 'Man is conceived in sin and born in corruption and he passeth from the stink of the didie to the stench of the shroud. There is always something.'"

Vankov retrieved his glass. "Hey, don't worry, though. You can't cheat an honest man, right, Paul?"

Thompson nodded and eased his grip on his briefcase.

Vankov also liked that Thompson had pegged him as a killer. Thompson worked with professional killers at DOD, and must recognize one. Vankov had often fantasized about killing someone, if only to earn a key merit badge, cross yet another line. Like losing his virginity when he was thirteen to a skank down the street, mostly for the rite of passage. He couldn't think about Alec Maynard without musing that Maynard had killed dozens or hundreds, even if the submariner never saw his victims, firing from underwater. Maynard had aimed the missiles and pulled the trigger, and that gave the weasel one up on him.

Now, maybe, Vankov had an opportunity for the perfect murder. He could smash this slug's skull with a rock and dump the body, just as he'd said, and nobody would ever suspect. That is, if Thompson hadn't told anybody about the trip and hadn't left, say, a tell-all note to be opened if he didn't return. Well, fun to think about.

Vankov reached under his chair and hefted a bulging Coach leather duffle bag onto the table. He unzipped the bag to reveal stacks of worn bills, hundreds and fifties, and angled it to give Thompson a direct view.

Thompson looked like a kid who'd just gotten a new pony. The paper pusher caught himself and for a moment seemed confused, eager to reach for the cash but sensing he shouldn't. He placed his precious briefcase on the table in front of him, unzipped it, and pulled out a thin manila folder. He studied the tableau and extended the folder to Vankov.

Vankov opened the folder to find a four-page form, stapled in one corner, signed on the back page.

"Look at page three," Thompson said.

Vankov did. There, toward the top, was the language Thompson had promised, in two dense paragraphs: ". . . Captain Jasper stated, in a formal interview, that during dinner in the officers' mess—a nonsecure location—Lieutenant Commander Moran revealed information that Captain Jasper recognized as top secret and beyond Lieutenant Commander Moran's security clearance." Moran was Maynard's paramour at the Dubai hotel. "Captain Jasper stated that he then asked Lieutenant Commander Moran how she had obtained this information that she had just revealed, and that Lieutenant Commander Moran replied that she had heard it directly from Admiral Maynard. Captain Jasper stated that he then cautioned Lieutenant Commander Moran that the information that she had revealed was highly classified and should not be discussed at the officers' mess. Captain Jasper stated that Lieutenant Commander Moran then grew agitated, that she refused to discuss the matter further with him, and that she promptly left the mess . . ."

The report then said that Maynard and Moran, in independent sworn interviews, each denied Jasper's allegations and that Moran said that Jasper must have misunderstood her in the noisy mess hall, because she didn't have access to top secret information. Maynard and Moran each also denied that they were engaged in an inappropriate relationship.

On the report's final page, the investigator wrote that he found both of Captain Jasper's allegations credible: that Maynard and Moran were engaged in an inappropriate sexual relationship and that Maynard had improperly revealed top secret information to Moran. But the investigator concluded that given the sworn denials from both Maynard and Moran, despite general confirmation from other officers that Maynard and Moran seemed inappropriately close, there was insufficient evidence to pursue either matter or to withhold Maynard's security clearance.

Vankov let a smile play. Even better than he'd hoped. The report had Maynard perjuring himself in denying his affair with Moran—an affair that the Dubai hotel audio tape had just proven, and that Maynard had then been forced to admit. Since that adultery charge against Maynard had proven true, the second charge also seemed credible, that Maynard had revealed top secret information to his lover, further exposing himself to blackmail by foreign interests, and exposing US national security to "exceptionally grave" damage. The report documented both Maynard's crime and his cover-up.

Vankov chuckled and slid the report back into the folder. He slid the duffle of cash across the table to Thompson.

26
AUTO-DA-FÉ

David Gruber yanked open the Georgetown tavern's door and faced a sea of marble, dark wood, and brass, dimly lit. The vibe was power and money, a redoubt for masters of the universe to plot conquests over cognac, not for college kids to pound shots or hoops fans to chug brews. Winter dusk was settling at 5:30 p.m., lending an aura of menace, like a vampire movie in which the undead await the dark. Gruber thought of Yogi Berra's line, "It gets late early out there."

Gruber had never been to this bar, but it looked like a place where, under other circumstances, he'd feel comfortable, where he'd enjoy an evening with friends. Maybe he'd come back, depending on how tonight went, to celebrate. This place might become one of his haunts, site of his greatest victory, like Eisenhower returning to Omaha Beach. Vankov had phoned Gruber a few hours earlier to suggest they meet here to negotiate an "armistice." Something in Vankov's tone suggested the Dark Angel thought he could dictate the terms.

Well, of course; Vankov thought he had his nuke, a Navy security report incriminating Maynard. That bogus document was a work of art. Paul Thompson had wound up doing most of the drafting; the Department of Defense official knew the military lingo. Thompson was thorough, even finding and forging the signature of a now-deceased Navy intelligence officer as the reviewer. Vankov had been hooked from the first phone call, Thompson had assured Gruber. And now Thompson had delivered the loot, all $1 million, in used bills. It had all gone perfectly.

Which meant that tonight Gruber might finally slay his dragon, might finally defeat Peter Vankov. Why, then, were his limbs jittery and his pulse pounding?

Gruber stepped into the tavern, his leather soles soft on the stone floor, and scanned the long, narrow chamber. There, at a small round table facing the bar, with an open ladder-back chair beside him. Vankov. The dim light caught the orange hair, the dyed strands iridescent. A tumbler waited on the table, probably with some exotic single malt. Good, Vankov would need it.

Gruber walked over and began to slide the empty chair around the table, to face Vankov. To look him in the eye, no fear, no weakness.

"No, leave it there. I want you to have a good view." Vankov pointed at a television screen above the bar. The TV was showing Fox News, a grainy shot of a locker room corridor, a segment about school violence.

Buck up, Gruber told himself. So far, consistent with what he'd expected. Vankov cocky, smug, the way the Dark Angel got when one of his scams was about to pay off. Vankov must have given the bogus security report to Fox News and was expecting Fox to air it this evening, soon. A Fox reporter would tout "evidence" that then-Admiral Alec Maynard had lied under oath about his now-proven affair with a subordinate. The reporter would gush that Maynard had also been accused of revealing top secret information to his lover, but that Maynard had gotten off the hook—until now—by perjuring himself in denying those charges, too.

Vankov waved two fingers, and a young blonde in a frilly white blouse and tight black pants soon appeared.

"Another one of these." Vankov swirled his near-empty tumbler. "And whatever my friend is having. My good friend."

Gruber scratched an eyebrow. Best to stay sharp. "A light beer would be great. Whatever you've got on tap."

The woman rattled off a few options and Gruber chose a Sam Adams Light.

Vankov reached into his tattersall vest—"waistcoat," he would call it—and checked his pocket watch. He pointed at the television. "History is about to be made."

"You've dressed for the occasion." Gruber couldn't help grinning at Vankov's outfit, down to the two-tone wingtips, the first pair he'd seen off a golf course.

Vankov gave a short, seated bow.

The waitress returned with a tray and set down the fresh drinks and took Vankov's empty with crisp, efficient movements, like a croupier. In a moment, she was gone again.

"At six o'clock," Vankov said as though beginning a briefing, "Senator Alec Maynard's bid for the presidency will effectively end. As will your mischief." Vankov sipped his whiskey and exhaled sharply. "And I will be canonized by Thomas Venable Hess, the next president of the United States. And duly handed the keys to the kingdom."

Gruber smiled along with Vankov. This was too good, too easy. "What happens at six o'clock?"

"The end of life as you know it."

Gruber nodded. "And you've invited me here so you can watch my face as you twist the knife?"

"That's a nice idea, and it may come to that. But no. I've invited you here to offer an armistice. I was born on Armistice Day, now known as Veterans Day. Which cheats me out of the spotlight anyone deserves on his big day. Well, tonight may become my new big day. Tonight's events may rival the events of November 11, 1918, in historical significance."

"And be known from this day forward as Peter Vankov Day?" Gruber felt himself slipping into Vankov's cadence and faux-soaring rhetoric. He was also looking at tonight as a cosmic triumph to be celebrated forever afterward.

Vankov grinned again. "I've invited you here to give the condemned man a last chance to repent, to renounce his naïve, pinko, weasel ways, and to join the forces of truth and freedom."

"Kind of like during the Inquisition, at the stake, when some Jews got a last chance to convert before the Spaniards lit the fire?"

Vankov cocked his head. "Yeah, something like that."

"And what's going to come on TV in ten minutes that's going change the world?"

Vankov grinned. "That'd kill the surprise. But I'll say this: It's a masterpiece, the apex of my artistic career."

"Come on, Pete, who are you kidding, your 'artistic career'? Even as an artist, you were a philistine, a glorified graphic designer for hire. You always drew dark, on canvas and then on K Street. When your last bonds to humanity began to fray, your work turned darker still. The Dark Angel."

Vankov's eyes narrowed as though he were sifting Gruber's words, followed by a dismissive shrug. "Let's just say at six o'clock there's going to be a knockout. There better be; I paid two million for it."

A hot spike shot through Gruber's guts. He tried to smile, hoping his eyes wouldn't betray his angst.

Was Vankov working some other scam for which he'd paid two million dollars? Because Paul Thompson had given one million dollars to Gruber, said that was the negotiated price with Vankov. No, the only scam in that price range was the Maynard security report. And Vankov wasn't made of money, as Gruber's mother might have put it.

Had Thompson charged Vankov two million, told Gruber the sale price was one million, and pocketed the other million? Thompson might have found the opportunity too tempting.

From Thompson's perspective, odds were that Gruber would never find out. It was a fluke that Vankov had just blurted the price. Well, not a fluke; it was Vankov being Vankov, being indiscreet because the alternative was too painful for the Dark Angel, having his work and his genius go unnoticed. The only thing worse than being talked about is not being talked about.

Thompson could have justified the theft, figured he'd done most of the work by crafting the bogus report and taken most of the risk by meeting with Vankov, which entitled him to at least half the profit. Thompson could have even told himself he was being generous with Gruber, taking only half the loot. No wonder Thompson had enlisted in the scheme so readily; he smelled money.

Or was it worse than that? Another pang shot through Gruber's middle. Maybe Vankov had indeed paid Thompson two million dollars: One million for the bogus security report and then another million to rat out Gruber as its author. Was Fox going to report at six o'clock that politico David Gruber had forged a Navy document falsely incriminating Maynard and then tried to sell it? As part of a nefarious plan, probably in cahoots with Maynard, to later expose the report as a forgery, impugning Hess and winning sympathy for Maynard?

No, a million was more than Vankov would have to pay for Thompson's rat. The Dark Angel might have pocketed some of the loot himself, given an inflated figure to his backer, probably Hess.

Or it might be still worse, or as bad in another way. Maybe Thompson, for Vankov's extra million, had arranged to make the phony Maynard security report appear genuine, maybe by paying Navy colleagues to place copies of the bogus report in Maynard's personnel files. Thompson had forged the Navy reviewer's signature; he could create as many "originals" of the report as he liked.

No, too complex. Your mind is going in sixteen different directions, Gruber chided himself. Focus. He swigged his beer.

"Something wrong?" Vankov asked.

Gruber forced another smile. No, Thompson must have stolen half the payoff loot, simple as that. The simplest explanation was usually right. There was even a scientific principle that said so, Occam's Razor.

Okay, if Vankov thought he had a knockout security report on Maynard, what did the Dark Angel want from Gruber? What was the purpose of tonight's antics? Well, Vankov had said he wanted Gruber's soul. That's what the devil usually wanted. Vankov might also want some or all of his two million dollars back.

Gruber checked his watch. Five minutes to six. He gulped some beer.

"Your time's running out." Vankov sipped his whiskey.

"Let's see this bombshell of yours. Then we can talk about whether I sign over my soul."

Vankov shook his head. "Too late then, Dave. Once the fire's lit, too late for the Jews to recant. No matter how much they scream."

Gruber blocked a gruesome image from a college textbook. Don't let Vankov jar you. "Why give me a chance to get off the hook at all? I didn't give you one, with that vote to kick you out of the firm."

Vankov nodded, a wistful smile playing. "That's right, you didn't. We may need to settle the books on that." He shrugged. "But right now, we could use you on Team Hess. You're the best apprentice I ever had." Another sip of whiskey. "Hess is going to be president. That's how it is, so come aboard. Help make Hess the best Ven Hess he can be. Do it for your country, for your principles." Vankov chuckled.

"I'm flattered." It was supposed to sound stony but came out tinny.

"I taught you everything you know, Dave. And you were good, until you became an ungrateful weenie. My scorched-earth negative ads magnified cynicism and tribalism? Small price. My coalitions divided people? So what? You want me to pick my fingers raw over it, like you do? You don't win the election, you can't do squat."

"Sure, Pete. So create a civic wasteland and grow more blasé as you do it. And measure your success by how much money and power you can bank and how much tail you can nail. Certainly not by some airy notion of moving the country or the party forward. A lot simpler your way."

On the TV, a stud with gleaming chestnut hair was sliding into second base as a blonde held a glove over his head for the throw. A shampoo's logo appeared in yellow script. One or two more ads, and the six o'clock news should begin.

Our Mutually-Assured-Destruction dance is about to crescendo, Gruber thought. Our MAD dance. Vankov was about to drop his nuke. Gruber had warned that he was China, had boasted that he could withstand the blast. Could he? But how could he back down now? He'd lose all credibility. Well, maybe not with Vankov. With the Dark Angel, principles and sermons didn't count for much.

Think! Gruber might have only seconds to change or cancel the biggest bet of his life before the roulette ball began spinning around the track.

Rebuff Vankov, and he will be in shackles by morning, charged with corrupting the democratic process. Which would be rich, coming at the Dark Angel's hands. Would Vankov also expose Jane Berglund? Did Vankov even know she was involved? Gruber had never mentioned Berglund to Paul Thompson. No, but he'd dangled to Thompson the prospect of a *New York Globe* exposé on the forgery, and Vankov could connect those dots. Dumb. Gruber had wanted to impress Thompson with the power of his plan, with his juice, to convince Thompson to join. Dumb.

What was Gruber's alternative? Sign on with Ven Hess now, then spend nine months putting that grotesque in the White House? How would it work—Gruber says "uncle" and Vankov whips out his phone and makes an emergency call to a Fox producer and kills the segment? Like a Spanish inquisitor extinguishing a match just before lighting the kindling? No, too dramatic. And Vankov wanted the segment aired, after what he'd paid for the report. No, Fox's six p.m. segment probably wouldn't name Gruber as author of the bogus document. That would come—if Gruber held out—on Fox's 6:30 or 7 p.m. show, after Vankov gave the producer an update.

Vankov had made the only viable argument for helping Hess: That Hess was going to be president, and a true American patriot did his part for his country, no matter who occupied the Oval Office. Salute the uniform, not the man.

The TV flashed to Fox's 6:00 p.m. anchor, severe in a white shirt and charcoal suit. Gruber's temples began pounding.

The anchor offered a teaser that Fox would air an exclusive on Alec Maynard at the top of the hour. "Stay tuned."

Vankov grinned.

The TV flashed to a middle-aged woman skipping through a hopscotch course, giddy over some new rheumatoid arthritis drug. Then a graying construction worker in a flannel shirt hefted a shovel, big grin.

How had Gruber misplayed this chess game with Vankov? No matter what Fox aired at six o'clock, the uncertainty alone proved he'd played poorly. Was Vankov truly more talented or savvier than Gruber, or just more ruthless?

Last commercial. Last chance.

"You think you're Superman, bulletproof, but you're just reading your own press, your own press releases," Gruber said. "The reality is, Maynard figured out your first big scam, Sistas for Sistas, which then collapsed." He smiled. "With a little help from me. Argentina blew up when Olga turned on you. Even your Dubai hotel-room audio fell flat; Maynard still got the nomination, and Yair ratted you out."

"You're not Superman, not anymore," Gruber continued. "You're Mr. Incredible, that cartoon superhero who can't squeeze into his costume anymore. You've gotten fat, sloppy, lazy, and even more warped. All that steroids and booze. You think I could have torpedoed you like that five years ago?" Gruber leaned across the table, until their faces were a foot apart. "And that's how I knew I could get you with the Navy security report."

Vankov recoiled as though Gruber had punched him.

"You didn't teach me everything I know." He kept his eyes locked on Vankov's. "You taught me everything you know." He pulled some folded pages from his jacket pocket and slapped them on the table.

On the TV, the Fox anchor was waving a document. Was Fox blasting Maynard for revealing top secret intel, or exposing a forged report that claimed Maynard had? The screen flashed to a close-up of Maynard.

"Wow, Fox also has a copy?" Gruber motioned at the pages on the table.

Vankov unfolded the pages and saw that Gruber had handed him the Navy security clearance report on Maynard, another signed "original." The same report that Fox was now showing in a full-screen close-up. The report for which Vankov said he'd paid two million dollars.

Vankov glanced at the television, at Gruber, and back at the TV, like a driver who'd bumbled into an intersection and now faced traffic from multiple directions. Vankov whipped out his cell phone. Was he going to order Fox to abort the segment?

"The fire's already lit, Pete."

On the TV, a talking head was intoning that the report spelled Maynard's doom: The end of his presidential bid, the end of his Senate career, and maybe the end of his freedom.

"For some real news," Gruber said, "read the *Atlantic* tonight."

A few hours later, Gruber's cell phone blared, alerting him that Berglund's "Vankov's Greatest Hits" story had posted on the *Atlantic* website. Gruber pounded the device with his thumbs and scanned through the piece. He spotted only two edits, minor for style, no change in the thrust.

Berglund's story focused on Vankov's enlisting Middle Eastern despots to dig up dirt on Maynard, taking a thing of value, committing felony violations of campaign finance laws. But Berglund opened with the latest news, the bogus Maynard security report. Fox hadn't named Vankov as its source. But Berglund did, amplified in a bright red subhead.

PART

TWO

27
GENERAL AVIATION

Ven Hess shifted in his desk chair to admire a jumbo photo of himself on the mound in Wrigley Field, snarling, winding up to deliver a haymaker. The pitch would be a ball, low and inside, on his way to walking the batter. On his way back to Triple-A. But that didn't lessen the photo. He turned to his lawyers, sitting in the matching office-supply-store chairs. A fat one and the thin one, Abbott and Costello. No, more like Laurel and Hardy.

"Anybody see you come into the building?" he asked them.

They looked at each other and Laurel shrugged.

"Were there any cameras outside, any reporters?"

They shook their heads.

"All right." He took another glance at the menacing mound photo. "What do the feds have on Vankov?"

The lawyers looked at each other and Laurel straightened in his chair. "That *Atlantic* story is a roadmap. From what we've gleaned, the feds are looking at campaign finance violations, money-laundering, racketeering, perjury, obstruction of justice, and foreign-agent charges. They're digging deep into Mr. Vankov's work for a Middle East dictator who paid him millions, including cash and a couple of houses, that Mr. Vankov allegedly did not report. From what our sources tell us—not confirmed—federal investigators have tracked some of Mr. Vankov's payments from his foreign clients to deposits in Cyprus and other money-laundering havens, also never reported to the IRS."

Hess swiveled his desk chair and gazed out at the Capitol, the marble and white-painted dome brilliant against a clear blue sky. Looked like a postcard shot. You'd never know it was frigid out, with this building's central air. He swiveled back.

"How did you leave things with Mr. Vankov?" Hardy asked.

"How? I sent him to the showers. Told him to clean out his locker." Hess grimaced. "What'd you expect me to do, after that *Atlantic* hit job?" And after Vankov flushed two million dollars of Hess's hard-earned money. Two million dollars. That put Vankov's ledger way into the red.

"Sure," Hardy said. "Of course. It's just a matter of, well, we don't want Mr. Vankov so . . . unhappy that he seeks retribution."

No kidding. If Re-Pete spilled to the feds about the Hessian's role in the Navy security report and the rest of it, game over.

Hess shook his head. He should have fired Re-Pete months ago, after that "Hess's Brain" *Time* magazine piece, before Re-Pete had so much on him. He'd nearly done it. Instead, he'd kept a running tally of how much he was getting from Vankov, versus how much the guy was costing him. As long as Re-Pete stayed in the black, Hess would keep him on the team. Meanwhile, Hess would make daily temperature checks of his manager, like telling him, 'Before you come into my office, Re-Pete, I need to know how hot you are.'" Jesus, how could he have left a wild pitcher on the mound, in a post-season game?

"How hot is this going to get for me?" he asked the lawyers.

They exchanged looks again and Hardy adjusted his suitcoat over his pudge and cleared his throat. "The feds probably won't question you about Mr. Vankov. Most of the violations that Mr. Vankov is accused of predate your campaign, so they shouldn't need you to make their case against him." Hardy shrugged. "Also, the feds are generally reluctant to intervene or interfere in a presidential campaign."

"Reluctant?" Hess nearly yelled. "Well, that's a comfort. That sounds like a contract clause that says Party A will 'thoroughly consider' before hosing Party B. I've done lots of things I was 'reluctant' to do, because in the end I had to do them."

Laurel gave him a smile, like a doc with bad news and good news. "Your firing Mr. Vankov has gone a long way toward keeping the feds off your neck."

The next morning, Hess strode toward Reagan National Airport's General Aviation terminal flanked by his secret service detail, severe in dark suits. This was the way to travel, escorted from a chauffeured Lincoln to a private jet, a flock of aides tending to your every whim, even carrying your briefcase. This first walk was short, no need to button his overcoat, even in the February frost with a breeze that scraped his face.

Hess allowed a smile. This was even grander than the Show. In the Majors, even if you were a star pitcher—and, face it, Hess hadn't been—you still dressed and showered in a packed locker room, still shared a bench in the dugout. Still crammed into a team plane or bus.

Not on Team Hess. He was the star and owner. All the accoutrements were his, had his name on them. The plane would take off when he said so. With those aboard he wanted. Then land where he said. With privacy at a wave of his hand and plenty of leg room.

He also had a winner's vibe and momentum, the Big Mo. It was so different playing on a winning team than a losing team; he'd seen that in his season with the Chicago Cubs—okay, in his two months with the Cubs—when they'd gone from contender to cellar dweller. Success bred success. A win in the Iowa caucuses, then an even bigger win in New Hampshire, and now Hess was the favorite to take South Carolina at the end of the month and sew up the GOP nomination by April, the pennant. Then onto the general election in November, the World Series. Against Alec Maynard.

"Sir." His traveling press aide sidled up. "There are some reporters on the tarmac. And one camera."

Hess turned, gave his press dweeb The Stare.

"The schedule we put out just listed your public events, we didn't say where you were leaving from. But they must have figured it out. Now they're waiting for us."

The press wasn't waiting for "us." They were waiting for him. For Hess. For the Hessian.

"Where's the camera from?" He didn't bother looking at the press dweeb.

"I don't know, sir."

They'd been laying on the "sirs" thick the last couple of days, since he'd canned Vankov. Cut your ace pitcher, and nobody in the dugout feels safe.

They filed into the general aviation terminal, which felt like a travel agency office, with institutional beige carpet, a couple of Formica desks, and posters of Caribbean beaches tacked to the walls. Low-end, for what these guys charged.

One of Hess's aides asked whether he wanted a coffee or a banana or to use the men's room. Before he could answer, another elbowed in to give him an update about some Podunk Bugle poll.

"Coffee, two sugars," Hess told the first aide. Not that he really wanted it, but if he kept refusing their overtures, they might figure he was low-maintenance and stop asking. And stop thinking about his needs. Well, if they wanted to collect a World Series ring, they'd better think about the Hessian's needs. Constantly.

A kid handed him a Styrofoam cup and he sipped the coffee, which tasted day-old. He slid the cup onto a plastic table, let the coffee slosh over. Hess motioned to his campaign manager—his new campaign manager, his third—for his briefcase. Hess didn't need the press seeing an aide toting his briefcase, then running some snarky piece on the imperial Hessian.

He buttoned his topcoat and signaled his lead secret service guy. The super-cop leaped to the far door, and Hess followed him into daylight, the sun bouncing off the tarmac and spiking into his eyes.

As Hess's vision cleared, an assault of voices hit his ears, like bleachers erupting. Except they weren't fans cheering as he took the mound or blew away a batter. They were shouting questions at him, demanding answers. About Pete Vankov.

He unwrapped a stick of Wrigley's Double-Mint and slid it into his mouth as he walked toward a gleaming Gulfstream idling about thirty feet away. Took the first bite and savored that mint blast.

A shrill voice cut through the din. "Has the FBI contacted you about Peter Vankov?"

He turned. A thin woman with streaked brown-blond hair and a small, pointed chin, her top-heavy face magnifying her anger. What was she so ticked about?

"Mr. Hess," she hollered again, even more shrill. "Did the FBI contact you about Peter Vankov?"

He spread his arms, gave her an innocent "Who, me?" gaze. Then he locked on her eyes. "No," he said, and kept walking toward the Gulfstream.

His press dweeb stepped between him and the media horde, which was comical and, in its way, touching. The press guy couldn't weigh more than 140 dripping wet, and a couple of the cameramen were nearly Hess's size. The streaky blonde could probably take him if it came to that. Gutsy little kid, taking one for the team.

The questions kept pelting him.

Hess cupped one hand to his ear, pointed the other hand at the idling jet, and gave the newsies a helpless, amused face. Hey, it had worked for Ronald Reagan. He turned back and continued toward the plane.

Oh, hell. These questions wouldn't just go away. Better get it over with. And now was a good time, on the move, keep it short, make it look like no big deal. He stopped and pivoted halfway around, as though preparing a pickoff throw to second. The press horde froze.

"Peter Vankov worked for me for a very short period of time," he began in the command voice he'd learned in the broadcast booth. "He started as my press aide and did some other work for us. Overall, a small and short-lived role on a big campaign."

They bleated that Vankov was Hess's campaign manager. A high voice yelled, "Come on!"

Hess raised his hand to quiet them, bunch of baying hounds. "Anybody who knows me will tell you that when I'm on the mound, I call the pitches."

A deep voice shouted something. Hess ignored the guy, talked over him. "These accusations against Pete Vankov have nothing to do with me. But I do feel bad for him, bad about what they're doing to him. First that magazine piece and now, according to you people in the press, federal investigations. They're picking through the guy's life, going back ten, fifteen years, through stuff he did then. Supposedly did."

They hurled more questions, accusations really, voices rising, railing against dirty politics. Yeah, and what about yellow journalism?

"Pete Vankov is a talented guy, a real savvy guy," he said in the command voice. "He built a top-notch network with the media, with 'the holy trinity of Republican taste making,' someone called it—*Fox News*, syndicated talk radio, and the Christian press—and that's why we brought him on our team. He also has a real feel for campaigns. He's helped Ronald Reagan and lots of other Republican stars over the years, the decades. His troubles don't involve me, but I don't like seeing what's happening to him. And I wish him well."

He waved at the press, the way the Gipper used to, and turned back to his plane. As he neared the steps, the din of questions faded into the engines' roar.

Late that night, as Hess was skimming some staff memos in a hotel room in Columbia, South Carolina, his cell phone rang with a blocked number. He knew who was calling. He'd been expecting to hear from him. This late-night call was perfect. No one would ever know they were still talking, or certainly not what they were talking about. And no one would overhear. The Verizon cache would show only an unknown number, and Hess wasn't president yet, so there were no formal call logs. He clicked the green answer icon.

"Mr. President," Vankov said.

"Pete."

"I'm glad you still remember me."

"Oh, come on, Pete. I had to say that to the press. You're kind of radioactive these days, kid."

"StormSpill is going to dump some emails to and from Maynard's campaign manager," Vankov said. "Tomorrow probably, Friday at the latest. Toxic work environment in that campaign, staffers complaining about favoritism and harassment, that kind of thing. And some Mickey Mouse stuff, like charging the taxpayers for campaign travel. Maynard went to Arizona and Nevada last month but made sure to stop in LA to take a dump so they could charge the airfare and hotel bills to the Senate, you know, a California senator's official business."

"Thank you, Pete." Hess added quickly, "For letting me know." He stepped to the window and gazed out at the South Carolina State Capitol, which looked quaint, lit against the night, like a miniature of the federal version. "You've always been savvy and tough, and I always liked that about you—I also said that to the press. Like an old pitcher who uses his smarts and maybe an occasional dab of Vaseline to get the job done."

Vankov coughed or cleared his throat, drilling Hess's ear. "I'm expecting to be indicted. The prosecutors haven't told me officially, but my lawyers say it's coming."

Hess expelled air. What do you want in return for your silence? "When?"

"The indictment?" A pause. "Who knows. My lawyers told me from now on, I'm in their bull's eye. Bunch of little weasel pinko pricks. They're enjoying this. You can see it in their smug Ivy League faces."

Hess tried to pick his next words carefully. His brain was straining at the end of another eighteen-hour day, and the effort drilled a pain through his right temple into his eye.

Silence scratched across the line.

"Listen, kid," Hess finally said. "I appreciate what you've done for us, what you're doing. And when I get to the White House, first order of business is to take care of you, make sure you're not a victim of some miscarriage of justice."

More silence.

"Thank you, Mr. President. Freedom and prosperity."

Hess hung up.

28
GUILE

The babe was wagging her finger at Pete Vankov, mock scolding, her brown locks cascading to her CD shoulders in shimmering waves, framing her perfect teeth, caramel eyes, moist cinnamon lips. She leaned forward, her breasts straining her camisole, and Vankov felt himself stiffen, in his fuzzy half-sleep. He heard a banging, wondered what it was, then saw it was the woman clapping her hands, beckoning him, the way she might summon a spaniel. He stepped toward her.

Then another bang, louder, followed by shouts, then heavy footsteps, and the world ignited, and Vankov realized the physical world had shattered his reverie.

He opened his eyes. Light poured through his bedroom window, not a soft morning desert glow, more like a solar flare. His iPhone showed 5:25 a.m. About half an hour before dawn. June in Albuquerque.

More footsteps, growing closer, louder. He sat up in his bed, tried to remember where he'd put his slippers. On the floor, or had he left them in the bathroom?

His bedroom door burst open and flashlights seared his eyes. He blinked, made out two men in helmets and blue windbreakers, flak jackets poking up from their collars, one wielding a rifle. Hard faces above sinewy necks. In a moment, one of them grabbed him and flattened him onto the bed, face into the duvet. Now pressing his arm up, like a wrestler working a chicken-wing.

"FBI," a voice barked. "We're here to execute warrants. You're under arrest."

Vankov felt a cold weight slide over his wrists, heard some metallic clicks and snaps, and then they rolled him onto his back, onto his bound hands. A spike shot through his left arm, his pinched nerve flaring, raw in the morning.

Now there was a squad in his bedroom in helmets and windbreakers and flak vests and guns, an assault of glares.

"You really need an army to take down a fifty-three-year-old consultant with a pinched nerve in his neck?" he shouted at the nearest agent.

Another thug hauled him to his feet as though Vankov were a tackling dummy. The guy was a head taller, partly from combat boots. Vankov saw "FBI" printed in bright yellow on the backs of their blue jackets, big enough for street signs.

The stormtrooper who'd hoisted him looked him over and gave him an odd grin, and Vankov realized that even amid all the furor he hadn't fully shrunk.

"Peter Vankov," one of them intoned, then barked the Miranda warning as though auditioning for some B cop movie.

Keep quiet and call the lawyer, he told himself. Run the script we prepared. Stay calm, that was key. Lucky, in a silver-lining way, he'd had to stop serious weightlifting after pinching the nerve. No risk now of a "roid rage."

They at least let him put on his slippers, which were by the bed, then led him out of his bedroom and onto the landing. Another blue-jacketed squad was tossing his study, one of them yanking cables from his computer, another studying a framed drawing on the wall, Vankov's recent piece showing horned demons ravishing nymphs, all of them on a raft floating toward the edge of the Earth.

The art critic turned, maybe at the sound of footsteps, and smiled at

Vankov. He glanced back at the demons floating toward the abyss, then again at Vankov. "Self-portrait?"

The stormtroopers walked Vankov downstairs to his stucco living room, where more feds in blue windbreakers were knocking cushions from his sofa and rooting through his cabinets. One nimrod was holding up a flash drive as though he could read its contents in better light.

"I'd like to put on some clothes," he told the fed hoisting his arm.

"Later."

Vankov looked down at his outfit. Sateen pajamas in maroon candy stripe with blue piping around the collar, pocket, and cuffs. Short sleeves, long pants. The best he'd been able to find at a local Target a couple of years ago when he'd needed something quick.

His hair must be a mess. It usually took him a few minutes to do the choreography in the morning, cover the thinning areas, fluff the bottle-brown thatch. No way now to even sweep the strands across his forehead, with his hands bound.

A fed was examining the French art deco chandelier as though Vankov had hidden diamonds or coke in one of the shades. His wife had found the lamp in a Georgetown gallery and had to have it. But she had no place for it, their other homes were already filled with chandeliers along with other bric-a-brac she'd had to have, so it wound up here in Albuquerque, an antique eyesore retrofitted into a contemporary split-level. Jesus, he hated that thing.

They hauled him toward his open front door. Dawn was breaking, a magenta and yellow glow rising over the mountains. The beginning of an idyllic day, a high over ninety but dry and crisp. He laughed to himself. He'd come to the desert to escape his troubles. He'd planned a morning sunning on his deck, catching up on emails, and then lunch in Old Town Albuquerque. He should have stayed in Washington. Although more jackboots were probably tossing his other places right now, in Florida, New York, and DC. Maybe even his flats in London and Paris.

He'd erased some of the most damaging stuff, but left enough on his phones, laptops, desktops, and external hard drives to make this a great day for the other side. He'd thought he had more time, that they'd give him a warning, a notice, like gentlemen.

They walked him onto his lawn and a klieg light ignited, blasting him in the face. A TV camera. He squinted. CNN. Jesus.

He straightened, arched his head back, maximizing his height, giving them his full, wide neck, like a peacock preening. But the display would have only so much effect in striped shorty pajamas. This was going to become his enduring image: unkempt hair, unwashed face, and Target pajamas. After a lifetime of attiring just so, of biweekly hair and nail sessions, of tans and bronzers. This is how the world would see him and remember him. Like a celebrity mug shot. Which must be coming, too.

Why was a TV camera here? Well, because some law-enforcement weasel, in the DOJ or FBI, must have tipped CNN. They weren't satisfied to leak these stormtroopers' body camera footage. They had to put Vankov's defrocking live on network TV in megapixels. Tune in, watch the Dark Angel go down. This investigation was enough of a circus, with enough feds involved, that Vankov would never find the leaker, get the prick's scalp.

How could this be happening? The US attorney for New Mexico must have gone to court, convinced a judge they'd likely find evidence of one or more federal crimes, and gotten a warrant to search Vankov's home. They'd gotten a no-knock warrant because, what, they had a reasonable fear that Vankov would flee or become violent? No, because he might destroy evidence in that moment between the agents knocking and entering. Damn right he would have.

Vankov knew why they were doing it. They were crippling him to make sure he couldn't recover in time to help Hess. Because they wanted Maynard to win. It wasn't just that they were Ivy League pricks who despised Hess and Vankov, envied their wealth and resented their clout. They were deep-state libs.

For years, Vankov had been signing off phone calls and meetings with "Freedom and prosperity." His signature. Now they were going to take both of those from him. A deep-state election stunt by Maynard-world. Lib-world. Weenie-world.

He turned to an agent beside him who was facing forward, jaw tight, mugging for the camera. Loud enough for the mics to pick up, Vankov told him, "You think I'm a bad guy? A dirty trickster? Well, you're a bunch of sadists. This live-TV perp walk is about as dirty as anything I've been accused of. Your hands are filthy—all of you—and covering them in rubber gloves won't hide the stains."

The agent gave a short laugh, didn't even look at him.

"No, I'm serious. The worst I've been accused of is nihilism, but you guys get off on this stuff. That's sadism, by definition. Look it up, prick." Come on, elbow me, or shove me or spit on me, with the camera rolling. Come on.

No response, not even a glance.

Today was the second time this year, within four months, that Vankov had been had, he mused. First, Gruber had beaten him, outplayed him, with that bogus Navy security report. In a way, that stunt bothered Vankov less because Gruber had guile. That was the Dark Angel's highest compliment, bestowed sparingly, stingily, rarely. Guile. It compensated for a lot of sins.

"You have no guile," he told the agent beside him. "You guys marching me through this perp walk? You're weasels. Weenies."

No response.

And yet even today's shaming made him feel a twinge of pride. He was a big enough player, had altered American politics enough to draw such force from the other side.

"You libs are playing my game," he told the agent. "I tell all my clients, my elected clients: Always use the powers of your office, the powers invested in you by 'the people,' to maximum effect, and with maximum drama. And always spin to Joe and Linda Sixpack that you're fighting to uphold 'justice and the American way.'" He spat on the ground, near the agent's shoe.

That got the agent to look at him. "Why don't you do yourself a favor and shut up?"

In the distance, black vans were racing up his street, dust clouding the pristine air, obscuring the distant hills. These ninjas had probably slunk in during darkness, driven up with their lights off, parked a few blocks away, then crept to Vankov's house so they could break down his door in cinematic glory in front of the CNN camera.

They led him to a clear spot on his lawn, made him stand there, let the cameras have at him.

A roadrunner ambled toward Vankov from around the bend, from his pool area. Looked like the same one he'd seen the last couple of days, had fed a slice of bread yesterday. The bird gave him a wary, puzzled look.

In the distance, Vankov heard a whirring, as though something was chopping the sky. Which is exactly what it was. A black helicopter was angling toward him. Was it going to land on his lawn? A cherry on CNN's treat?

They'd probably sent the helicopter because they didn't want to hold Vankov in a local tank. They'd whirl him to a more distant holding facility. Maybe to the federal courthouse for arraignment. And for more humiliation. For a more formal defrocking.

The roadrunner raised a wing against the approaching helicopter, gave Vankov what looked like a farewell glance, and darted off.

29
CENTREVILLE

The ground was soft after recent rains, and David Gruber tried to set his Italian loafers down gently, so they didn't sink into the mud. He leaned against an oak tree, satisfied that the trunk's girth would hide him from the street, from a car's view. A golden dusk was settling over Centreville, Virginia, helping to obscure him.

Gruber was a few feet from a concrete path to the one-story rambler, a generic box in red brick and white wood siding. The place had a wide wooden porch, though, which must be nice for summer nights and cookouts. If Paul Thompson had any friends. The bureaucrat seemed a loner.

Gruber looked at his watch again. Nearly 7:30 p.m., around the time Thompson got home. Thompson finished his shift at the Navy offices in Crystal City at 6 p.m., then usually grabbed a bite at a local diner or restaurant to wait out rush hour, then drove twenty-five miles home, arriving around now. Jake had given Gruber the intel, the most they'd agreed Jake would do without knowing more about the situation, which they'd both seemed glad not to discuss.

Gruber buttoned his topcoat. Around 40 degrees, but it felt colder here in the suburbs, away from the urban canyons that retained heat and blocked breezes. He smelled some type of wildflower and maybe cut grass, homeowners greeting the new Spring.

He let his thoughts drift, and Pete Vankov's now-iconic image floated into his head, the Dark Angel on courthouse steps after a procedural hearing, wearing a black cape and a black fedora, Al Capone meets Dracula. He felt a smile form but ached with a sense of loss that drowned his glee.

He scanned Thompson's lawn, saw what looked like dried dog turds at the curb. How did I get here? Ivy League law graduates turned partners at bigfoot K Street public affairs firms weren't supposed to spend their evenings ambushing henchmen in suburban Virginia. Maybe tonight was the apotheosis of Gruber's quest to prove something when he moved to Washington, and certainly when he joined DNFV. He'd completed the metamorphosis his eighth-grade teacher had promised, that the scrawny teen having trouble with girls would be fighting them off with sticks at thirty. But he'd kept hunting and acquiring and consuming long past his thirtieth birthday, long past making his point. Maybe now he was proving, as the years passed, that he still had mojo.

He checked his watch again. Nearly 7:40 p.m. Maybe Thompson had joined some coworkers for drinks or gone to a movie. What did a single, middle-aged man do on a weekday evening? He laughed. What did Gruber do? Maybe Thompson also sat in his living room reading political thrillers and literary fiction.

Headlights bounced in the distance, then neared. Looked like a large American car, maybe a station wagon. Gruber angled around the tree trunk, keeping the oak between himself and the car.

The car slowed—it was a station wagon, looked like a blue Buick—and turned into Thompson's driveway. Gruber watched as the car illuminated the red tricycle a few feet in front of the garage door, then lurched to a stop. Gruber had bought that trike thirty years ago, had taught both his daughters to ride it, and hadn't been able to part with it, figuring he'd find another use for it. And tonight, he had.

The Buick's driver's door opened, and Thompson stepped out. More like waddled out. He looked even heavier than Gruber remembered.

Gruber stepped out from the oak and walked over.

Thompson was reaching down to lift the tricycle when he startled and snapped around, maybe hearing Gruber's footsteps or seeing his shadow.

"Hey, Paul."

"Dave?"

"I couldn't seem to reach you by phone—I left at least six messages. Maybe your devices aren't working, your office or your cell. So I thought I'd give it the personal touch."

Thompson squared and stepped back from the tricycle. "It's been crazy. I've been meaning to call you back."

Gruber nodded. "Well, you probably know what this is about. Kind of our version of *On the Waterfront*. You know, the scene in Johnny Friendly's bar when Charlie tells the stooge, 'You're fifty short, Skins.' Then Johnny—Lee J. Cobb—turns to Skins and says, 'Gimme.' You want to do Skins's lines?"

Thompson just stared at him.

"Okay, I'll do both parts. He affected a soft, obsequious tone: 'I—I musta counted wrong, boss, I—'Then he sneered and grunted, 'Gimme!'"

"Dave, you must be mixed up."

"No, Paul, that's another film, that's Carlo in *The Godfather* when Michael comes for him. 'Mike, you've got it all wrong . . . I'm innocent.' Which, of course, Carlo wasn't. And Mike tells him to stop saying he's innocent, that it insults Mike's intelligence and makes him very angry."

Thomson scrunched his face, as though confused. He scanned his yard.

"You're asking me if that's an argument?" Gruber said. "No, that's a fact. The argument's leaning over there against that tree." Gruber pointed toward the oak. Then he laughed. "Relax, Paul, just kidding. Nobody here but me. But you do recognize the lines? Ah, come on, Paul, *The Cincinnati Kid*, Steve McQueen and Rip Torn."

Gruber had considered bringing muscle but didn't want anybody seeing him with Thompson. He dropped his grin. "Let's go inside and talk, Paul."

Thompson seemed to consider, then his face loosened. "Sure, I've got a couple of brews in the fridge."

They settled in a wood-paneled living room with a plaid sofa and matching green leather chair and ottoman.

"That new?" Gruber asked, pointing at a massive 4K television set, at least seventy inches, wedged between two windows. "Nice."

Gruber ignored a bottle of Amstel that Thompson placed on a scarred coffee table before him. "Paul, imagine my surprise when I learned that you got two million dollars from Mr. Vankov, not the one million you returned to me."

"Dave, I got one million, just like I told you."

Gruber glared at him.

"I don't know who you've been talking to, but why would you take their word over mine? Who told you that, Vankov? The guy's a professional sleaze. You said so yourself. How do you know he didn't take two million from whoever and pocket half? Why would you look at me?"

Gruber shook his head. "I told you, don't tell me you're innocent." He shifted forward on the couch, wondering what stains were adhering to his suit pants. He glared at Thompson again until the other man looked away.

"I'll let you keep fifty thousand, but I want the rest. Tonight, now." Gruber shoved the beer bottle away from him.

They looked at each other for a few beats, and Thompson took a swig from his Amstel.

"You must be familiar with the concept of Mutually Assured Destruction." That gambit hadn't swayed Vankov but should work better with this apparatchik.

Thompson nodded, wary.

"Good. We've both done something we shouldn't have done. But I'm the crazy one who can take the explosion; you can't. So give me the fucking money, or I'll turn your cubicle into a cell." Gruber narrowed his glare, felt himself trembling.

Thompson studied Gruber, then raised his arms at his sides. "Okay. I'll get it." He stood and walked out of the living room.

A blast of relief surged through Gruber. He must look crazed, for Thompson to back down so quickly. "I'm not in this league," Thompson seemed to be thinking. "I'm done, I'll take my fifty grand and buy an RV."

Then it hit Gruber that Thompson might return with a gun or a baseball bat, or might not come back at all. Gruber dashed to the side of the doorframe Thompson had walked through, the way Bogie did in some film.

A minute later, Thompson waddled back into the living room lugging a large leather duffle bag. He plopped the bag onto the coffee table with a thud. The bag was Coach, in a supple brown leather, Gruber noticed. Far more elegant than the blue canvas travel bag in which Thompson had delivered the initial loot.

As Gruber watched, Thompson unzipped the Coach duffle and pulled the sides open. The bag was half-filled with stacks of cash.

30
"WHAT'S GOING ON?"

Alec Maynard eased back into a sofa in his suite at the Moscone Center, San Francisco's premier convention center. Two decks below in the glass-and-steel colossus, twenty thousand revelers were gathering in a space the size of an airplane hangar to celebrate what every major poll was predicting, Maynard's election as president of the United States.

November already. What do they say, the days crawl but the months fly by?

Maynard looked across the room at Claudia, sipping coffee at a round oak table, back straight, arms stiff. She returned a forced smile. But her message—her reminder—was clear enough: Even after the public shaming for his philandering, she had stood by him, held his hand, suspended her teaching career to join him in countless cross-country slogs, forced down corn dogs and cheese steaks and funnel cakes, all in a wager that this day would come, that she would become First Lady, and now he'd better deliver.

He nodded to her. Roger that.

He looked at his watch. Five p.m., Pacific time. Eight eastern. The first polls closing. He thrummed with the same mix of anticipation and giddiness he'd felt when he was selected for admiral, knowing that only a formality—in that case a Senate confirmation vote—separated him from glory, but that the appointment was still not official, that there was still a chance to get derailed by a foe or a fluke.

Some polls had him beating Hess by double digits. Tonight might deliver a landslide and a mandate. Within four hours, Maynard should be crowned leader of the free world, commander-in-chief, president. Well, president-elect. Then, soon enough, president. Mr. President. President Maynard.

A slew of new titles. Maynard had held more titles than anybody he knew. Seven grades in the Navy, from ensign through Rear Admiral, and "Captain" when he was in command at sea, no matter his actual rank. Then Senator and sometimes "Mr. Chairman" when he led a committee. Now, soon, President. A lifetime of titles had forced him to equate occupation with identity, rank with status, forced the mindset "You are what you do." And now he was going to sit atop it all.

A cheer rose, and he turned to the television mounted on a wall above a credenza. The first returns were in. A swath of cornflower blue erupted on the right side of a gray map of the United States, along with a couple of splotches of red. Numbers appeared in bright yellow. Maynard was leading Hess 65-34, with some third-party ciphers sharing the remaining one percent. Steady. They'd have to count through six time zones tonight, but this seemed a solid start. He glanced at Claudia and saw, for the first time in weeks, that gleam of pride that had long warmed him, sustained him.

Around the suite, champagne flutes rose and clinked. This field sanctum bustled with donors he'd met once or twice, a host of pols who'd endorsed him on the hustings, some top campaign apparatchiks, a few Senate colleagues, and some Senate aides and former aides. Climbers who'd bought a ticket for this victory or wangled in, some after the work was done, like goldbrickers arriving at Normandy Beach in time to pose for newsreel cameras. Most beaming, as though they'd fought and triumphed together, shipmates all. But their grinning faces showed none of the fatigue or angst or other battle scars that stared back at Maynard in the mirror. Where were they, most of them, when he was exposed and lampooned as an adulterer? When pundits were spouting his political epitaph?

He spotted his orange-bearded digital whiz, Scott, across the room. The kid nodded to him and turned back to a sandwich. Refreshing aloofness amid all these suck-ups. He beckoned Scott over.

"So far, so good?" Maynard asked.

Scott shrugged. "Yeah, overall. But this is mostly the Northeast, where you're strongest. And the polls—even the exit polls—aren't jibing with the actual tallies in some ways."

"Meaning what?"

Scott shrugged again. "Well, some people may be voting for Hess but not admitting it."

Maynard nodded. Sure, nice to see your 401K swell, but who wanted to admit to supporting an unfit reactionary?

More howls and clinking glasses. Maynard looked at the television. Other eastern states had come in, blue spreading across the gray map. His lead was holding above sixty percent.

Maynard felt something strike his shoulder, and he turned to see a flushed, beefy guy in a plaid sports coat patting him, nearly punching him, in boozy euphoria. The guy's anorexic wife laid a claw with long coral nails on Maynard's forearm, as though making her own claim.

Others swept by to congratulate him, to chat, to touch, to mark their places in history and in his memory, for the trove of patronage jobs and contracts and grants and titles he'd soon have to dispense. There must be a dozen would-be ambassadors in this suite, Maynard figured, along with several would-be cabinet secretaries, and maybe an aspiring Librarian of Congress or even a poet laureate.

A collective gasp shot through the room, and Maynard looked at the television to see a large gray rectangle turn bright red, joining a spreading Midwest wound. An ache clawed up his leg from an old parachute mishap, a quixotic quest to earn jump wings at the age of 41.

He saw his campaign manager, Jeff, working a heaping plate of grilled shrimp. Jeff turned away before their eyes could meet, like a pet spaniel diving under the kitchen table. Jeff's leaked emails about the campaign's strife and chiseling hadn't helped, especially in a close race.

Maynard heard a champagne cork pop and turned to see smiles returning to now redder and wetter faces.

"A one-off," he heard one reveler assure another, pointing to the latest splotch of red on the TV's national map.

Maynard found himself compiling data points, ingrained Navy training, noting the tallies and trends and reactions. For Sit-Reps, or situation reports, to issue tonight and for after-action reports to draft tomorrow. Always press to improve performance. He smiled and shook his head.

An alcohol haze wafted his way. The champagne was still flowing even as the dominoes kept falling the wrong way. Even as smiles gave way to frowns and tears, his loyal legions would stick with him, at least for a couple more hours.

The entire political class seemed shocked, many mortified, judging by the ashen talking heads on the television and by his aides pacing the suite like zombies. Pros who earned their livings speaking were speechless. Some wept. His press secretary had to gather himself before he could deliver a recent tally.

Finally, the red wound spread across much of the TV's gray national map and a graphic burst up showing that Ven Hess had captured the magic 270 electoral votes. The room settled into a stunned silence, punctuated by sobs and sniffles. Maynard also felt stunned, frozen in the sofa as prickles ran down his neck.

He slid into a deep, silent place in his head and zoomed out from the suite. This wasn't supposed to happen. Not according to the polls. Not according to the pundits. And not according to a majority of those who had actually voted. Maynard had won the popular vote, like Al Gore not so long ago. By a margin of several million this time. Most voters wanted him. It didn't matter. Hess had won the electoral college, taking five swing states by minute margins. By several hundred counties out of America's many thousands. Ven Hess would move into the White House on the strength of a football stadium's capacity of voters, spread perfectly across several decisive corners of America. With a nearly impossible electoral inside straight.

Maynard felt the sofa shift and turned to see Claudia joining him, but at the other end, too far away to reach for her hand. He gave her a clenched smile.

She sighed. "Admiral."

The title, for which he had strived most of his adult life, had never sounded so tinny.

Jeff was at his side, face sagging as though in mourning.

"Sir," Jeff said, and Maynard couldn't help smiling. The simplest, safest address.

"Time for the eulogy?" Maynard asked.

His campaign manager nodded.

When Maynard stood, his legs were nearly numb, and he supposed he was in some form of shock. He'd felt a sensation—or lack of sensation—like this once before, on a fast-attack sub after a long standoff with a Soviet boat. He'd been a lieutenant junior grade then, twenty-four years old, and had performed well enough during the death dance to earn a commendation, but had crashed when the tension ended. He'd been alone in his stateroom, crawled into his rack for fifteen minutes, and nobody ever knew.

Maynard hadn't prepared a concession speech because he hadn't thought he'd need one, hadn't wanted to consider the possibility that he'd need one, or that Ven Hess was actually going to be President of the United States. Maynard would wing it; what was the worst that could happen, at this point?

Before he went downstairs, he placed the obligatory call to Hess.

America's next president told him, "You ran a hell of a race." Which Maynard supposed could be taken two ways.

By the time Maynard headed down, the crowd was sparse. Most of the revelers turned mourners had abandoned the ship, leaving behind a tableau of soiled paper plates and half-filled plastic cups. The bunting and banners, some hanging and glimmering in twenty-foot strips, mocked him from three sides. Still, enough stalwarts remained that a sea of bleary eyes gazed at him, beseeching him for some answer, some hope, some assurance. A few hands clapped, and then some more, and soon the cavern thundered and echoed with applause. He waved, but they wouldn't stop. He felt sensation return to his limbs and resolve charge his body.

They kept clapping, and Maynard knew the only way to stop them was to begin speaking. He couldn't open by saying that the people had spoken, because they hadn't. Or, rather, they had; most of them had said they wanted Alec Maynard in the White House. But the Electoral College had overruled them, through a byzantine process that few understood and many wanted to abolish, but that was the verdict that counted tonight.

"The American constitutional system for two hundred and fifty years has worked its way," Maynard was saying when the din died enough for him to hear his own voice. "And we congratulate President-elect Hess and we wish him well on behalf of the country."

He went on, predictable but important pabulum, a nation united behind its duly elected new leader. He summoned all his military discipline and every better angel of his nature to concede gracefully. The most underrated song in Lin Manuel Miranda's book for *Hamilton*, Maynard had long thought, was Washington singing, "We're gonna teach them how to say goodbye," celebrating the beauty and majesty of America's tradition of peaceful transfer of power.

As Maynard recited the lyrics, a thought kept swirling through his head, that the country was fucked.

Maynard lurched out half asleep as his Amazon Alexa blasted the song he'd programmed after returning home from the Moscone Center a couple of hours earlier: Marvin Gaye's "What's Going On?" lamenting the crying and dying it proclaimed.

Maynard's mind had been churning through the short, fuzzy night, and thoughts pinged off his skull as he sat up in bed, on how and why. He coiled to bolt to the bathroom, to prepare for the day, but reminded himself that the war was over. He heard silence now, as Gaye's outro ended. No beeping messages, no ringing phones, no yapping drivers waiting to whisk him to an airport or a news conference. No secret service agents checking his house. Silence. The sound of defeat.

Maynard threw on jeans and a cotton V-neck sweater; should be warm enough for November in California. He stepped into a pair of boat shoes and trotted down to his garage. He gazed at his 1962 Studebaker GT Hawk, a gleaming symphony of chrome and black lacquer that he'd spent two years restoring but hadn't driven in months, hadn't even seen in weeks. A neighbor had been giving the car a weekly workout, keeping the hoses and engine clear and lubricated, the pistons and gears smooth.

Maynard slid into a bucket seat and cranked the ignition, smiled as the V8 growled, admired the circular instrument cluster on the textured aluminum dash, the Golden Hawk emblem in the two-tone steering wheel. He fished a garage door remote from the center console, aimed, and fired. He didn't know where he was going, how long he'd be gone, when he'd be back. He was just going. For the first time Alec Maynard could recall, he was going to be spontaneous.

He pulled out, his foot poised over the brake, braced for secret service agents to dash over. Nobody came. There were still some reporters camped on his block but they must have been snoozing, or maybe they just no longer cared.

He squinted against the morning sun, bright in a clear turquoise-blue sky. A bracing breeze hit his cheek through the open window. He turned onto his street in the heart of Telegraph Hill, accelerated up the block, and spotted a feral parrot perched on a lamppost, insouciant and free. He made a couple of turns and was soon cruising the Embarcadero with its view of the water. His mind was still churning, along with his empty stomach, and he couldn't savor the scenery.

The election was over and Ven Hess, the Hessian, was President-elect. Despite Maynard's lifetime of service, in uniform and out, and the peace and prosperity he'd helped deliver, the country had rejected his bid as its leader in favor of an erratic, incompetent huckster. Maynard laughed at his own naive efforts to transcend race, at his lifetime playing the clean-cut exemplar of the colored male. Turns out Obama hadn't broken through a ceiling, Maynard mused. Obama had been allowed through, an exception that had just proven the rule.

Maynard steered onto the San Francisco-Oakland Bay Bridge and gazed down the Hawk's long black hood to the top of its chrome grill. On Interstate 80, he eased into the passing lane.

He sensed other cars slowing, as they often did, to admire the Hawk, its lines and chrome and whitewalls. The other motorists didn't seem to notice the Hawk's driver, their own senior US senator, who eight hours earlier had won the popular vote for president of the United States. Do we all look alike to them?

Until Hess's victory, it hadn't been clear how many had been seduced by Hess's promise of an American "Revival." Revival of what? Revival of who? Hess's platform—if you could call the Republican's scattered musings, dog whistles, and racial resentments a platform—couldn't tap a vein of racism deep enough in contemporary American culture, in post-Obama culture, to win the big prize, Maynard had thought, had hoped.

"But now we know better, right?" he muttered to himself.

All right, Move! A blue minivan was blocking him in the passing lane, another self-righteous prick doing five miles over the speed limit, figuring nobody had any need, or any legal right, to go any faster. Maynard put his hand on the horn and noticed he was trembling. He reminded himself he was still a US senator, this prick's US senator. He took and held a deep breath and eased off the gas.

Maynard's numbers crunchers had shown him in the wee hours how the election had come down to a few hundred counties that Obama had won but this time went for Hess. Such a narrow margin proved, some would argue, that racism could not have decided the election. Maynard was growing sure that election microanalysis missed the bigger picture.

He placed his trembling hand back on the horn and gave a gentle, quick beep. Nothing. The minivan just kept puttering along.

Would the van move for a white driver? Maynard thought of the regular assault of glances, clutched purses, and other micro-aggressions that had left his gut perpetually tight. Even now, as he yearned to let the GT Hawk loose, let the V8 roar and pant, he knew not to tempt the Highway Patrol with a

Black man speeding in a shiny classic car.

Another memory gripped his mind. An old bit by a favorite comic, Chris Rock, when Rock made his mostly white audience acknowledge that they wouldn't trade lives with him, even though he was rich and famous, cuz he was still Black.

Hell with it. Maynard whipped around the minivan, into the center lane, the Hawk's 289-cubic-inch V8 and two-barrel carburetor roaring. This was driving. He felt looser, freer, seeing open highway. Ahead of him, three thousand miles of road, until Interstate 80 ended in Teaneck, New Jersey. Maybe he'd drive on to Sacramento, to Reno, to Omaha, maybe all the way east to Teaneck. Drive through the day and through the night, he'd done eighteen-hour shifts in the Navy, he could do twenty-four hours now, easy. He was just sitting, after all. Maybe he'd turn north in New Jersey and take I-95 into Canada. Then just keep driving, wherever the roads took him. He felt the ache slicing into an eyeball fade.

Maybe the progressives were right, after all. Or maybe—more likely—they'd created a self-fulfilling prophecy in which their vision of America as a zero-sum struggle among groups for slices of the pie had frightened just enough whites toward Ven Hess as their savior.

Yet racism didn't entirely explain Maynard's loss. Some of the fault lay with himself and not with his stars. He hadn't run a perfect campaign. And then there were Pete Vankov's thousand cuts. That's who Maynard had really been running against, Vankov. Ven Hess was a vessel for Vankov's venom, an unworthy and uncompelling opponent without his puppet master, his Brain.

Stop. He had to banish these thoughts spinning around his skull before they sent him into a frenzy or sent the Hawk into a guardrail. Life is only a series of days, and this is a new one.

As the Studebaker passed a pickup, Maynard spotted a Hess bumper sticker, and his hands tightened on the wheel, quivering to ram the bigger vehicle. He held another deep breath until he'd passed the truck.

He'd come so close, the election had been so tight, the result could have shifted so easily. The whizzes were right about that. Maybe racism wasn't the explanation, or not the sole explanation. Maybe Maynard had achieved more than exposing America's ugly truths. Maybe America was moving toward a Martin Luther King content-of-your-character society. The change would be gradual; it took miles to turn a battleship. Maynard might yet be that transformational figure to deliver the promised land. Maybe even in four years; how much of Ven Hess could America take?

Maynard eased back into the passing lane and pointed the Studebaker Hawk down the open road, toward the rising sun.

31
PASTA SALAD

Around ten on a late November morning, Ezra Fitch's assistant buzzed Gruber on the intercom to say that Mr. Fitch would like to see him in his office. She omitted the "prompt-lay," but any summons from the senior partner made Gruber's stomach tighten. He heard a howl followed by his window rattling and turned to see bare trees on K Street shaking in the wind.

Gruber arrived in the mahogany throne room to find Fitch with a rag in one hand and a plastic bottle in the other, dabbing at the gilt frame of a seascape. Fitch was tall enough to see the top of the frame without a stepstool, and his long arm extended to buff the gold leaf.

"Sit down, David." Fitch sounded calm, peaceful.

Gruber padded across the Isfahan rug and sat in the leather chair in front of Fitch's massive desk. Today was his first summons from Fitch since Vankov had blackmailed them with Gruber's stolen email.

Fitch finished his housekeeping and folded his long frame into his throne.

"I'm retiring," Fitch said and smiled. "At the end of the year, officially."

Gruber studied the older man. "You're okay? I mean, nothing wrong, physically?"

Fitch smiled again. "No, no, nothing like that. It's time. My next chapter will be set in Harpswell, Maine, the family homestead." He pointed to one of his seascapes.

Gruber nodded.

"I'm not letting Ven Hess or Pete Vankov chase me. I'm waiting a few months to make that clear. Though I'll allow that running this firm is going to be a head-banger with Hess in the White House." He gazed at the Maine seascape. "It's time."

Gruber nodded again.

"You're the first one I've told—in the firm. I'd appreciate it if you'd keep it to yourself until I make an announcement."

"Sure." Gruber searched for words to express his dismay and thought of a congressional candidate who'd challenged one of his clients years earlier, then caught Lyme disease and dropped out of the race. "This isn't how I wanted to win," Gruber had told his client to say, when in fact it was a terrific way to win, saving money and energy and angst. Then Gruber recalled one of Vankov's frequent warnings, "Don't bullshit a bullshitter."

"Well, as you can imagine, I'm very sorry to hear that, Ezra. But the only scenario I can think of that approaches working for you is succeeding you. Which should also be the next-best scenario for the firm."

Fitch grinned. "Well, ambition is a virtue. I was coming to that, my replacement. Or, as you put it, my successor. Which has a more regal ring." Fitch's smile faded. "You've had some bumps in the road recently, to mix metaphors. Some serious bumps that impugn your judgment and raise questions about your stewardship."

"Who among us is without sin?"

Fitch cocked head in a half-nod.

Gruber's big "bump" had to be his aborted play to oust Vankov. Fitch had told him that he would cancel the vote from the agenda. "Anybody has a question, he can take it up with me." On its face, Fitch had said he'd do the dirty work, spare Gruber the indignity. But that's not really what he was saying. Fitch was saying that he was going to clean up Gruber's mess and was going to do it his way. That Fitch would let the other partners know the vote was off. Maybe he'd told them, in that authoritative Ezra Fitch way, "I've decided there won't be a vote on Pete Vankov," and left it at that. And the others hadn't asked why because the DNFV code held that you talked only about matters that had to be decided. But maybe Fitch had said more to the other partners. Gruber had been living with that uncertainty. Well, he trusted Fitch. Besides, what choice did he have? Was Fitch now telling him that the oust-Vankov "bump" was bigger than Gruber might have thought?

They danced for a bit, or jousted, until Fitch finally bolted upright in his throne and said, "I want you running the firm." Then he had held up a hand. "Look, I'll do everything I can, but I'm a lame duck. We're just going to have to count votes."

That evening, Gruber got to his Connecticut Avenue condo early, around dusk, and got to work in his kitchen. Was it still his kitchen and his apartment, or had it become their condo? No, this slice of pre-war grandeur was still his. As Berglund had reminded—or threatened—him a couple of times, she could fold down the backseat of her VW, load in everything she kept here, and bolt in half an hour. She'd brought one piece of décor, her Felix the Cat plushie, which now sat on a side table in their den, his den. The modern prints hanging on the thick plaster walls, the various statues and nicknacks throughout the three-bedroom place, were all his.

A breeze rustled past some bare elms and through an open window, chasing the onion smell.

Gruber twirled a measuring cup around his thumb. He was soon in a creative fury, unleashing scents and flavors, concocting manna.

He had perfected this recipe twenty-five years ago, a staple of bachelor cuisine easily varied with a range of meats, vegetables, pastas, and sauces. He'd gotten as exotic as squid over black fettucine, but Jane Berglund was a Corn Belt girl, so tonight it was grilled chicken, zucchini, onions, and tomatoes over whole-wheat fusilli.

Gruber found himself jouncing with euphoria, thinking about his meeting with Fitch that morning, then thrumming with fury and frustration. Then itching with uncertainty. He tried to focus on slicing zucchini and made several slow, even cuts before tiring and pounding the knife through the rest of the vegetable.

Gruber slid the peeled veggies into a saucepan on a burner. Oil and garlic crackled and spat. He couldn't focus on the cooking. The last time he'd counted partners' votes, to oust Vankov from the firm, he'd nearly lost his own job. This next vote, to elect a new managing partner, would certainly spell his fate. He wouldn't stay at DNFV, couldn't stay, if he lost the spot and had to answer to one of those overgrown frat boys who'd nixed him. Then what? With Hess in the White House, Gruber might find all of Washington chilly.

He had enough cash to cruise for a while, with the two million from the Navy documents ploy. Well, one million, nine hundred and fifty thousand, after paying off Paul Thompson. When Gruber returned from Centreville that night, he'd crammed Thompson's first payment, from the blue canvas travel bag, into the Coach duffel. He'd shoved the bulging Coach bag into the back of his bedroom closet. He'd been wrestling over what to do with it since.

He'd told Berglund, only half kidding, that they could charter a jet and take the duffel to any number of banking havens around the world that would gladly deposit the cash without questions. Some would credit their deposit toward easy citizenship in a country that might guard them from the arm of American justice, if it came to that.

"That would make you just like him," she'd said. "Him," the name she would not speak, meant Vankov. Except when it occasionally meant Hess.

When the front door clacked open, the whole-wheat fusilli had boiled for nine minutes. Perfect timing. Berglund strutted in with an airy "Howdy!" Gruber strained the pasta and poured it into the saucepan over the vegetables and chicken, now nearly tender, his symphony coming together. He stirred the mixture with a spatula.

By the time Berglund had washed and sat at the granite-topped kitchen table, the entree was ready. Gruber filled two bowls with pasta salad, drizzled light Italian dressing over each, and stirred.

He padded over in bare feet and joined her at the table with his manna. He admired his work. Show value every day, a consultant on an early campaign had instructed. Domestic bliss, Gruber thought, surveying his queen and their feast in their palace.

She was brooding again. Looking away, ignoring the bowl before her.

"It's best when it's hot," he said, with more of an edge than he'd intended. Well, she'd groused about his poker-faced reticence. Why, she implored, wouldn't he communicate?

He poured Chablis into glasses. "Tonight's a celebration." He told her about his meeting with Fitch, about his pending triumph and ascension.

She raised her glass. "Congratulations. Though I hope it's not premature. When he's involved, nothing is over until it's over."

"He is not involved. He is busy trying to stay out of prison for the next twenty years."

"On top of everything else, it means more money," he said. "Substantially more."

She scrunched her features into a confused mien. "Don't you already have all the money you'll need for years?" She angled her head toward the bedroom.

He began eating his pasta salad. Just the right mix of textures, of tang and saltiness, the right temperature. But no resonance, no afterglow. He swallowed a bite, and it was gone.

"How can you keep that thing on the wall?" She pointed to a framed drawing by the kitchen door of two men in business suits standing atop the *Globe*, sharing a magnum of Champagne. Gruber and Vankov, drawn by the Dark Angel himself.

He shrugged. "A memento of better times."

She turned to study the piece, grinding her chair on the stone floor. "From this distance, it's hard to tell the two of you apart—who's who."

He laughed. Yes, Pete Vankov had not only tutored Gruber, he'd also shown him much of who he was. There but for the grace of something, went he. He tried to summon a clever riposte, but nothing came to him.

"You can't possibly feel bad for him. After all he's done."

"We beat him, and it's a supremely sweet victory. Our victory. But I don't take sadistic joy in his arrest or indictment or in the spectacles of his court and media prosecutions, if that's what you're getting at."

She speared a zucchini slice with her fork and slid it around the rim of her bowl.

"Did I enjoy the mano a mano combat with the Dark Angel?" he went on. "As Pete might put it, 'You bet.' But not just for me, for justice."

She rolled her eyes, and he felt his hands tremble, as though eager to punch something. He took a deep breath, a miniature Breath of Fire. In a couple of months, he mused, he might be running a major Washington public affairs firm and have his dream girl, or he might be an unemployed, twice-divorced has-been.

He glanced at the page posted on the refrigerator and went through what was usually his morning ritual, reciting the words his mother, and generations of others, had hung on their refrigerator doors, Reinhold Niebuhr's Serenity Prayer. He chanted to himself, like a mantra:

God grant me the serenity
to accept the things I cannot change;
courage to change the things I can;
and wisdom to know the difference.

Berglund had poised the speared zucchini slice above her bowl, but she still hadn't taken a bite. He sighed silently and shoveled from his own bowl. Pretty good.

He reminded himself that Jane Berglund had crossed so many bright lines to be with him and join him to bring down Vankov and stop Hess in a scheme that had, at best, only partially succeeded. She'd endured so much for their partnership, professional and romantic. He tried to still the thrum in his head.

"What's eating you?" he blurted. A phrase his mother had thrown at him when he'd gone through a sullen teenage phase.

She looked up. "How can you be a Republican? You did vote for Maynard, right?" She'd picked up a portentous cable TV cadence after landing an MSNBC contributor gig and doing some high-profile freelancing after her *Atlantic* exposé made her a star.

He nodded, sensing a setup.

"Why don't you just switch and become a Democrat?"

"Is that a question or a request?"

She shrugged. "It's not like I'm asking you to change your religion."

He laughed. "Does that bother you, too, my being a Christ-killer?"

"Forget it." She poked again at her pasta.

The thrum in his head now echoed in his ears. "No, I can't forget it. I need you to understand me. After all our time together, you still didn't fully appreciate who I am, what I believe. You don't have to agree, but you have to understand." Without that validation, what we have will wither, like my earlier relationships. And part of me will wither, and I'll be alone again. Maybe forever.

She was holding her fork, waiting.

He took a deep breath. "Contrary to what your lefty media bubble preaches as gospel," he began, feeling himself slip into pitch mode, "the pre-Hess GOP was so much more right than wrong about both the country's problems and its opportunities. There was simply more about America—in its culture, it's economy and its system of government—that needed to be conserved rather than radically transformed."

A sad smile began playing on her face.

"That party—go back a few years—didn't deny climate change and shared the goal of getting all Americans health insurance. It just believed that those things were better addressed through the genius of American markets and innovation than by ever-greater power and control in Washington. They didn't want to abandon folks in poverty amid America's general plenty, but they wanted to empower them to succeed, not make them dependent on entitlements from the state. And that party understood that America's serving as global 'policeman' for seventy-five years had given the world the freest, richest, least violent seventy-five years in all of history. That especially needed conserving."

She shoved her pasta aside, barely eaten. "So how did Pete Vankov and Ven Hess soil Abraham Lincoln's brand?"

"Don't overread it, Janey, bad as it is. Hess is in the White House because of a tiny sliver of the hundred and thirty million votes cast, a freak mutation in the genetic code of America's democracy. You misread it, you can transform that fluke, tragic as it is, into something even worse, and something repeatable. If the intelligentsia insists too loud and too long that Hess's election reveals ignorance and darkness at the heart of nearly half the American people, you may get stuck with Hessism for a long time."

She scowled, but then gave the barest shrug, which he took as a grudging nod to his insight.

"As much as I despise Hess and Vankov, I still can't become a Democrat because pretty much ever since Martin Luther King so wrongly declared in 1967 that America was 'the greatest purveyor of violence in the world,' the Democrats have been a left-wing party, not a liberal party. And we have a hundred and fifty years of evidence that whenever this lefty Word is made flesh, it can give the world only the equality of shared poverty and only the peace of the dead or the defeated, surrendered, and compliant."

He stopped and let his breathing slow. He swept a knuckle across his temple, wiping sweat. Too much cayenne on the chicken?

They eyed each other across the table, a divide of a few feet that felt like miles. Finally, she gave him that wise nod of hers, which he took as the affirmation he'd begged, even if not complete agreement. It was the most he'd hoped for. And he deemed it enough to keep their little household tumultuous—but solid—in these tumultuous times.

32

THE RESISTANCE

Pete Vankov paused before the unmarked steel door in the suburban Dallas office park to do some quick isometrics, to pump his biceps so the veins would bulge when he shucked his sportscoat. He'd lost serious muscle mass since he stopped lifting heavily, but his aging skin had more vascularity, giving him a vibe of a grizzled warrior. His veins would protrude even more in the Texas heat. Well, relative heat; nearly sixty in December.

Show gratitude, he reminded himself. They thought they were honoring him, offering this rare visit, trusting him with the address of their "undisclosed location," which they'd somehow managed to keep private. Vankov knocked, waited for the buzzer, and stepped into the studio.

There she was, inside a big glass booth, wearing a red-and-white Santa hat and an "I am the Resistance" T-shirt. Amanda Jenks, afternoon drivetime star of MindBattle, syndicated on radio stations across the country and live-streamed, darling of conspiracy theorists, evangelicals, right-wingers, dark fantasists. Vankov's peeps, especially since he'd seen the Light, found the Way.

Jenks had aged since he'd last seen her, only a few months earlier, when he'd enlisted her to help take down a pandering socialist Democrat wannabe-senator. She looked smaller and softer. Dumpling-shaped now, with cat eyeglasses on her round face below her thinning scarlet mop. She looked all of her forty-five years, and then some. A bearded guy in a sleeveless plaid flannel shirt, could have been an out-of-shape lumberjack except for his goth tattoos, was manning a mounted camera. MindBattle's website drew more hits than *Newsweek*.

Jenks bounded out of her chair for a hug. Then stepped back to look him over.

"You look pretty good," she said. "Considering."

He took off his tweed herringbone jacket, revealing a garland over his blue "Pete Vankov is Innocent" T-shirt. "Whole new perspective." He flashed a beatific smile.

"This is going to be a great show," she gushed. "And you'll get way more contributions because this is the end of year. When people divvy up to give to causes."

He nodded, as though it was nice to hear about the mammon, but he was on a higher plane. "I wanted to make my announcement on your show, Amanda, because your audience will understand, they'll have the right perspective. I don't want to go on some mainstream outlet, with pagan reporters, who'll give it the wrong spin." He shook his head. "Actually, I didn't want to say anything publicly at all, because some people would say I'm using Jesus to stay out of jail. But I've been testifying, mostly small churches but some bigger ones, too, and the pagan reporters have begun sniffing around, so I figured I better put it out there before they do."

Jenks pointed to a large digital clock that showed 3:55 p.m. and motioned Vankov to the set. She slid into her chair like a pilot into a cockpit, and Vankov took the open opposite seat before a large mic. Jenks went into some pre-flight routine, tapping her keyboard, doing soundchecks, sucking from a bottle of water. The cameraman was testing and coaxing his machine.

Soon a red light came on, a deep disembodied voice counted down from eight, and Jenks leaned toward her mic.

"There's a battle on for your mind!" she began. "If you're listening to this feed, you are the resistance."

She turned to Vankov. Here in the studio with her, she told her listeners, was Pete Vankov, bad boy of Republican politics turned good boy. "Pete, I've never seen you looking so relaxed."

"I've found Jesus Christ. It's that simple." He angled toward his mic. "I don't hate anybody anymore. For the first time in my life, I don't hate somebody. I have nothing but good feelings toward people. There's just no mileage in fighting and feuding."

"Well, Pete, that's nice to hear. But there's lots of people out there who still have a jones for you. Your trial's scheduled for February, two months from now. Campaign finance violations for allegedly colluding with foreigners to hurt Senator Alec Maynard, money-laundering, racketeering, perjury, obstruction of justice, and foreign-agent charges. They're throwing the book at you, and they can put you away for twenty years."

Yeah, tell me about it. Vankov was going broke preparing for the trial, maybe trials. He was hemorrhaging ten thousand dollars per billable hour, paying every high-priced lawyer in Washington and New York.

The feds were focusing on the Maynard hotel-room audio, Vankov's lawyers had told him in a two-thousand-dollar primer. But Vankov was only Hess's campaign manager, which made it tricky to hold him personally liable. So prosecutors had charged Vankov with conspiracy to get the UAE tape, then lying about it. Conspiracy with who? With "Individual Number One," never named. Ven Hess, of course.

"The deep state wanted to prosecute—to persecute—both President Hess and me. But they got cute—too cute, my lawyers say. The feds didn't go after Hess because they didn't want to look like they were interfering in an election. They figured they'd wait until he lost, which seemed to them a good bet. But they underestimated us, underestimated the people, and Hess won. And now the deep staters didn't think they could prosecute a sitting president. Which left them only with me."

He shrugged. "I sort of feel like Job, like I'm being tested. My trials—in every sense—have taught me something about the nature of humanity, love, brotherhood, and relationships that I never understood, and probably never would have. So, from that standpoint, there's some good in it. Maybe that's part of the test, learning that."

She was looking at him, waiting for more. Like a couple of ministers where he'd testified. More heart, more soul, more revelation.

"My persecution has let me see that what's missing in society was missing in me: a little heart, a lot of brotherhood. These past decades, since I got into the political game, have been about acquiring and consuming—acquiring wealth, power, prestige. Consuming clothes, cars, homes, even flesh. I acquired and consumed more than most. But you can acquire and consume all you want and still feel empty. What power wouldn't I trade for a little more time with my friends? What house wouldn't I trade for my freedom? It took a persecution—looking at years behind bars—to drive home that truth, but it's a truth that the country can learn on my nickel."

"So what does that mean, for a guy in your line of work? No more campaigns? No more negative campaigning?"

"Well, I don't call it 'negative campaigning,' because I'm just revealing truths about the other guy. I call it 'comparative campaigning.' But, bigger picture, I've adopted the Golden Rule as my credo, 'Do unto others as you would have them do unto you.'" He gave the camera a soulful glance. "I wish more people would think about the Golden Rule. I wish I had."

Jenks hunched over her mic, and Vankov braced for a devil's-advocate question. The newly converted often needed to prove themselves, like bangers getting "jumped in" to a street gang. But she launched into a pitch for a diet supplement that promised to "sharpen your thinking, extend your memory, and boost your mojo," all in three pills a day.

Vankov rotated his neck and pictured the West Virginia church where he'd testified the previous weekend, and tried to recapture the spirit, the rapture.

"So you've forgiven your enemies," Jenks said. "The prosecutors who are putting you on trial, your former partner you say set you up, all of them?"

"In the old days, I would have taken revenge against every one of them. I've got a long memory, and I'm patient. I've lain in the weeds for years before springing the perfect trap. But I've come to understand that vengeance is God's, not mine."

An image of Gruber's grinning face floated into Vankov's head. "That's not to say, even as I strive to love my enemies, that I don't see them for what they are. The deep-state prosecutors are dishonest and politically motivated. They're trying to get me to bear false witness against President-elect Hess, for some type of leniency. But I won't bear false witness." He clenched his jaw. "I do believe they're satanic. Especially the twerp who set me up."

"Nerds are one of the most dangerous groups in this country, because they end up running things." Jenks shifted in her seat. "But they still hate everybody, because they weren't the jocks in high school. So they play little dirty games on everybody. They use their brains to hurt people. And we're onto them. I see you, you little rats!"

She leaned forward until her lips brushed her mic. "Sure, your prosecution is political, Pete. The New World Order doesn't do anything unless it passes their cost-benefit analysis, unless it helps all of their major operations. That's their tyranny. I know they staged those terror attacks. 9/11 was an inside job. These wicked globalists are so threatened by human potential they poison the water and the food, and spray the sky with those jet contrails, even unleash novel virus bioweapons to turn us into a bunch of slugs, a bunch of lobotomized sloths so they can control us." She pointed at some invisible enemy. "You think your evil is invincible? You're not invincible, and God is going to deal with you, and you are cursed to hell!"

She turned to him, her face nearly as red as her Santa hat.

"I was a sinner, I'm admitting that," Vankov said. "But I'm not going to apologize for anything I did on Ven Hess's campaign, because I didn't do anything wrong." He tugged his "Pete Vankov is Innocent" T-shirt. "By the way, Hess likes your show."

Jenks smiled. "It's surreal to talk about issues here on the air, and then hear Hess say it two days later, word for word." She laughed. "Listen, the elite hate Hess. I'm not saying he's perfect. I never expected Hess to go charging into a goblin's nest and not get some goblin vomit and goop and blood on him. I just don't want to catch him in bed with a goblin. But if he's in there rolling around hacking them up and he's got a goblin guide taking him into the cave, I'm not expecting him to not get dirty."

Vankov nodded. "Nobody ever said life was fair." Get back on message. "The Living Bible has given me faith." He touted The Living Bible as an accessible, plain-English, church-approved translation that made the Word clear. Then he went into his bit about two former hardcore Reagan aides who had shown him the Light. "One spent ten hours with me praying, counseling, and reading The Living Bible. The other, who runs a lay ministry, led me to the Lord."

"He showed me the work that had to be done," Vankov went on. "I had made it my life's work to understand my enemies—but not to empathize with them, because then I couldn't do what I had to do. Only so that I could manipulate them and defeat them. Now I had to truly understand them, so I could love them."

He told her about the "forgiveness calls" he'd been making to those he'd wronged over the decades, about the "forgiveness letters" he'd been mailing and emailing, about the books he'd been sending with scribbled notes about love and family.

"I went through six months of hell before I found the way," he said softer. "And I know the worst is yet to come, but now I'm ready for it. I only wish I'd rediscovered the church sooner. And I'm trying to do the tough task the Bible requires, praying for my enemies. It's easier, really, because God will deal with them, so it's not as though the deep state is going to go unpunished."

She broke in, another pitch, this one for a miracle balm. Just rub it into your arms twice a day, and you'll beat any disease, even cancer.

"Sometimes I think my sister was lucky, she was the lucky one." Vankov let his voice break. "Taken when she was only five years old."

The segment was nearly over, and Jenks launched into what seemed a benediction.

"I admire your attitude, Pete, but I've had enough of these people. They're a bunch of Christian-murdering scum who run giant death factories, keeping babies alive and selling their body parts. What more do you need to know about these people, they literally crawl out from under rocks, and they run around screaming, 'We love Satan, we want to eat babies.' I have them on video at the Texas statehouse, women going, 'Hail Satan.'

"We're going to return the republic," Jenks continued, spittle flying. "We'll never be perfect, but my God, we're not going to keep babies alive and harvest their organs. We're not going to sell their parts for women's cosmetics. We're not going to have Pepsi with baby flavoring in it. I mean, what the hell have we become?"

Her glare shifted to a faraway gaze. "I ask you to look in the mirror, and ask yourselves what are you doing in this time of great challenge? What are you doing to unlock minds? Once the mind is unlocked, once the intellect is turned on, then comes the discernment, then comes the awakening of the soul, then comes true enlightenment and empowerment. The globalists seek to make you a bunch of jealous, stunted, weak, backstabbing, gibbering demons. All of us have the lower elements and the higher. We must strive for the higher. Stay with us! Resist! Resistance is victory!"

After the red studio light went off, Vankov gave Jenks a goodbye hug, a lot of muscle under all that flab. She promised she'd link MindBattle's website to Vankov's legal defense fund site so that her listeners could buy his T-shirts and other "Pete Vankov is Innocent" merch.

Vankov walked to the steel door and unzipped his bag to slide in his garland. He noticed his copy of The Living Bible, which he'd meant to use as a prop on Jenks's show, and then thanked his stars, or God or whoever, that he hadn't. He kept forgetting to take the cellophane wrapper off the book and at least skim it.

33
THINGS OF VALUE

Gruber was rinsing and loading the breakfast dishes into the dishwasher and Berglund was taking her vitamin pills as the radio gave the traffic and weather. Clear roads, balmy for early February with an afternoon high near fifty degrees, and sunny. Perfect driving for a commute from Annapolis to the District.

A Saturday, but Berglund and Gruber both had to go in to work. She to discuss the evils of money in politics live on MSNBC for her "contributor" gig, and he to finish a proposal for a Japanese furniture consortium looking to expand in US markets.

He could have worked remotely, she figured, now that he was the big cheese at his firm. Managing partner at DNG, the outfit's latest iteration, now that Pete Vankov and Ezra Fitch had left the masthead. But he had an old-fashioned taste for offices and live exchanges.

From a Carrera counter, the radio chimed for its top-of-the-hour network news feed. A lilting tenor began with an alert. "President Hess this morning issued a full pardon to his former campaign manager, Peter Vankov."

She sprayed water.

"Vankov was scheduled to go on trial in two weeks in federal court on a variety of felony charges including campaign finance violations, racketeering, money-laundering, perjury, and obstruction of justice," the tenor intoned. "President Hess also issued pardons to three men convicted of nonviolent, drug-related offenses and commuted the sentence of two other nonviolent drug offenders."

She gripped a bottle of multivitamins. "You've got to be kidding me!"

Gruber met her eyes, his mouth agape. Then he laughed, slowly at first, then a wet-eyed howl.

She glared at him, waiting for him to finish. Eventually he stopped, issued a few puttering sounds, breathed deeply, and wiped his eyes.

"Wow," he said.

"Yeah, wow."

All their efforts were for naught. Well, all her efforts. Gruber was running a big K Street consulting firm while her consolation prize was, as Gruber sometimes called himself, an aging nebbish.

Neither of them spoke as the radio voice prattled on about immigration rules, or maybe visa statistics, she wasn't catching it. Finally, she said, "It's like a horror movie when someone frees the devil from a dungeon cell. To usher in a new era of darkness and corruption."

He laughed again, this time like a truck releasing its air brakes. "Pete gets more credit—or blame—than he deserves. We're pretty good in Washington at gumming up the works all by ourselves. Remember what Napoleon said: 'Never ascribe to malice that which can adequately be explained by incompetence.'"

He gave her a smile, then a thought seemed to hit him, and he marched out of the kitchen. She heard him pad down the parquet corridor and open the bedroom door, and then his sounds stopped as he hit the carpet.

She took her last vitamin, put her water glass in the dishwasher, and placed the pill bottles back in the kitchen cabinet.

Gruber marched back into the kitchen lugging the leather duffle bag from the closet with both hands. He plopped it on the floor. So that's what two million dollars in cash sounded like. Minus the fifty-thousand-dollar payoff to Paul Thompson. So much for honor among thieves, or whatever they were.

She squinted at him.

"I've been trying for six months to figure out what do with the money. Now I know." He was beaming. "Well, I have a bizarre idea of what to do. We can talk about it in a bit."

The money was his to spend, she supposed. But she'd been tallying his points, and if this scheme sent him into too deep a deficit, she could always load up her VW and move back to Old Town, Alexandria. She was still paying rent on her apartment.

They headed out the back door for a brisk walk along the shore. She thought this jaunt might serve as his "in a bit" for discussing the cash, but he plodded silently. She pointed out a colorful shell, and a few minutes later they agreed to call a local repair service for the washing machine.

Back in the house, they changed their shoes and exchanged their nylon jackets for a tweed sportscoat and a pearl-button cardigan.

She gave him an odd look as he hefted the leather duffel to the garage and into the trunk of his Jaguar XJ. He slid the big bag toward a corner, behind his emergency kit of flares and bandages, as though hiding it.

"We can talk about this on the way," he said.

They rode in silence through Epping Forest and onto Route 50 West. The Jaguar gobbled the highway, the big cat issuing only a low humming growl. Like riding in a tank, compared to her VW. They'd left half an hour earlier than she needed for her MSNBC hit, maybe for whatever he had planned.

"When I took the managing director gig, I promised you I'd use my talents for good, not evil." He grinned at her. "That's Batman's line, from the 1960s TV show."

"Well, that's about the most one could ask of a Republican operative."

His grin died and he turned back to the road. "I learned a lot from that show. Such as: Proper dental hygiene is essential to effective crime fighting. Holy cavity!"

He turned to her again.

She gave him a mock smile.

They were nearing Interstate 395 and Washington when Gruber spoke again. "The key question is, 'What is a Thing of Value?' That would've been the question at Vankov's trial, if we'd gotten there."

"Well, not his artwork." She pictured the drawing in his kitchen.

Gruber was in one of his grooves and ignored her remark. "To Illinois Governor Rod Blagojevich, naming someone to the senate seat that Obama vacated to become president was a thing of value. Or, as Blago put it, "It's 'a fucking valuable thing, you just don't give it away for nothing.'" He smiled again.

Fine. A Democratic jerk; the GOP didn't have a monopoly. She gave him a half-nod.

"The presidency is a thing of value," he went on. "Having America's democratic process driven by Americans, without undue influence from foreign actors pursuing their own agendas, is also a thing of value. Which is why colluding with foreigners is a crime."

"Got it." Lots of value out there.

He steered onto I-395, the highway taking on an urban intensity.

"Which all gets us to the two million dollars in the leather bag. Or close enough." He glanced at her. "What's its value? What is its highest value, in terms of its buying power? And why is it in the trunk?"

At last. She gestured for his answer.

His head jolted as a sign for the South Capitol Street exit came into view, and he steered into the right lane. He slowed behind a line of cars, and his face loosened. "Whatever else, our conversations would be pretty boring if we agreed on everything, don't you think?"

"Yes, my dearest. But the question is, do we agree on enough?"

His face tightened again. He cruised down South Capitol Street, along a boulevard recently gentrified by construction of Nationals Park, home of Washington's baseball team, the Nats, back in its third iteration. He turned left onto Virginia Avenue and steered his $90,000 Jaguar XJ into one of the most blighted areas in the nation's capital.

She pressed the door-lock button and inched down in her seat.

After a few blocks, Gruber pulled over. The Jag's tires crunched bottle shards, cans, needles, who knew what. He parked behind an old Chevy missing hubcaps.

"Trust me, just for a minute," he implored.

She crossed her arms.

He stepped out in his Harris Tweed herringbone, khakis, and rubber-soled bucks. He walked around the car, and she heard the trunk open and soon close. When he came around her side, he was hefting the leather duffel.

"Jesus," she said. Well, can't be any more dangerous than Afghanistan during the war. She opened her door and stepped out of the Jag.

He headed toward the underpasses for the Southeast Freeway, a stretch of Interstate 695 rumbling above them, wealthy politicos and professionals zipping from their Navy Yard condos and beyond to Capitol Hill and downtown offices.

He led her beneath one of the expressway bridges and she saw a group of homeless clustered around a trashcan fire. She turned to him and saw a look almost of relief.

She knew, at that moment, what he was planning. Would he really go through with it? It was crazy. Empowered by a pile of cash, wouldn't they kill themselves with booze and drugs, or die defending their loot? But wasn't that basically what Gruber and his frat-firm buddies had been doing for years? Which must be his point.

Gruber angled his head at the group of figures beneath the overpass.

She studied the tableau, then nodded.

They stepped closer to the encampment, their soles crunching debris. The homeless eyed them.

Gruber shouted a cheery "Hello!" His voice sounded an octave high.

He set down the leather duffel bag about fifteen feet from the fire and turned to her.

She took his hand and they walked off, to pursue new kinds of value.

ACKNOWLEDGEMENTS

G uile was conceived and written by me with my co-author, Charles Robbins. Charlie has been a friend, colleague, and partner in (figurative) political crime since Arlen Specter was throwing early model cell phones at him in the skies above, well, somewhere.

He's a far more talented writer than am I, so anything a reader does not like about this book is solely my responsibility.

While very much a work of fiction, *Guile* does draw inspiration from many real life individuals and events. To all those who have been either mentors or exemplars of roads better not taken in my long career in politics, policy and government, I send the appropriate measure and variety of gratitude.

Mostly, of course, acknowledgement is due to my primary sources, gone a decade now, but never not with me for a moment:

For those who worked, that I could live learning,

For those who loved, that I could learn living,

For everything, and for always,

For my parents.

Printed in the USA
CPSIA information can be obtained
at www.ICGtesting.com
CBHW070755170824
13314CB00008B/147